Early praise for *You Again*

"The author does an excellent job answering the question that many wonder as they grow older: what am I going to do with the rest of my life? Am I doomed to just continue living out the same routines, day after day, week after week? This book is not just a love story, but an exploration of self. The title not only echoes Rosalee's encounter with a past love, but also of her own experience in finding her way back to the person she used to be."

- Kelsey Edwards, library director, Bladen County Public Library

"This is a sweet, down-to-earth story with just the right touch of wry humor. I loved caring about Waters' characters; she's crafted them to feel like the reader's old friends."

- Dr. Sonya Sawyer Fritz, associate professor, English, University of Central Arkansas

AMANDA WATERS

Orange Hat Publishing
www.orangehatpublishing.com - Waukesha, WI

You Again
Copyrighted © 2020, 2019 Amanda Waters
ISBN 978-1-64538-070-2
Second Edition

You Again
by Amanda Waters

For information, please contact:

Orange Hat Publishing
www.orangehatpublishing.com
Waukesha, WI

Editing by Carolyn Kott Washburne
Proofreading by Margaret Dwyer
Cover design by Rachel Hardy

www.orangehatpublishing.com

Dedicated to Ruth Pauline Blair and L'Wana Jo Rush

chapter *1*

October 2018

Something was wrong.

The autumn sun glinted off of the water below the trail, birds sang tirelessly, and squirrels rustled through red and gold leaves searching for their winter stash. Rosalee turned to her right. Tommy stood a few paces in front of her, looking over his shoulder, a smile on his face. "Why'd you stop?" he asked.

Rosalee shook her head. "Something's wrong here."

"Yeah, you're being weird," a different voice said from her left.

She turned and saw George, hands stuffed in his jeans pockets, an unlit cigarette hanging from his lips. Rosalee glanced between the two of them. "This isn't right. It's not the way it happened," she repeated.

The sound of a bell rang loudly through the air, but neither Tommy nor George seemed to notice.

"Do you hear that?" Rosalee asked. Maybe the bell was giving her that unsettled feeling. It was certainly getting louder. And more annoying. But even the squirrels and birds seemed unphased.

Rosalee put her hands on her ears as the bell got louder. "Seriously?" she shouted at Tommy. "You don't hear that?"

Tommy turned all the way around and walked up next to her. He leaned forward, gently removing one of her hands from her ear and putting his lips next to her ear. "Answer your phone."

Rosalee jerked awake in her bed, disoriented and still wishing the ringing would stop. She glanced at her bedside clock and sighed, knowing only one person who would be calling her this early. She reached for the phone.

"Hello."

"Mother? Are you sick?"

Rosalee cleared her throat. "No, honey, you just woke me up is all. I haven't talked yet."

"Why are you still in bed?"

Rosalee rolled her eyes. "Because it's only 7:15 in the morning, Elizabeth, and I don't work on Thursdays. I stayed up late reading a book last night because sleeping in is a perk of being 63, darling. Something to look forward to."

"Well, I'm sorry I woke you. I was checking out Macy's website before work this morning, and noticed they're having a sale on boots and sweaters this week. Did you tell me you wanted some new boots this fall?"

"I did! That's perfect. And I have time today to stop by. Thank you for thinking of me, sweetheart."

They chatted for a few more minutes then said goodbye when Elizabeth got to work. Rosalee hung up the phone and set it down on the bed next to her. She snuggled under her quilt and closed her eyes, debating whether or not she wanted to go back to sleep. She really had stayed up much later than normal last night, but that dream she was having when the phone rang was unsettling. She often dreamed of Tommy, especially in the fall when they used to go camping and hiking all the time. But why on earth was George in her dream?

The feeling of something damp and cold on her face solved Rosalee's sleep-or-wake dilemma. She opened her eyes and turned to see a furry brown-and-white face right next to hers.

"Hey, Billy," she said to her big mutt. "Need to go out?"

Billy wagged his tail and Rosalee sat up, slipping her arms into her flannel robe and her feet into her fuzzy slippers. As Billy galloped around the backyard, Rosalee settled into her morning routine, a routine that hadn't varied much for years. Get the coffee started, put food in Billy's bowl, get her own breakfast ready, let Billy back inside, sit down at the tiny table that sat under the kitchen window.

She sat for a moment, listening to Billy's crunching and the dry leaves rustling outside the window. She could hear a garbage truck a few blocks away, and the sounds of the children who waited for the bus down at the corner, just one house down from her own. They were good, homey sounds. Rosalee breathed a prayer of thankfulness for the morning—for the blessing of routine, the company of her loyal and sweet dog, and even the fact of being awakened by a daughter who cared enough to think of her mom.

But for a moment, Rosalee was also just sad. She always felt lonelier in the morning. Maybe it was something about that single coffee cup. Tommy had been gone almost four years now, but she missed him so much some days. She missed him even when she didn't have dreams about him, but especially then.

The doorbell chimes startled Rosalee out of her reverie, and she went to answer the door. "Oh, hello, Tripp!" she said to her youngest neighbor. (*Where do people come up with these names? Tripp? What kind of name is that?*). "How are you?"

"I'm fine, Mrs. McDonnell," the eight-year-old said. "Um, I just saw your paper at the end of the drive while I was waiting for the bus." He held out his hand holding her newspaper just as the big yellow school bus rumbled around the corner.

"Oh, hey, there's the bus," he said, turning to run across her yard and through his own. "Bye, Mrs. McDonnell!" he called over his shoulder as he sprinted away.

Rosalee waved, a smile on her face, and her earlier sadness abated. That was one sweet boy. She didn't care what nonsense his parents were thinking when they named him; the Blairs may not know how to name children, but they clearly knew how to raise them. As she closed the front door and walked back to her breakfast, paper in hand, Rosalee decided to bake some cookies to take to Celia Blair today. Or maybe some cranberry muffins. Or a cake. Oh! Or a pie. How long had it been since she'd baked a pie? She probably had the ingredients for coconut cream, and she knew she had the ingredients for chocolate cream. There might also be a bag of frozen berries in her freezer. She preferred fresh fruit for pies, of course, but you couldn't really be picky sometimes.

"Billy, we're baking pies today," she said as she sat down at the table.

Rosalee opened the *Riverton Daily Journal* and spread it out on the table to read while she ate.

Rosalee had started reading the newspaper when her kids were small and she was desperate to think about things other than diapers, toys, and the not-so-exciting adventures of Dick and Jane. She read the paper cover to cover, even now, even the high school sports pages. People were surprised to find out that she actually enjoyed sports, but after so many years of attending her son's and then her grandchildren's sports games, it was inevitable that she'd grow to enjoy sports now and then. When she'd finished, Rosalee re-folded the paper and set it on the edge of the table; she'd throw it in her compost pile later. She opened the back door for Billy who was whining to go out again—"we'll go for a walk later, I promise"—then went to the sink to rinse her breakfast dishes.

She turned on the radio mounted to the kitchen cabinet and tuned it to the AM country station. It had a bit of static, but it played everything that she liked: Waylon Jennings, Charley Pride, Loretta Lynn, Dolly Parton, Hank Williams. Her granddaughter Jessica liked more of the modern country music, but Rosalee stuck with the classics most of the time. Made her forget how old she was. Not that her sometimes achy bones, dry skin, and wrinkles ever let her forget that. Or her need to get up and use the bathroom at least two or three times a night. Or her reading glasses. But what was the use of thinking about all that? At the very least, listening to her music while baking in the kitchen made her feel like herself.

Rosalee took off her robe and hung it across the back of a kitchen chair, then tied an apron on over her pajamas. She pulled out two glass pie plates and set them on her counter, then made her way around the kitchen, pulling out ingredients and utensils as she went around. Flour, salt, sugar, chocolate, shaved coconut, coconut milk, eggs, shortening, butter, measuring cups, rolling pin, measuring spoons, a small mixing bowl, a glass mixing bowl, a wooden spoon, a fork, and her frying pan for toasting the coconut. Chocolate cream pie and coconut cream pie. Surely Celia liked at least one of those. She hummed along with Johnny Cash as she floured her counter then measured and poured more flour, salt, and shortening into a bowl and worked it into a crumbly mixture with her fork. She added a tiny bit of ice water, and mixed it just barely into the flour-and-shortening mixture before setting the ball of dough onto her floured counter.

While the crusts baked, Rosalee mixed up the filling, beat the meringue for the chocolate pie, and whipped the cream for the coconut. While the meringue baked on the chocolate pie Rossalee got dressed, ran a comb through her hair, and brushed her teeth. She applied just a little mascara and some lipstick. No need to go all out for a neighborly trip next door, but Rosalee never could shake the habit of putting forth at least a little effort when one went visiting.

A few minutes later Rosalee knocked on the front door of her neighbor's house, her other arm holding a tray with two delicious pies resting on it. Celia must have been near the door, because it opened almost as soon as Rosalee knocked.

"Rosalee!" Celia said, delight in her voice and a big smile on her face. "How are you?"

"I'm doing well," Rosalee said, returning the smile. "I was just in the mood to bake this morning, but the Lord knows I don't need baked goods lying around my house." She held out the tray slightly. "So I brought you some pies."

"Oooohhh," Celia said. "Those look amazing. Please come in and have a piece with me; I just started a pot of coffee, and Aislin just went down for her nap. Perfect timing."

"That sounds lovely," Rosalee responded. She followed Celia into the house, through the hall and back to the kitchen. The Blairs' house was laid out similarly to her own, although they had knocked out part of the wall between the hallway and kitchen, and then again between the hallway and the living room. It didn't quite create an open floor plan like you find in newer homes, but it was definitely a more spacious look.

"Have you painted recently?" Rosalee asked as she set her tray down on the kitchen table and looked around at the sage-green walls.

"Just last weekend," Celia said as she pulled down two dessert plates and two coffee mugs from a glass-front cabinet. "I was originally going to go with yellow—I've always wanted a yellow kitchen—but I saw this color and just fell in love. Plus, it goes with my dishes really well." She gestured to the chocolate-brown-and cream-colored pottery dishes.

"I love it," Rosalee said. "Makes me think of a garden in springtime."

"That's what Levi said," Celia replied as she opened a drawer. She pulled out two forks, a pie server, and two tiny teaspoons for the coffee. The sugar bowl was already sitting on the table, and she turned toward the refrigerator. "Do you like milk or cream in your coffee, Rosalee?" she asked, hand on the door. "I have 2% milk or half-and-half."

"A little half-and-half would be lovely," Rosalee answered, pulling out a chair at the table and sitting down.

Celia set the half-and-half on the table then went to check the coffee. "Excellent," she said, flipping the power switch and pulling out the insulated carafe. She poured Rosalee a cupful, then filled her own mug before setting the carafe on the table and sitting down in one of the kitchen chairs, pulling one of her jeans-clad legs up underneath her.

"So," she said picking up the pie server. "Which kind would you like? I, myself, plan on having a little slice of both, so don't be shy." Her brown eyes twinkled.

Rosalee laughed. "A piece of each sounds perfect. Clearly I couldn't make up my mind even when I was baking them!"

As Celia served them their slices of pie, Rosalee asked about the children and about Celia's husband Levi's job. Levi was the lead mechanic at the best repair shop in town. It was actually how Rosalee had gotten to know the Blairs. Tripp was about three when they'd moved in next door. Rosalee remembers looking out her kitchen window as Celia and Levi and a group of young people had carried in the loads of boxes and furniture from the moving truck, trying the whole time not to trip over and crush the little blur of energy running around the front yard. As she'd been taught, Rosalee had put together a casserole and carried it over that evening to meet her new neighbors.

Normally Tommy came with her, but he'd been bedridden by that time, and she'd made the short walk across the yard by herself while he watched *Jeopardy!*. The Blairs had been friendly and pleasant, and they'd all chatted a few minutes on the deep front porch. Tripp had eagerly shown her his seashell collection that he'd just unpacked, and told her that he was starting preschool next week and she should come with him.

Rosalee had smiled at his enthusiasm, thanked him sincerely but told him that she needed to stay home to take care of her husband, Mr. McDonnell.

"Why?" Tripp had asked with the frankness of youth.

"Tripp," Celia had sighed. "It's not really any of your business. I'm sorry, Mrs. McDonnell."

"Oh, it's fine," Rosalee said with a smile. "We're neighbors after all. Makes sense that we'd know each other a little. She'd turned toward the boy. "Mr. McDonnell is very sick with cancer. It makes him tired and hurt a lot. And he can't move around very well anymore. So I take care of him."

Tripp nodded. "Oh," he said. "That's very nice of you."

Rosalee smiled, "Well, he's my husband and I love him very much."

She'd soon said goodbye. The sun was going down and the Blairs' had had a long day. Rosalee hadn't really seen them again except in passing until a few weeks later when she'd gone out to get the car started to take Tommy to the doctor and it wouldn't start. She'd been trying for several minutes and had finally gotten out of the car, frustrated. She was standing in the driveway, hands on her hips and staring at the car, trying to decide which of her children to bother with a phone call when she'd heard someone walking toward her.

"Mrs. McDonnell?" a male voice said.

Rosalee turned to see Levi standing behind her. "Rosalee," she'd corrected automatically. "Hello, Levi, how are you."

"Well, I'm fine," he'd said, smiling. "But are you okay? I noticed you've been standing out here for a while."

"Oh," Rosalee had blushed slightly. "Well, the car won't start and Tommy's got an appointment this morning. I'm just trying to figure out who to call."

"Why don't you let me take a look," Levi said. He set a small cooler down on the driveway, pocketed his own keys, and walked toward Rosalee's old Buick. "Just pop the hood for me and try to crank it again."

Fifteen minutes later, Rosalee was waving as Levi pulled his truck out of the driveway, her own car humming away. She had a business card in her other hand, Certified Car Care printed in clear block letters on its front. Levi had told her that's where he worked, and if she ever had any car problems and Levi wasn't home, she should just call him at work and he'd take care of things for her. Such a nice young man, Rosalee thought. She knew he was probably going to be late to work for stopping to help her. But it meant the world to her that he'd done that small kindness for her. And it strengthened her heart to know that God had blessed her with kind neighbors.

"So how are the grandkids?" Celia's question brought Rosalee back into the present.

"Perfect, of course," Rosalee broke off another bite of pie with her fork as she elaborated, talking about Corbin's college classes and his new girlfriend, Jessica's excitement to be back in school, Austin's first girlfriend, Chris' latest backpacking adventure with his Boy Scout Troop, and Keira's latest dance recital. Celia mentioned she'd been thinking of putting Aislinn in dance, but just couldn't find a class that fit her schedule.

"It's such a balancing act," she said, standing up to top off her coffee mug for the third time, then sitting back at the big farm table. "I mean, we've already got school and homework, Boy Scouts on Tuesdays, Bible study on Wednesdays, and guitar lessons on Thursdays after school. Tripp really wants to play basketball this year, but we've always had a one-thing-at-a-time policy." She shook her head, her brown ponytail swaying slightly. "I want the kids to have things they enjoy doing, but I want to have time for…spontaneity, you know? And down time—playing and exploring and reading and just being together. I don't want to teach my kids that being harried and busy and overscheduled is the norm, you know?"

Rosalee nodded, thinking back to when her own kids were young and in school. She didn't know if there just weren't as many options, not as much homework, or she'd just forgotten how busy they were. "You'll figure it out," she assured Celia, smiling and patting her hand. She'd just opened her mouth to ask Celia how Tripp was enjoying his guitar lessons when they heard a soft sound from the hallway. Rosalee looked up to see a small, dark-haired person coming down the hallway dragging a faded orange blanket.

"Hey, sweet girl," Celia said, reaching out her arms to Aislinn as she walked closer and pulling her up in her lap. "Did you have a good nap?"

Rosalee looked up at the retro diner clock hanging next the refrigerator. "Oh, my!" she said. "I can't believe I've taken up so much of your time."

"Whatever," Celia said with a smile. "I've enjoyed every minute of your visit. And since you're already here, do you want to stay for lunch?"

"Oh, I shouldn't," Rosalee replied, although secretly she was really enjoying the company.

"No, you should stay." Celia turned to Aislinn and asked the two-year-old what they should have for lunch. The verdict was grilled cheese sandwiches and tomato soup. Celia declared that they needed music while fixing lunch, and she put an iPod into a set of small speakers sitting on the kitchen counter.

"Any requests?" she asked.

"Marley!" Aislinn said from her spot at the table, waving her purple crayon for emphasis.

Celia grinned at Rosalee's puzzled expression. "Bob Marley," Celia clarified. "The reggae singer? Some friends of ours got the kids a Bob Marley CD one year for Christmas as a kind of joke, and they actually really love it."

Rosalee shrugged and smiled. "I'm game. I'm fairly certain none of my kids or grandkids has gone through a reggae phase, but it's always good to try new things."

The cheerful music made its way through the kitchen as Celia and Rosalee put together the simple lunch and Aislinn colored at the table. Rosalee smiled to herself as she whisked the soup in the saucepan on the stove. What an unexpected afternoon! Rosalee had become a creature of habit, she knew. She wasn't sure if she'd always been that way—no doubt when the children were small, routine had been a big part of their lives—but she knew for sure that life had developed a distinct pattern during the years Tommy was sick. Of course, now that pattern was different, but still. Every day was essentially a variation of the same theme: eat, walk the dog, work in her garden, work at the library, spend time with her family. Read, watch TV, take care of errands. She'd become quite the broken record. It had never really bothered her before, so what was it about spending the morning with her neighbor that had made her suddenly feel so amazing? Like walking into room and opening the blinds, finally noticing how dusty everything was.

Lunch was a delight, and after helping clean up, Rosalee finally made her way home, empty handed during her return trip, as she'd left the pies for the Blairs to continue to enjoy. Billy wagged his tail and woofed once when she walked in the door, which, in Billy-speak was the equivalent to jumping up and down in a frenzy. She ran a hand over his head as she snapped the leash on his collar.

"How about a walk, boy?" she asked. Billy didn't seem too perturbed at having missed his morning walk, but he was definitely excited to head out the door. It was funny how different her usual neighborhood route was at this time of day. In some ways quieter—no one heading off for work or school, just the occasional car. As she approached her house at the end of the walk, the school bus came rumbling around the corner. Billy observed the boisterous crowd exiting the bus with his usual placidity.

Rosalee felt particularly invigorated as she watched the kids run home and walked up her own paved walkway. Maybe she should change up her routine more often. Lately she'd been feeling old—she figured it was just normal. After all, she was 63. But really, was 63 all that old? Think of the actresses who were in their 60s—Meryl Streep, Helen Mirren, Glenn Close—all beautiful and vibrant and successful. And wasn't Corbin telling her the other day about his girlfriend's mother who did triathlons? Amazing! Rosalee realized she'd been feeling more and more like someone older than even 63, wrung out and dried up. But today she felt fresh and energetic. Her soul felt young. And she liked it.

chapter 2

June 1973

In 1973 Carlton, Missouri was a small town, and still old-fashioned in that way that Midwestern small towns tend to be. Sure, the outside world came calling in the form of TV and movies and magazines and boys gone off to war, but most people who wanted to experience the big and changing world left and didn't come back all that often. Traditional values still ruled in Carlton, at least for a while yet.

A lot of people thought I was shy, but I think they mistook quiet for shy. I knew that I was a simple country girl, so I tended to observe before acting and speaking, wanting to make sure I said and did the right things. And I didn't see the need to talk for the sake of talking. I was comfortable in my skin, for the most part, and comfortable with my little world. I was happy to stick around Carlton, help my momma, read my books, and hang out with the friends I'd known since we were all in diapers.

George Bowen made quite a splash that summer, mostly because he was new and different and drop-dead gorgeous. He was in town visiting an aunt and uncle, home for the summer from his first year at college. Which, of course, was so glamorous.

His uncle was a local carpenter, so George had come to work for the summer with his uncle. I met him first at the pharmacy candy counter, and pretty much daydreamed about his blue eyes non-stop until I saw him again almost a week later.

I'd come to town with my best friend Betty; I'd finished my work at home helping momma and just wanted to get out of the house. I'd done some mending for one of the neighbors and had a little money, so I thought I might look at a new bracelet or maybe some lipstick. And Betty was always up for a trip to town. She had a crush on the gas station attendant; he was a senior at our school and the star forward of the basketball team. So we headed down the hill to town. Betty beelined for the gas station and started talking to Phillip, so I went across the street to Tom's Drug Store. I was standing in the makeup aisle trying to decide between Cinnamon Delight and Peachy Cream when I felt someone walk up behind me.

"So, do you always hang out in drug stores?" a deep voice said.

I felt my face flush just a little but made myself turn slowly and tried not to look like a naïve country bumpkin awed by the attention of a handsome college man—which, of course, I was.

"You're here, too," I said, raising one eyebrow.

George laughed—it was a great laugh. I felt that laugh all the way in the bottom of my toes. And when he laughed, his eyes sparkled like big, blue diamonds.

"Touché," he said. He leaned shoulder against the wall and smiled at me. "So, Rosalee Barnes. What are you doing at Tom's Drug Store on a Saturday afternoon?"

I held up the tube of Cinnamon Delight. "Buying lipstick." Then I blushed again. I noticed that George was standing less than an arm's length away from me, wearing faded jeans that fit just right and a white t-shirt that looked incredibly soft. He had a plaid shirt on over the t-shirt, unbuttoned and with the sleeves rolled up. He was at least six inches taller than me, lean and muscular. All man, as my momma used to say. And all of a sudden, talking about lipstick made me think about kissing. And I had a thought that George Bowen could probably kiss my socks off.

"And what about you?" I asked, trying to hide the fact that my body temperature had just spiked.

His smile turned sheepish and he held up a packet of cigarettes. I wrinkled my nose but didn't say anything.

"How is business with your uncle?" I asked, hoping to extend our conversation.

"Good," he said with a shrug. "We're busy, if that's what you mean."

"What made you come to stay with them?" I asked.

"Well, Uncle Jim needed some help and I needed a job. I could have found a job in Kansas City, but, you know, they're family. And we get along just fine." George grinned. "Plus, Aunt Ruth is a really good cook."

I smiled back at him.

"Say, what are you doing later?" he asked, standing up straight. "You know…after you buy your lipstick."

Why, do you want to help me test it out? Good grief, where had that thought come from? Now I was staring at his mouth. It was a really nice mouth.

I forced myself to look up at his eyes and shrugged in what I hoped was a casual way. "Not sure," I said. "Betty might come over to listen to records. She got a few new ones last week."

He took a step closer to me. "Do you like pie?" he asked.

"Doesn't everyone?"

"I hear the diner has the best pie in Missouri."

"It's probably true. And their coffee's pretty great, too." Was I sweating? Could he tell I was sweating?

"Sounds like I need to try it. Would you like to go get some pie and coffee with me this evening?"

Is there a word more emphatic than yes? I settled for the yes. I knew my momma would have a few things to say about me going on a date with a near stranger. Part of my brain was already working out my responses to my mother's protests— which included the fact that we'd known Jim and Ruth for ages so George really wasn't a stranger—while the other part made arrangements with George. He'd come to my house at 7:30, and I told him my parents were pretty old fashioned, so he should plan on coming in to meet them. We finished making our plans and I put one of the lipsticks back without even checking to see which one I'd kept. But I knew if I didn't get out of there soon, I was going to collapse into a big puddle. Clean-up in aisle 7.

"See you tonight, George," I said.

He reached out and touched my arm. "See you tonight, Rosalee Barnes."

I floated up to the cash register and set what turned out to be Cinnamon Delight down on the counter.

"Hey, Tommy," I said.

"Hey, Rosalee," Tommy replied, setting his book to the side. He reached for my purchase, glancing behind me as George walked out the door with his already-purchased cigarettes.

Tommy frowned slightly before turning back to me and taking my money. He said something, but I was busy dreaming about my date and missed it.

"I'm sorry," I said with a smile. "My brain is in la-la land. What'd you say?"

"I asked if you heard about the bonfire next week. First cookout of the summer."

"I did, thanks!" I said. "Should be fun. Your dad going to let you off work early?"

"Hope so."

Tommy handed me my change, and I slipped the lipstick into my pocket. "Well, see ya around."

He nodded as I walked out the door and crossed to the gas station. Betty could see my anxiety—I was bouncing on the balls of my feet after all—and wrapped up her conversation with Phillip. We walked home with our heads together, and I told her all about my date with George. She, of course, squealed in all the right places and offered to come over early and help me do my hair and makeup and pick out what I was going to wear.

Momma didn't put up as much of a protest as I expected her to; I think it helped that I'd prepared myself for the worst. She asked if the "young man" was planning to get out of his car be respectful, and I said of course, this wasn't some Ryan O'Neal movie or something. She told me I should warn my father and that he was out in the barn. Daddy just grunted when I told him. His head was deep under the hood of his truck, so I stayed out for a few minutes handing him tools and chatting about the bonfire next week down at the swimming hole, and the new pizza place going in downtown.

I helped Momma with supper but was too nervous to eat more than a piece of cornbread. So I asked to be excused and went to get ready. My younger brothers started teasing me once they found out I was getting ready for a date, but I just waved my hand in their direction and raced to my room. It took me a good hour of trying on clothes to settle on an outfit—jeans and a blue-and-white peasant top with sandals I'd bought with my birthday money. Betty arrived while I was choosing what to wear and she loaned me a bead necklace to go with a pair of big silver hoop earrings. Betty did my makeup—she was always better with that kind of thing—and I used a curling iron to make my hair kind of wavy. I even used my new Cinnamon Delight lipstick. I kept getting more nervous, mostly because Betty kept asking me questions like "What if he wants to share? Do you think he'll sit next to you or across from you? What if he tries to hold your hand? Will you let him put his arm around you? What if he tries to kiss you?"

"Betty!" I said, slapping at her playfully. "You have got to hush. You're making me all nervous. Now just spray me and get on out of here."

She laughed and hit my hair with a blast of Aqua Net. "Have fun tonight."

I rolled my eyes but gave her a quick hug on her way out the door. "Thanks again."

"You're welcome. You look totally hot, so just be prepared!" She laughed again as she waved to my parents and brothers and headed home.

It was 7:20. I picked up the book I'd been reading but couldn't concentrate, so I settled on a copy of Momma's *Better*

Homes and Gardens instead. The doorbell rang right on time, but I let Momma answer it before coming out of my bedroom. George was even better looking than I remembered from just that morning. He was still wearing jeans but had cleaned up his boots and traded his t-shirt and plaid shirt for a blue button-up shirt that made his eyes practically glow. He sat in the living room and made small talk with my parents for a few minutes—how did he like college…what was he studying…how were his parents…My dad finally said, "Well, better get on down to the diner before they run out of chocolate cream. We'll see you by 10:30."

"Yes, sir," George answered.

I grabbed my purse and gave my parents each a quick kiss on the cheek before following George out the door.

I was nervous as George backed out of the driveway, so I distracted myself by asking George about his family. It turns out they used to live in Carlton, but they had moved to Kansas City when George was a baby so his dad could find a better job. Now Mr. Bowen was a manager at a hardware store, and Mrs. Bowen stayed home with George's younger sister. George was the first in his family to go to college, something you could see he was proud of.

Before I could ask him anything else, he was parking in front of the diner. My favorite corner booth was empty, so I led him back there and we slid into the booth--across from each other, for the record.

Peggy Wilson—a friend of my momma's I'd known my whole life—gave me a wink as she took our order for two coffees and two slices of chocolate pie. I resisted the urge to roll my eyes and turned back to George instead. Again I was struck by just how comfortable George looked. He looked like he belonged in that red vinyl booth, his body turned slightly so that his back rested against the glossy white wall, his head just below the black-and-white photograph of Carlton's Main Street that hung on the diner walls. His right arm rested on the black formica table, his long, strong-looking fingers curled lightly around the white coffee mug, and his other arm stretched along the back of the low booth. But he'd also looked like he belonged in my parents' living room, sitting on the plaid sofa surrounded by family photos and hand-made doilies. I wondered if it had something to do with the fact that he was good looking. He was undoubtedly one of the best-looking people I'd ever met, but it seemed to me that beautiful people were more confident and sure of themselves. George wasn't cocky, but he could have been.

"So, what are you studying in college?" I asked.

"Well," he said, "this first year I'm just taking general classes. Algebra, English composition, Philosophy 101…that kind of thing. I don't have to pick a course of study until next year, but I think I'm going to study accounting. I like numbers, and it will give me a lot of options for work."

He grinned, flashing his dimple. "I like the idea of making money, you know? Not worrying about it."

I smiled back. "Who doesn't?"

Peggy walked by then, setting our slices of pie on the table and topping off our coffee.

"What about you?" he asked after we'd each taken a bite of our creamy desserts. "You planning to head to college?"

I shrugged. "I'm not sure. It's a lot of money, and I don't really know right now what I'd study. I might just get a job, work for a while, see what happens."

I took another bite of pie, my fingers gripping my fork a little too hard.

George nodded. "That's cool," he said. "Never hurts to give yourself time to figure your life out, that's for sure."

My grip on the fork relaxed. I'd only left sleepy, old-fashioned little Carlton a few times in my life, and George was not only from a big city but had been to college, too. I'd been worried that I'd see condescension in his eyes, but he'd surprised me. I leaned forward a little, my dark hair falling over my shoulder.

"You know what I'd really like to do?" I asked.

George shook his head and smiled at me over his coffee mug.

"I'd really like to get a job, save my money, then travel."

George raised his eyebrows. "Oh, yeah? Where do you want to go?"

"Anywhere!" I said with a laugh. "Everywhere! I'd love to get in the car and take a road trip to the East Coast, or head west and hike in the Rockies and see the redwood forests. Or go to Europe and sit in cafes and tour cathedrals and castles. Or walk on the Great Wall of China…" I laughed again, blushing a little. "Sorry, I got a little carried away. I just…I think that's what I'd love to do more than go to college."

In my excitement and enthusiasm, I'd pressed my hands into the top of the table and George reached his own across the black Formica and rested it gently on one of my own. "I think that sounds pretty amazing," he said. "You should do it. Save your money and go."

"But where should I go first?" I asked, slightly breathless.

His midnight eyes crinkled, and my heart and stomach and

all the rest of my insides clenched. "Now that's a good question," George said, drawing his vowels out. "Not to be taken lightly. And since you need to be home in 20 minutes, I'm thinking we should figure it out over another cup of coffee. Maybe in a couple of days?"

I glanced at the black-and-white cat clock hanging behind the cash register and was surprised to see that George was right about the time. I took one last sip of coffee and thought about my schedule for the week—predictable and boring—and what Mom and Dad might say about me going on another date just a few days after my first one.

"Sure," I said, smiling what I hoped was a casual smile, like I did this kind of thing all the time. "I'm babysitting Tuesday evening until about 7, so maybe we could meet here after that?"

George pulled his arm off the back of the booth and nodded, draining the last of his coffee before replying. "Sounds good," he said. "You want me to pick you up from babysitting?"

"Oh, no, I'll have the car," I said. "But thanks."

He slid out of the booth and held out his hand. I thought about good girls and fast girls and Betty and my mom and then mentally kicked myself and my overthinking. I slid toward the edge of the booth and placed my—thankfully not sweaty—hand in his. He smiled again as I stood up, and we walked out to his car.

chapter 3

October 2018

Despite her revelations and spontaneous determination to mix things up in her life, the rest of Rosalee's week went pretty much according to schedule. Although Justine, one of her co-workers at the library, asked her if she'd changed her hair, the standard question when someone seemed different and you just couldn't quite put your finger on it. And on Friday, Rosalee called her granddaughter Jessica to talk about changing their usual Friday night plans.

"What do you think about going out for a change?" Rosalee asked.

"Going out?" Jessica sounded surprised but not opposed to the idea.

"Sure. We could go see a movie in the theater or something. Maybe grab dinner if you want."

"Are you sure?" Jessica asked. "I bought some new foot scrub for pedicures."

"Jessica," Rosalee said. "The only thing I care about is having a Friday night date with my granddaughter. The details are really irrelevant. And I enjoy going out. I do it periodically, you know."

"Oh, I didn't mean anything by it," Jessica said, with a laugh.

"It just surprised me, that's all. I don't remember the last time we changed up Friday nights. But yeah, that sounds great. Let me get online real quick and see what's playing."

They ended up deciding on a romantic comedy that had just come out, and breakfast-for-dinner at a diner just a few blocks from the theater.

"You know," Rosalee said as she dug into her French toast after the movie. "I've always loved going to a diner. It reminds me of being a teenager."

"Did Grandpa take you to a diner when you dated?" Jessica asked, eating another forkful of pancakes.

"Actually, yes," Rosalee said, "But the first time I ever went on a date to a diner was with a boy named George Bowen. I met him at your great-grandpa's store. I was picking out some lipstick and he was…well, I guess you would say he was trying to pick me up. At the very least he was certainly flirting with me."

Jessica smiled. "And what did you do?"

Rosalee shook her head and smiled. "What do you think? I went out with him, of course! The only other boy who'd ever asked me out was Charles Martin, and that was to a basketball game at the school. George was very comfortable with himself and girls, and I was easily flattered."

"So, a hot summer fling," Jessica said, her mouth quirking as she took a sip of coffee. "Who knew, Gram? And all these years, you had us believing you were some kind of country mouse."

"Oh, let me assure you," Rosalee said, "I was. He was bored and, like I said, he was good looking and interested in me—and absolutely exotic and interesting compared to all the boys I'd grown up with."

As she spoke, Rosalee picked up the check and glanced at the big old silver watch of Tommy's that she'd never gotten rid of, pulling her wallet out of her purse. Jessica started to ask some more questions about what she was already referring to in her mind as "The Summer of George," but a sadness had crept into Rosalee's eyes, and Jessica kept her questions to herself.

"You ready to head home?" Jessica asked the obvious question.

"Time to get this old lady to bed," Rosalee said, as she placed her cash on the table.

"Grandma!" Jessica exclaimed. "You are not old."

"Well, some days it sure feels like it, sweetie."

Rosalee hummed to herself as she watered the flowers on her front porch the next morning. She was wearing a sweater against the morning chill, but the bright sunshine promised another lovely day. Perfect for a Saturday soccer game. Both of her youngest grandkids played in a community soccer league, and most of their games were on Saturdays.

"Hi!"

Rosalee started slightly—she'd been lost in thought and hadn't heard Tripp run up. But she smiled down at her cheerful little neighbor.

"Well, hello," she said, setting down her watering jug.

"Momma wants to ask you to babysit," Tripp said as he bounced up and down between the ground and the bottom porch step.

"Sorry, Rosalee," Celia said, rounding the corner with a toddling Aislinn in front of her. "He's a little too fast for me and his little sister."

Rosalee waved a hand. "Nothing to be sorry about. What's this about babysitting?"

"Well, Levi and I had made plans to meet a few friends for supper tonight, but our babysitter is sick. I know it's last minute, but I wondered if you'd be up for watching the kids? They both go to bed pretty early, and we won't be gone long at any rate."

Rosalee rested a hand on her hip and glanced down at Tripp, who had graduated to hopping up two steps and back down again. "I think that would be fine," she said. "What time? I'm headed out to a couple of soccer games, but that's all I've really got going on today."

Celia's face lit up. "Perfect!" she said. "We're not meeting them until 7:30. Would you be all right to come over around 7:00? I can show you where things are and everything. Explain the remote controls." She rolled her eyes, but grinned.

"Oh, that sounds fine," she said.

"Yay!" Tripp took a flying leap off the third porch step. "Can we go to the park now, Momma?" He took off toward his own driveway before waiting for a response. Rosalee laughed as Celia once again rolled her eyes and picked up Aislinn.

"I'm sorry," she said again. "I'll run all his energy out at the park, I promise."

Rosalee waved her on with a smile and finished watering her mums and asters and ferns. She made a mental note to drag the ferns back into the house before babysitting. She'd pulled them out to enjoy the sunshiny day but knew the overnight air would get too cold for them. After she emptied her watering can on the last plant, Rosalee paused before walking around to the utility room door and sat on the top porch step. Billy trotted over from his sunny spot in the driveway and sat next to her, nudging for an ear scratch. Rosalee obliged.

She glanced around the sunny Saturday street and smiled. She could hear laughter from a few doors down and saw a couple of school-aged boys tossing a football in their lawn. Two bicycles raced down the street in front of her, and a dog barked in the distance. She loved this street. Loved her neighborhood. It wasn't fancy, but it was homey and settled and...okay, she'd admit it... almost clichéd in its Americana. She'd been around long enough to know that there was probably some real hardship happening behind the painted wooden doors that lined the block, but she also knew that in some homes there was real love and hope and happiness, too. Like the Blairs. And the Tanners who lived across the street. And, yes, even in her house, too. Rosalee smiled and took a deep breath, enjoying the smell of fall air and this sense of contentment she was feeling.

"Come on, Billy," she said, patting the dog's shoulder. "I've got to get ready to go watch some soccer."

She walked around the side of her house, Billy behind her. She'd just set her watering can down inside the sink in her utility room when she heard the phone ring.

"Hello?" she said.

"Hi, Mom," Elizabeth answered. As usual, she sounded slightly distracted. Rosalee smiled, knowing Elizabeth was probably doing about 10 things at once. God knows she got that kind of energy and drive from her father.

"Hi, dear," Rosalee said. "Are you coming out to the soccer games today?"

"We are. That's why I'm calling. I'm putting some chili in the crockpot, and I thought you could come over after and eat with us."

"Oh, that sounds nice," Rosalee said, "and normally you know I would, but I'm actually babysitting tonight."

"Babysitting?" she couldn't see her stop everything, but Elizabeth's voice certainly took on a stop-everything kind of tone. The full energy of her attention was now on Rosalee. "Who on earth are you babysitting?"

"The neighbors." Rosalee walked to the counter and selected an apple from the wooden fruit bowl. Only two more left, and no bananas, she thought. Time to go to the grocery store.

"Mother, are you listening?" Elizabeth's voice finally penetrated Rosalee's fruit thoughts.

"Sorry, honey, I was thinking about grocery shopping."

Rosalee thought they could probably hear Elizabeth's patented Mother-you're-so-exasperating sigh all the way down the street.

"I asked why you're babysitting the neighbors. Is this a good idea? How old are they?"

"Their babysitter got sick, they are very nice neighbors, it's a great idea, and they are eight and two years old."

"Hmm," Rosalee could hear Elizabeth getting back to putting her chili together. "Well, I guess next time, then. See you in a bit. I'm bringing snacks."

"Bye."

Rosalee chuckled as she turned off her phone and pulled out a paring knife to slice the apple. Elizabeth was all energy and opinion and had been since she'd discovered her vocal chords... so essentially the day she was born. Rosalee had never understood exhaustion until after she'd given birth to Elizabeth. Fortunately, Charles had been more laid back. Then again, what chance did he have with a big sister like Elizabeth?

Several hours later, Rosalee knocked on the Blairs' front door and was greeted by a bouncing Tripp. "Hi!" he said. "I answered the door because I could see it was you through the window. I'm not supposed to answer the door if it's a stranger."

"Good plan," Rosalee said with a nod of her head. She stepped inside and closed the door behind her.

"Momma said we can watch a movie after Aislinn goes to bed if you want to. She said I can pick and we can have popcorn and chocolate milk and *eat it in the living room*."

Rosalee clapped her hands and smiled. "That sounds perfect."

Tripp raced off shouting "Momma! Daddy! Mrs. McDonnell is here!"

Rosalee smiled and chuckled to herself. She barely remembered when her kids went through the running-and-shouting-everywhere stage. Of course, grandkids were a different story. One could argue—especially after the afternoon's games—that a few of them were still in that stage. But it was fun. Much more fun than the I'm-too-cool-for-anyone-and-anything stage. Fortunately, even if a couple of her grandkids were in that stage, they were never too cool for Gramma.

Celia followed the unmistakable sound of a wooden spoon on a pot, and met Celia just as she turned the corner into the kitchen.

"Hi!" she said with a bright smile. "I've got sandwiches and fruit all ready for the kids. And I heard Tripp fill you in on the evening snack plans."

"Indeed," Rosalee nodded with her own smile.

"Aislinn will go to bed in about an hour. Here, let me show you her bedtime stuff."

Celia walked Rosalee back to the bedrooms and pointed out diapers and pajamas and books and the bedtime lovey.

"Tripp can do all his bedtime stuff himself if you just point him in the right direction and get him going. Teeth, pj's, toilet, the usual." She laughed and touched Rosalee's arm. "You have children and grandkids—I'm sure you know the drill."

"Well, everyone's got their own routine."

Levi stepped out into the hall from his and Celia's bedroom, fastening on a watch. Rosalee assured them she and the kids would be fine. Celia took a few more minutes before they left to point out the emergency numbers and to remind Tripp to be helpful and sweet.

Several hours later, both children were tucked into bed after blocks and cars and books and the promised popcorn and a movie. Rosalee rinsed the children's supper dishes and put them in the dishwasher, then sat down on the living room couch and picked up the magazine she'd tucked in her purse. She took a deep, contented breath, but her magazine sat unopened on her lap. What a sweet family. She hoped that Celia and Levi were enjoying their night out. She'd always loved being able to watch her grandkids so her own children could have date nights. Although she didn't get to do that as much once Tommy had gotten so sick. He always told her to just leave him at home and he'd be fine for a few hours. But it was hard.

A pewter-framed photograph on the fireplace mantel caught Rosalee's eye. It was a picture of Celia and Levi standing by a beat-up pickup truck. Well, Levi was standing next to it, and Celia was perched on the hood in ripped jeans and a bright red tank top. Levi was leaning a bit toward her, his arm wrapped around her waist, his eyes shaded by a ratty Kansas City Royals baseball cap. Rosalee could tell that Celia was laughing at something; from the mischievous grin on Levi's face, it was probably something he'd done or said.

Rosalee smiled. From what she remembered of boys, he'd probably done or said something mildly shocking or scandalous just for that express purpose of getting Celia to laugh like that. Tommy hadn't done that much—he'd always been slightly more serious…and kind, thoughtful, and stubborn, too. But he definitely had a sense of humor, and sometimes she thought his seriousness made him that much funnier because his humor seemed to come out of nowhere.

Rosalee smiled at the photo, and the thought of Tommy… then sighed. She'd be the first to admit that toward the end— when he'd been so sick and caregiving had become her life— it was almost a relief when he'd finally passed on. Oh, she felt plenty of guilt at that thought, and it certainly made her grief that much more intense. She'd finally blurted the thought out guiltily at knitting club one day when one of the ladies had asked her how she was doing. Instead of appalled faces, her comment had been met with nothing but sympathy. They all knew. They knew how many months of knitting club she'd missed and how many sleepless nights she'd had. A few of them had lived through a similar situation themselves. Sara had reached over and taken her hand.

"Honey," she'd said. "We all know you're not happy to have lost your husband. Because you lost him before he died. You've been through part of that grief already. And as much as you hated seeing him in pain and not himself, don't you think he hated those bags under your eyes? Don't you think he hated the fact that he was no longer your husband but your patient? It's okay, Rosalee. It's okay to be sad, and it's okay to move on. To take a breath. To rest and be thankful for that rest."

It'd been exactly what she needed to hear. After that, she'd allowed herself to let go of Tommy the patient and remember Tommy her husband and best friend. She'd let herself enjoy being her own woman again, creating her own schedule and getting up when she wanted, not when Tommy needed to be fed or moved or given more medicine. For a while, she even enjoyed being alone. Of course, that had worn off. Conveniently, Jessica was taking a year before college to work and really wanted to get out of her parents' house. So she'd come to live with Rosalee and keep her company. By the time she'd moved out, Rosalee had gotten used to being alone again. She could ignore the loneliness most of the time. Until lately, it seemed.

Rosalee shook her head. So what if she was feeling lonely. It would do her no good to dwell on it. She reached over to the coffee table and picked up the television remote control and turned it on just for a little noise—she didn't see a stereo anywhere, just one of those mp3 speaker things. She found what appeared to be the public television station playing a Ken Burns documentary that she'd already seen and turned the volume high enough to hear but low enough that it was more in the background. She picked up her magazine again, turning to an article on herb gardens. Hmm…maybe she should try her hand at growing some herbs next spring. A few easy vegetables. It'd been forever since she'd grown anything more than perennial flowers. Rosalee smiled and settled back against the pillows.

chapter 4

June 1973

The phone was ringing when I walked in the door. Momma was in the garden, Dad wasn't home from work yet, and I figured the boys were out in the woods, so I threw my keys on the hall table and hurried to the kitchen, hoping it hadn't been ringing long. And hoping that a certain blue-eyed someone was on the other end.

"Hello," I said, breathless.

"Hey there."

My skin tingled. "Hey," I said, still breathless, but not from the sprint. "What's up?"

"I'm taking a smoke break. What are you up to?"

I set my purse on the kitchen table and leaned one hip against it.

"Just got home from the Wallace's."

"The who?" I heard him take a deep breath, and could picture him sitting on Jim and Ruth's back porch with his cigarette in his mouth and the phone cord stretched as far as it would reach.

"The Wallaces. My standard summer gig. Mr. Wallace manages the gas station and Mrs. Wallace works part time doing filing at the doctor's office, so they need someone to watch their kids in the mornings during the summer."

"Sounds fun."

I couldn't quite tell if he was mocking me, but I chose to believe he was making genuine conversation.

"It is. They're good kids, so it feels like easy money." I wound the long phone cord around my finger.

"Saving up for your around-the-world ticket."

I laughed. "You know it."

We chatted for another minute, then George said he had to get back to work. He asked if I was busy after supper.

"Nope," I said. "Want to do something?" My hands felt shaky as I said this, completely shocking myself with the bold words coming out of my mouth. Betty would be proud—my mother would be horrified.

"Absolutely," he said. "Want to just head to the diner for some coffee."

"And pie?"

"Goes without saying."

I laughed again. George said he'd pick me up at 8 p.m. I think I managed to keep my cool long enough for us both to hang up the phone. But then I proceeded to dance and leap around the kitchen, pumping my arms in the air. I called Betty. She squealed, excited as only a best friend can be, and we discussed what I should wear and all the reasons George was so hot. She told me about the latest sweet thing Phillip said to her, and I took my turn listening. We'd been talking for a while when my mom came in, her face shaded with her big straw hat. She'd left her gardening gloves in the mudroom, but she still had a few smears of dirt on her face and arms.

"Hi, sweetheart," she said, smiling. She pulled a glass from the cabinet and filled it with water. "How was your morning?"

"Great," I said. "We went to the library and the pool for a bit." I leaned against the counter and pulled an apple from the fruit bowl. "I'm going to go get coffee with George tonight," I said.

She raised one eyebrow at me and just stared. I caved.

"If that's all right with you," I said. Mom was old fashioned, and I found it was better to just roll with it. Fighting Mom just made her dig in.

"Of course," she said, proving my point. "You'll be home for supper then?"

"Yeah," I said. "He's coming by at 8 p.m."

I went upstairs to tear apart my closet before it was time to help mom fix supper. I was pretty distracted all evening, and I know mom picked up on it. Daddy may have noticed, but he tended to ignore my "moods," even though I'm pretty sure I didn't have all that many. I tried to eat, but only managed a few bites of potatoes and half a glass of milk before I was nervously tapping my finger on the table and trying to join in on the dinner conversation. Even with the talking—the boys were full of stories today—I could hear the kitchen clock ticking, like a countdown in my head. Once everyone else was done eating, Mom was quick to remind the boys that it was their turn to wash dishes. They were still groaning and making a racket when I gave mom a quick kiss on the cheek of thanks and tore up the stairs to get ready.

This time, I was trying to go for a casual "I-didn't-really-try" cool-girl look. I settled on my favorite jeans, a Willie Nelson t-shirt, and my red espadrilles. I freshened up my hair and makeup with a quick go at the curling iron and a little more mascara and lipgloss. Mom would probably shake her head at my date attire, but she still thought it was a shame people didn't still leave the house wearing gloves and a hat. I'd just grabbed my purse when the doorbell rang. I took a deep breath and grinned. There was a crazy good-looking guy downstairs. A college guy. A smart guy. And he was waiting for me.

When I got downstairs, George was sitting and talking with my dad and brothers about the St. Louis Cardinals. My mom wasn't around, but I could hear her knocking around in the kitchen. I walked into the living room and stood by the door, waiting for Dad to finish his comments on the Cardinals pitching staff.

"Ready?" I asked, as soon as there was a pause in the conversation.

"If you are," he said with a smile, standing up off the plaid couch.

"You guys have fun," Dad said, standing up to shake George's hand. "See you at 10:30."

"Sure thing, Dad," I said, giving him a quick kiss on the cheek. "Bye, Mom!" I hollered toward the back of the house.

It was a perfect hazy and purple late June evening, the air cooling as the sun set. Fireflies were winking under the oak trees and over the vegetable garden, and I could hear frogs singing in our neighbor's pond. I took a deep breath as I walked to George's car, smelling the heavy scents of the lilac bushes by the front porch and the honeysuckle that ran along the back fence. We drove the short distance to the diner with the windows down, talking idly about music and our favorite radio stations. There wasn't much to choose from in Carlton. We only picked up a few Springfield stations and one AM Christian station run out of the basement of the Baptist church. I confessed that I liked the country station best.

"Ah," George said, grinning and flashing his dimple at me. "So you're a country girl. Boots and broken hearts and all that."

I shrugged. "Might as well stay true to my roots, right?" I said.

"Never pegged you for a rhinestone girl," he said.

"Well, I prefer the more folksy stuff—banjos and mandolins and haunting harmonies."

"Oh, you mean hippie music."

I smacked his arm but laughed at the same time. "Come on, it's good stuff! And you have to admit, folk and country music have some of the best songwriters around. I mean…some of those songs really tell a story, you know?"

George shrugged. "I'll have to take your word for it. I'm more of a rock-and-roll guy."

"Well," I said. "Challenge accepted."

George raised his eyebrows. "I'm ready," he said.

He pulled into the parking lot at the diner, and I thought about how much FUN it was to talk with George. I'd mentioned that to Betty when I'd called her earlier today, and she laughed over the phone.

"It's called flirting, you goose."

I thought about that as we slid into the corner booth we'd sat in last weekend and wondered if Betty was right. I guess I'd never really flirted before. I'd known most of the boys in Carlton since we were in grade school. When I talked to my friends and acquaintances who were boys, it was just relaxed and easy conversation—but nothing to write home about. Not memorable. But with George…I felt fully engaged in the conversation. He made me feel funny and interesting and witty. Was that flirting? From the outside, when I'd watched other girls flirt, it had seemed either fake or forced or like at least someone involved was nervous. I didn't feel at all nervous with George. Well, maybe a little.

"Coffee?" Peggy walked up with her glass pot and winked at me.

"Yes, please." We turned our cups over on their saucers.

"Anything to eat?" she asked as she poured the steamy, fragrant drink into our cups.

"I'd like a slice of lemon meringue pie," George said. He looked at me and smiled. "Rosalee?"

"Umm…any strawberry pie today?"

"Sure thing, honey." She walked off to get our pies and we looked at each other. We picked up our conversation about music. I told him about some of my favorite musicians, and he told me about concerts he'd been to. I asked him if he worked on Saturdays, and when he said no, I invited him to come over Saturday afternoon to let me expand his musical education. Our conversation moved on to more stories of his year at college. He told me about some of his classes, and how everyone wanted to philosophize during class discussions.

"So far," he said, swallowing a bite of his pie. "I've managed to avoid it in my algebra class. But one of my buddies says stay out of any of the advanced math classes, because a lot of them get into theory too…which, of course, leads to some joker wanting to talk about the meaning of life or something. Or you know… Vietnam."

We were both quiet. Talk of Vietnam had a tendency to halt

any conversation because everyone either had an opinion or a story or both—it was part of everyone's life. I thought about what to say to fill this particular silence. I didn't want to blow off the serious topic if it was something he wanted to talk about, but I didn't want to push it either.

"I think people in general just like to hear themselves talk," George said eventually. "Especially in college. Everyone thinks their ideas are the most important."

I tilted my head. "And do you enjoy big deep college discussions?"

He shrugged. "Not really. I'm there to learn and get a degree that will help me get a good job."

"Smart."

He grinned and leaned across the table, lowering his voice. "Well…I'm also there to…socialize."

I mirrored his movement and lowered my own voice. "You mean…party?" I asked with my own grin.

He laughed this time. "You know, Rosalee, I can't quite figure you out, but I like it. We should definitely keep hanging out."

Would he still say that if he knew that half of it was pure bravado, that I was forcing myself to act relaxed and nonchalant and…well, cool?

"You know, it's all an act." Did I just say that?!

He raised an eyebrow and stretched his arms across the back of the booth.

"What do you mean?" he replied, a smile playing at the corners of his mouth.

"This…casualness." I waved my hand in the air as though I were trying to illustrate the word. "I'm not experienced with guys."

Again, why was I playing true confession again? Did I WANT him to stop hanging out with me? I picked up my coffee spoon and put it back down again, my eyes focused on a crumb from my pie.

"Rosalee," George said, reaching out and touching my hand briefly, causing me look up. He was smiling, but in a friendly way. Not mocking, like I was afraid it might be.

"Don't worry," he said. "You're not interviewing for a job here. No experience necessary."

I laughed.

"You're pretty, and funny, and I was intrigued by the wholesome small-town girl vibe you've got going on."

Was that a compliment?

He put his hand on mine again, lightly, "I'm still intrigued because, like I said, I can't fit you in a neat little box. I like talking to you. You have real conversations and actually share your real opinions. You're not fake, and that's pretty awesome. I'm sorry if I made you nervous."

I blushed. "Well...thanks."

He leaned back again, leaving my hand bereft and cold. "Now," he said, shifting the conversation. "We have 45 minutes and unlimited coffee. I need some background before you start subjecting me to this hippie music of yours. Tell me about your top three favorite singers."

I smiled.

chapter 5

October 2018

Rosalee double-checked the cart of books that she had finished putting in order, then glanced at the clock. Thirty minutes until closing, just enough time to get these books shelved. She wheeled the black metal cart from behind the desk and headed to the chapter book section of the children's room at the library. Things were pretty quiet this evening—Mondays often were. Rosalee loved this little library. There were two public libraries in town now, but this was her favorite. It had originally been just a converted old farmhouse. Eventually the town had added on a nice, modern building, but had left the farmhouse. First floor was now a coffee shop, and the second floor housed offices and administrative staff. Sometimes Rosalee would come to work early and treat herself to a pastry and cup of coffee at the coffee shop. Jessica had even worked there for a while in high school.

Caroline, the full-time children's librarian, was laying out material in the corner, prepping for Tuesday's regular story time. That corner of the room was slightly sunken, with three steps leading down to a good-sized, wedge-shaped area with a rocking chair at the point. A pile of pillows sat along one wall. Sometimes the kids pulled them out for story time, and sometimes they'd just pull them out and read for a while when nothing else was going on. A low table lined the other wall, where Caroline or one of the other librarians would set up crafts. Some front-facing bookshelves were built into both walls, providing a place to display books relating to that week's story time theme, or just books the librarians wanted to display and highlight.

Stephanie, one of the other part-time staff, was at the desk in the opposite corner doing some work on the computer. Rosalee was about halfway through shelving her cart when Stephanie looked up from her work and called out.

"Rosalee" she said. "Caroline and I and a few of the reference staff are headed to Brick Oven tonight. It's Beth's birthday. Would you like to join us?"

Rosalee turned toward her. "Well…" she said, her first instinct to politely decline, although she wasn't sure why.

"I know it's last minute," she said, waving her hand. "Beth wasn't sure her sitter could stay late, so we didn't have final plans until this afternoon. If you can't, I understand."

"Actually," Rosalee said, "that sounds great. I'd love to." *After all*, she thought to herself. *What plans do you have? None, that's what. And weren't you just thinking the other day that you had become a hermit?*

She finished shelving her cart of books while the other two began getting everything in order for closing. Twenty minutes later Rosalee was climbing in her car to calls of "See you there!" and pulling out onto the relatively quiet street. She smiled to herself, looking forward to a nice dinner with her co-workers. She made a quick stop on the way at a dollar store, grabbing a cute birthday card and gift bag. At the restaurant, she took a moment in her car to sign the card and put the bag of coffee she'd purchased that day into the gift bag. It'd been an impulse buy— she'd had a thought of giving it to Celia Blair. But she could always buy another bag; she knew Beth liked coffee as well—she always had a mug in her hand—so it worked out nicely.

Rosalee was the last to walk in, but the other ladies were still taking off sweaters and jackets. They'd snagged a table against the wall, much preferable, in Rosalee's opinion, to sitting in the middle of the room. She set her purse down in an empty chair, then dropped her small bag in front of Beth's place. "Happy birthday!" she said, leaning in for a quick hug.

"Oh, thank you!" Beth said, returning the hug. "Rosalee, how sweet. You didn't have to get me anything. This is all so last minute and casual."

Rosalee waved away Beth's protests. "It's not much," she said, smiling. "But I can still hear my mother's voice in my head: 'Rosalee, never go to a party empty-handed.'"

Beth laughed. "My mom says the same thing."

Rosalee moved back down the table a few chairs to her own spot and, after a quick check to make sure the hardwood floors weren't too grimy, slid her purse under her chair. In addition to Rosalee, there were five women of varying ages around the table: Alysia, head of information services; Donna from technical services; Beth and Stephanie from the reference department, and Caroline, one of the children's librarians. Rosalee was pretty sure Donna and Caroline were around her own age, Beth and Stephanie in their mid-to early 40s, and Alysia somewhere between 25 and 35. Rosalee was terrible with ages. She only guessed Beth and

Stephanie's because she knew how old their kids were.

Either way, it was a comfortable group. Everyone except Rosalee had been working at the Woodson Public Library for at least 10 years. Rosalee had only been at the library for a couple of years, but the staff had been more than welcoming. This was the first time she'd ever accepted any offer for out-of-work socializing, though, and she found herself to be a bit nervous. But, as she'd been realizing more and more lately, it'd been a long time since she'd done any kind of non-family related socializing. Which, since she genuinely enjoyed the company of her co-workers, was one reason she'd said yes to the invitation.

Rosalee gave herself a little mental pep talk and picked up her menu, glancing around the restaurant as she did. She'd never been to Brick Oven before, although she heard various members of her family talk about it all the time. The décor reminded her a bit of a pub—lots of dark wood, warm light, and high-backed booths. Since the restaurant had the benefit of being a stand-alone building, there were a lot of windows. Rosalee could imagine how bright and cheery it looked in the daytime, but with no less warmth. There was a long bar at one end of the building, and behind the bar you could catch a glimpse of the big, wood-burning pizza ovens.

She glanced down at her menu, then turned to Caroline, who was sitting beside her.

"Have you been here before?" she asked. "What's good?"

"Oh, we come all the time," she said. "My favorite is the caramelized onion, pear, and gorgonzola. My husband's favorite is the barbecue chicken, and my daughter usually sticks with the margarita."

"Hmm," Rosalee mused. "Those all sound delicious."

"You can't really go wrong with anything," Stephanie chimed in from across the table. "It's all pretty outstanding."

Their server arrived a moment later and took drink orders. Rosalee heard Beth ask who was driving her home because she was definitely planning on some birthday drinks. Rosalee laughed along with the rest and joined in the general conversation about wine and beer preferences and which pizza they were all going to order. She and Caroline ended up deciding to split a pizza, and before too long, their waiter had slipped off to place orders and conversation turned to other topics.

"So, Rosalee have you always lived in Riverton?" Caroline asked, taking a sip of her red wine.

"No, my husband and I moved here not too long after we got married. I grew up in Carlton," Rosalee answered.

"No way!" Stephanie exclaimed. "My grandmother's from Carlton. I didn't think anyone else even knew where it was."

Rosalee cocked her head slightly. "Who's your grandmother?" she asked. "I'm sure I know her."

"Susan Mason."

"Mrs. Mason, of course!" Rosalee said, smiling. "She lived two blocks from the pharmacy and always had the most beautiful flowers in her front yard."

"Sounds like Gramma," Stephanie said. "We used to go visit every summer and every Thanksgiving. What a small world!"

"What about you ladies?" Rosalee asked. "Who's from around here?" All but Donna admitted they'd grown up in Missouri, if not in Riverton. Caroline had moved to Riverton with her husband's job. They'd both grown up in California.

Rosalee raised her eyebrows. "That must have been quite a culture shock," she said. She looked at Caroline with new eyes, noting the sleek and expertly colored hair, easy but flawless makeup, and casual but stylish clothing. She could see it clearly—Caroline may not have lived in California for 15 years, but she exuded West Coast.

Caroline laughed, her brown eyes warm. "In some ways, yes," she said. "I'll admit I miss being equidistant from the mountains and the beach. And I don't know that I'll ever get used to Midwestern weather. But Riverton is a great home. I felt welcome the moment we rolled into town, and that's never changed."

Rosalee felt proud of her home state.

"So, what have you all been reading lately?" Stephanie asked, shifting gears.

Caroline's eyes lit up, "I just finished the best book! I've been in a reading slump for weeks, so I took a chance on a recommendation from Kelly and it was perfect! I'd never have picked up this book on my own. I don't usually read romance novels, but Kelly assured me that I would enjoy this one and I absolutely did."

"I love a good romance novel," Donna said from across the table. "Who was the author?"

Caroline mentioned an author Rosalee had never heard of—not too surprising, since she tended to stick to mysteries and historical fiction—but she made a mental note to branch out.

"What did you like about the book?" she asked.

Caroline rested her chin in her hand and thought for a minute. "It was smart," she said. "Smart and funny, but not silly. And the characters seemed very real. I tend to like character-

driven fiction, and this story was as much about the characters as
people as it was about their love story."

Rosalee nodded in understanding. "I try to find those authors
when it comes to mysteries too," she said. "I love a good mystery,
but there needs to be as much character development as there is
plot development. Fortunately, a lot of my favorite authors write
series, so I can usually find something I like."

Donna asked her if she'd read a certain author, and the
women around the table kept up an animated discussion about
books and authors until the pizza arrived. Rosalee breathed
deeply, enjoying the variety of scents coming from the table.
Garlic and tomatoes and savory meat. She smelled the tang of
barbecue sauce from the barbecue chicken pizza that Donna had
ordered, and while Rosalee would have expected it to seem out
of place the scent was delicious —savory and rich. Her stomach
growled, and she laughed.

"I didn't realize I was so hungry," Rosalee said.

The women continued to chat as they pulled slices of hot
pizza from the oversized plates in front of them. The waiter
refilled drinks and took orders for new ones. Rosalee took a bite
of pizza—the crust was thin and crispy, with a charred flavor that
she assumed came from the wood-burning oven it had cooked in.
She had picked simple toppings—tomatoes, prosciutto, spinach,
and fresh mozzarella.

"I think I've been ruined forever," she said after swallowing.
"This is amazing!"

Caroline smiled. "I felt the same way after my first taste of
wood-fired pizza. They've been popular in California for a while.
That may have been the hardest part about moving to Missouri!"

They all laughed, and Rosalee lifted her piece for another bite. She glanced around the table as she chewed, a slight smile on her face. She was so glad that she'd accepted the invitation. Clearly her homebody ways were starting to lose their appeal, because she was having a lot of fun, more fun than she usually had on a Monday night. She was turning her attention to a funny story Beth was telling when she felt someone walk behind her chair and pause.

"Rosalee?" a deep voice asked. "Rosalee Barnes?"

Rosalee froze, her hand halfway to her face, her mouth hanging open. No one had called her Rosalee Barnes in a long time. And she hadn't heard that voice in a very, very long time.

Rosalee set her half-eaten slice of pizza on her plate with a trembling hand and wiped her fingers on the napkin in her lap. She placed the napkin on the table and slid her chair back. She could see the other ladies glancing behind and above her head then back at her, and she could see them wondering why she still hadn't responded, why she was taking so long to say anything.

Her knees felt like jello, and her hands started trembling as she stood up, then turned around. She willed her body to start cooperating, and she cleared her throat before smiling.

"George Bowen, you sure do know how to surprise a person."

The eyes that smiled back at her were exactly the same midnight blue as they'd been in 1973. The smile lines that crinkled in the corners were deeper and more numerous, but Rosalee noted the same straight nose and strong chin, the same confident grin and lopsided dimple, and the thick blonde hair that had turned a beautiful silver. George was dressed casually in dark jeans, brown leather loafers, and a white, button-up shirt with a navy pin stripe and the sleeves rolled up. As she reached out to meet George's outstretched hand with her own, Rosalee also noted that he had clearly been taking care of himself, as he was as trim and fit as he'd been 40 years ago. *Men*, Rosalee thought, instinctively sucking in her 62-year-old-post-child-bearing belly. *The bastards.*

"I can't believe it's actually you," he said, his hand lingering in hers, his whole face lit up with a smile. "I heard your voice and it was like a ghost from the past."

"Ghost…yes, that sounds about right," she kept a smile on her own face but inwardly cringed at her response. Her brain felt like that time she and Betty had gotten her daddy's car stuck in the mud down by the creek. They'd spent 20 minutes spinning those tires.

"So, how long have you lived here in Riverton?" George was asking.

"Over 30 years now," she replied. "How long have you been here?"

The question sounded wrong, and slightly accusatory to her ears, but if George thought so, he didn't let on. He just kept on smiling.

"Three days. I've been living in Chicago and just retired a few weeks ago. I was looking for a change of pace, and here I am."

"Retirement. Wow, that sounds nice." *Brilliant, Rosalee*, she thought to herself. *He's going to think you're getting dementia.*

"Well, I'm still doing contract work for the same company," he said with shrug, "but being an independent contractor is a lot more flexible."

"Mmm…" she said, nodding. "But why here?" She winced as soon as the words left her mouth, but she really did need to know.

George looked like he was holding in a laugh, which made her want to smack him just a little. "It's kind of a long story," he said. "But the short version is that my brother lives less than an hour away, and my daughter is thinking of moving here once she sells her house. So I'm scoping it out for her."

Rosalee's sluggish brain was suddenly aware that she was standing in a crowded restaurant, having an unsettling and highly personal experience. People were weaving around them, and although she could hear that the ladies behind her had continued their conversation, it seemed muted. Like they were talking to give her privacy, but kind of wished they were listening in. She didn't blame them…she'd be curious too.

"Well," she said, "isn't it a small world."

At that moment a family of five appeared to Rosalee's right, clearly needing to get around these two odd people who chose a very in-the-way place to have a conversation.

"Can I call you?" he asked after moving to let the people by. "I'd love to catch up, and aside from the crowd factor it looks like neither of us are free at the moment." He nodded at the table full of her co-workers.

Rosalee hesitated. Why shouldn't he call her? Her too-slow brain fired off a million reasons, starting with "he's a lying liar." But somehow, with the words "I don't think so" poised on her tongue, another part of her realized that particular wound wasn't…so much of a wound anymore. It didn't hurt, it wasn't tender. It was more of a scar really. So the question really was… why not? It'd been a long time since she'd thought about George Bowen, and she found that her overwhelming thought was simply curiosity.

Okay, and, *maybe, perhaps,* a slight flush of warmth, because good grief, that man was still too good looking for his own good.

"Sure," she replied with a hesitant smile. "Any time."

He started to reach out as though to touch her hand or shoulder, but she took a very tiny step back. She may not have been hurt anymore, but she hadn't seen George in decades. She wasn't ready for that easy familiarity. He must have read her signals, because he quickly dropped his hand and settled for another heart-stopping smile.

"Great," he said. "I'm glad." He pulled out his phone and tapped a few buttons before passing it over to her. "Just put in your number."

Rosalee was impressed that her shaking fingers didn't hinder her too much, and she typed her number as quickly as possible. She handed him the phone.

"I'll call you sometime next week," he said with a small wave and another flash of that damn dimple.

Rosalee watched George walk toward his table, joining a curly-haired woman who was doing her best not to look in their direction. He seemed sincere, she thought, but then again, he always had. She turned away from the crowded restaurant and back to her table, where the ladies were also doing their best not to act like anything interesting had just happened. Rosalee sat down, placed her napkin in her lap, and took a bite of her pizza. She chewed, swallowed, and took pity on her friends.

"Go ahead," she said with a smile. "Ask away."

chapter 6

June 1973

Saturday afternoon we were sitting on the porch swing, the warm summer air making me a little drowsy. We'd been listening to records in the living room—just as he'd promised George had let me introduce him to some of my favorite folk and country singers, and he'd brought over a couple of his favorite records too—but George had asked if I minded if we took a smoke break. I'd said sure, and grabbed a couple of cokes from the refrigerator before joining him outside.

"That's kind of gross, you know," I said, handing him a coke and sitting down.

He shrugged but didn't seem offended. "Peer pressure. It's not just for high school."

I thought about that for a minute. "So tell me about this partying you do." I said. The offhand comment he'd made about college "socializing" had stuck in my brain the past few days, and I was curious. One moment I imagined a free-for-all of drugs and alcohol and sex, and the next I imagined the kind of parties my friends and I had—snacks and music and sometimes dancing and almost always a rotating game of Hearts or Euchre.

He took a drag on his cigarette and exhaled away from me. "You can find about any kind of party you can imagine on or near campus," he said. "But the ones I go to tend to be pretty mild. Music, smoking, talking—you remember what I said about the talking, right?—sometimes weed. A little making out here and there." I saw him glance at me from the corner of his eye, and I could tell by his stillness he was waiting for my reaction to his openness. The good-girl part of me cringed a little at the weed and the making out, but also respected his honesty. Another part of me shrugged and thought *what's the big deal? Is this such a surprise?*

"Not too much different than what my friends and I do," I said with a smile. "Minus the weed and making out."

"No making out in Carlton?"

"Well…not publicly. I'm pretty sure Betty and Phillip have a special spot behind the gas station where he works."

George laughed.

We swayed in silence for a few minutes before George spoke. "I've only tried weed once," he said. "Didn't like it. And to be honest, that was in high school anyway. A good friend of mine was a stoner, so I finally tried it just to make him shut up about it. But I saw how it just kind of sucked the life out of him, so I was never really motivated to give it more than one chance."

I nodded, quiet as I processed our conversation. I took a sip of my coke so my silence would seem more natural. The cigarette smoking was kind of gross, like I'd told him, and my parents had always drilled into us that smoking was a dirty, expensive, and unhealthy habit. But my Uncle Lloyd smoked all the time, and while my mom made him take the cigarettes outside, it wasn't really a big deal.

My parents were REALLY against drugs though, pot included. But George did say he didn't like it and hadn't smoked it more than the one time. But I don't think he cared if other people did. And then I just kept thinking about girls. He downplayed it for the most part—except when he was flirting—but I knew he was more experienced than me. I could tell his…expectations were probably different than mine, too. I wasn't a prude necessarily, but I wasn't going to have sex with every guy I dated either. I went to church, and I believed in God, and I believed it when the Bible said it was better to guard your sexuality. I was pretty sure George didn't feel quite the same way.

But who cares? I heard Betty's voice in my head. He's just here for the summer! Summer fling! Practice flirting, kiss a boy, hold his hand, have a little fun.

"Do you like to read?" I asked.

He raised his eyebrows at me. "I'd like to be honest with you, but I have a feeling you're going to judge me if I say not really."

"Oh, without a doubt," I teased. "But I guess I'll go easy on you since we're still getting to know each other."

We talked for a while out on the porch. I asked him what he'd thought of my Dolly Parton record, and he admitted it wasn't bad. He asked how I'd liked The Grateful Dead, and I said it was pretty great, and seemed like the kind of record that would just get better every time you listened to it. He agreed, his eyes lighting up. He offered to loan me the record for a few more days. "Until our next date," he said with a wink. I rolled my eyes but blushed, too, before turning the subject back to different music lessons we'd each had to take as children. I'd taken several years of piano and stuck with that. George said his mom and made him take piano as a kid for a few years, but he'd quit in junior high for sports.

"But one of my friends started teaching me guitar last year," he said. "I'm digging it."

"That's cool!" I said. "You'll have to bring it out some time and play for me."

He was noncommittal about it, saying he wasn't really that great yet. I was trying to convince him I wasn't going to judge him when my mom pulled up in the car. She'd been getting her hair done, taking my brothers to their own required piano lessons, and grocery shopping. I was glad that George had finished his cigarette—I'd been surprised when he'd wrapped it up, stubbed out end in a handkerchief, and stuffed it in his pocket, but he said he didn't like to leave them around when he was at someone's house who didn't smoke. We both went out and helped my mom carry groceries in. George and his dimples were charming and polite, and my mom gave me a look that said *He's a cutie, but I think he knows it.* My own look responded, *Well, at least he's nice and polite, too.* Her return look conceded my point.

George said he had to go after that. I walked him to his car to say goodbye, and we made plans for coffee on Tuesday after work. I waved to him as he drove off, then went back inside, a huge smile on my face. I tried to look less like an idiot when I stuck my head in the kitchen and asked Mom if she wanted help with supper yet. She said no, so I quickly told her I was headed to my room and just call when she needed me. I grabbed the Grateful Dead record from the living room and ran up the stairs before she could snag me for a mother-daughter chat.

I liked talking to my mom, even about things like boys, but

right then I just felt more like keeping the afternoon tucked close for a little longer. In my room, I put the record down on my turntable—it was a really nice one I'd saved up to get—and gently set the needle down. The volume was already turned pretty low from listening to music at night, so I just stretched out on the floor by the speaker and closed my eyes, the smile back on my face. I replayed the afternoon over in my head, trying not to be too critical of myself or overanalyze our conversation. I thought about the realities of dating someone with seemingly so much more experience than me—grew up in a city, already in college, dating, smoking, drinking—just lots of different experiences that you just don't get in a small town like Carlton. Did it matter? At the moment, I thought probably not. It was just the summer.

I thought about music, and how when we were inside listening or talking about what we liked and didn't like and analyzing lyrics and style and talent, it was the most...genuine that George had seemed. Like he'd taken off his metaphorical cool-guy jacket for a little bit. I liked it. I liked the guy who seemed to care about something.

chapter 7

October 2018

Rosalee sat at a red traffic light, fiddling with her radio. None of the stations seemed to suit her today. The classical station she enjoyed was playing opera—definitely not her favorite—the oldies station seemed too loud, the country station too whiny. She felt like Goldilocks. She turned the radio off completely as the light turned green. After only one block, she felt antsy with only the sound of her breathing for company. She rolled down the window a bit, breathing in the cool, fresh autumn air. The road noise, something she generally couldn't stand, seemed to soothe her today.

After a few minutes, she turned into her daughter's neighborhood, and the road sounds gave way to more gentle neighborhood sounds. She wound her way through the tree-covered streets to the back of the neighborhood where Elizabeth's house sat. She and Jonathan had lived in this house for almost ten years now. It was an attractive, two-story farmhouse that sat at the end of a dead-end street. Their backyard butted up to an apple orchard, which Rosalee always thought seemed like the perfect backyard. It was far enough away from the main part of the orchard that the kids could play in there quite a bit as long as they didn't touch any of the trees.

Rosalee smiled as she drove down the driveway, remembering the one time Jessica and Corbin got caught climbing the apple trees. They'd been put to work for a weekend—hard work—and didn't eat another apple for years. But the owner never minded if they played in the orchard after that. Keira had never been much for mischief, so by the time she was old enough to run around the orchard, she was more into sitting underneath a tree and daydreaming. These days if you couldn't find the 16-year-old bookworm and her car was in the driveway, she was most likely out in the orchard with a blanket and a book. She and Rosalee were kindred spirits in this way.

This afternoon Keira was stretched out on the front porch glider wrapped up in a colorful granny-square blanket her other grandma had crocheted years ago. She waved as Rosalee walked up the path.

"Hi, Gram," she said, standing up to give Rosalee a hug. They were about the same height. Jonathan called them two peas in a pod. And it was true that Keira was the most like Rosalee out of anyone else in the family, in both looks and personality.

"Hi, sweetheart," she said. "How are you?"

Keira shrugged but smiled. "Fine. Nothing exciting to report, good or bad."

"What are you reading today?"

Keira reached behind her and picked up the battered paperback she'd left on the glider. "It's a fantasy novel of Eli's. He's trying to get me to give fantasy a chance, and he said this is the series to hook me."

Rosalee looked at the title, and although she recognized the author from the library shelves, she wasn't familiar with her work. "So...are you hooked?"

This time Keira grinned. "It's really good, Gram. I think you might like it. It's more about the characters really than the fantasy stuff. But even that I like better than I thought I would."

Rosalee was about to politely decline to try the author, but different words came out of her mouth. "Well, if Eli is willing to part with it for a while longer, pass it on once you're finished."

Keira said she didn't think Eli would mind and promised to give it to Rosalee when she was finished. Keira sat back down on the glider, and Rosalee had a thought to just sit down and enjoy the nice day on the porch with her granddaughter.

"Mom? Is that you?" Elizabeth's voice drifted through the open windows.

Rosalee smiled at Keira and squeezed her shoulder as she walked up to the front door.

"Sure is," she said as she walked inside. She set her purse on the hall table and walked toward the kitchen, where she knew she would find Elizabeth elbow deep in some kind of delicious dish. She walked into the large, sunny room. Rosalee took a deep breath. Rosemary, garlic, and coffee.

"Smells delicious, as usual," she said, walking to the coffee pot and pulling a big green mug down from the cabinet.

Elizabeth looked up from the pastry dough she was rolling and smiled. "Thanks. We're having chicken pot pie and spinach salad, and I'm going to whip some chocolate mousse once the pie's in the oven."

Rosalee always marveled at how her normally full-speed-ahead, seriously uptight daughter completely relaxed while cooking. Elizabeth had always been intense: student council president, valedictorian. Even though she and Jonathan had surprised everyone and married right out of high school, Elizabeth had gone straight to college while Jonathan started working for his dad's landscaping company. Thanks to summer sessions and Jonathan's unwavering support, Elizabeth had earned her Bachelor's degree in 3 years, just before having the twins. She'd put her education plans on hold while the twins and Keira were in pre-school, but enrolled in a Ph.D. program the same month she enrolled Keira in kindergarten. Rosalee was always so proud of Elizabeth, even when she didn't quite understand her.

"What can I help with?" Rosalee asked as she poured a bit of milk into her coffee.

"You could chop and toast some pecans for the salad," Elizabeth replied, and nodded her head toward the pantry. "There should be a bag on the top shelf."

Rosalee took a sip of coffee—mmm. Jonathan was a coffee fanatic, and they always had something delicious in their coffee pot—then set her mug down and walked to the pantry. She quickly found the bag of pecans, a knife, and a cutting board and stationed herself on the corner of the island where Elizabeth was now putting her crusts on top of steaming dishes of chicken, carrots, potatoes, peas, and gravy.

"Anybody missing tonight?" Rosalee asked as she gave the nuts a rough chop.

"Jessica has to work, but otherwise, everyone should be here."

Most Sunday evenings Elizabeth cooked a big dinner for her family, Rosalee, and Charles and Mary, and their kids. When

Elizabeth and Charles were young, Sundays had always been a family day. They went to church together, ate lunch together, and generally just spent the day as a family. When the kids were little, sometimes they'd go to the park, play board games, go fishing or hiking. As they got older, Rosalee and Tommy would help the kids finish up their weekend homework, or sometimes they'd have a family movie night. Some days they'd all take naps, then wake up gradually and putter around the house until Tommy picked up take-out pizza. The routine continued until the kids went to college, but once they all ended up back in Riverton, Elizabeth had declared she was reclaiming Sundays as family day.

"Did you ever think about cooking for a living?" Rosalee asked her daughter as she chopped pecans.

"What do you mean?" she asked, crimping the last piecrust and turning to open the oven door behind her.

"You know, become a chef or a baker or something."

Elizabeth placed the pies in the oven and closed the door, quickly setting a timer, then turning back to her mom. She tucked a stray bit of hair behind her ear.

"Not really," she said. "Why do you ask?"

"Oh, just you seem really happy when you're cooking, that's all. Relaxed."

Elizabeth raised her eyebrows. She reached over and grabbed a skillet, setting it on the stove and dumping in Rosalee's pecans, then lit the burner.

"I thought about it once," she said, gently shaking the skillet a few inches above the flame. "About six months into writing my dissertation, I thought I was going to go crazy. Jonathan swears he gained 20 pounds. I'd get stuck or frustrated and bake a cake or pie or try a new recipe. I learned to make sushi and crème brûlée. The kids loved it, of course." She laughed again. "Jonathan also says we almost went broke buying groceries, but I still knew how to shop a bargain."

"So why didn't you?" Rosalee had picked up her coffee and settled on a barstool. Elizabeth shrugged.

"I kept thinking about what Dad would say, you know? Not that he wouldn't have supported whatever career I chose, but just the thought of not finishing something I'd started."

Rosalee smiled. That sounded about right.

Elizabeth turned off the burner and set the skillet down. "Anyway," she continued, "that phase only lasted about six months. I faked-it-'til-I-made it long enough that I had a genuine breakthrough and was able to find my groove and finish that thing. I mean, I think I would have been happy as a chef, but I love teaching, too."

"Well, that's what matters," Rosalee said.

Elizabeth picked up her own mug of coffee and leaned back against the counter. "I know everyone says that cooking is the only time that I'm not uptight." She waved her hand dismissively as Rosalee opened her mouth to protest, even though she had just thought that exact thing. Mother's reflex, she supposed. "It's okay, Mom," Elizabeth said. "I am self-aware at times. I know I'm uptight. And yes, being in the kitchen relaxes me. But maybe if I did it for a living, it wouldn't be that for me anymore. So... everyone eats better this way." She grinned—her father's grin, Rosalee thought. "Plus, everyone knows exactly when to ask me a favor, or permission for something. I always knew when they had something really important to talk about because they'd come help me with dinner."

"Like I said, as long as you're happy."

The patio door into the kitchen opened at that moment, and Elizabeth's husband Jonathan walked in wearing athletic shorts, a long sleeved t-shirt, and running shoes. His gray t-shirt sported dark spots on his back and under his arms, and his thick, dark hair was mussed and damp.

"Hi, mom," he said, walking to Rosalee and planting a kiss on her cheek.

"Eew, Jonathan, you're all gross," Elizabeth said.

Jonathan grinned. "You mean you don't want a little post-run affection?" he asked, then walked up to Elizabeth and wrapped his arms around her in a bear hug. She squealed but was laughing too hard to get away. Jonathan gave her a loud, lip-smacking kiss, then let her go and headed toward the sink to get a glass of water. Elizabeth swatted him as he walked away, still laughing.

"So, Mom, what's new with you this week?" Jonathan asked.

"Actually, I ran into an old friend a couple of days ago," Rosalee said. She gripped her coffee cup.

"Someone from Carlton?" Elizabeth asked.

"Umm...sort of," Rosalee replied. "He was working there one summer and we became friends." Did she pause too long on the word friends?

A few thought wrinkles appeared on Elizabeth's forehead as she studied Rosalee. "I feel like there's more to this story," she said.

Jonathan grinned. "What, you think your mom's hiding some deep, dark secret?" he teased.

Rosalee felt her body temperature rise under Elizabeth's

piercing gaze. She shrugged, working hard to keep her voice level and relaxed, as though it wasn't a huge deal that she'd run into the first boy she'd fallen in love with. The boy who broke her heart, the boy she hadn't seen in more than 40 years.

Rosalee regretted opening her mouth. There was just so much on her mind today. She was finding it difficult to think about anything else, and the words just came out. Jonathan had asked what was new, and this was what was new. But were her confusing emotions and thoughts anything she wanted to share with her daughter? Yes…but not right now. She couldn't get her thoughts to make sense to herself, let alone her high-strung and opinionated daughter. She took a breath, wondering how little she could get away with saying.

Luckily, the front door burst open at that moment, welcoming her son and daughter-in-law and the elephant-like stomping of her two teenage grandsons. She set her mug on the bar and stood up to greet her family. She smiled at the boys and wrapped her arms around them as they both talked at once, but when she glanced up to see Elizabeth watching her, she knew that the subject had not been dropped just…temporarily put down.

For about 15 minutes, the house was in a pleasant state of mild chaos. Austin and Chris set the table, arguing in a way that reminded Rosalee of her brothers, and Rosalee poured herself, Mary, and Elizabeth glasses of wine while Elizabeth directed traffic and kept an eye on dinner. Jonathan ran upstairs for a quick shower, and Keira came in from the porch, setting her book on the hall table as she made her way to the rest of the family in the big kitchen and tried to talk Elizabeth into letting her have a glass of wine. Elizabeth reminded her that she was underage, and Keira winked at Rosalee as she grabbed a pop out of the refrigerator instead.

Once the food was on the table, Mary went to the back door and called for Jonathan and Charles, and everyone quickly took their seats around Elizabeth and Jonathan's big dining room table. After the typical shuffling and "Chris! Don't be so grabby and wait until we're all ready," the table was quiet, all eyes turning toward Jonathan. He smiled, held out his hands and they all did the same, taking the hands of their neighbors and bowing their heads as Jonathan said grace. After the "amen," Rosalee saw Chris's hand shoot out toward one of the two dishes of pot pie. She smiled as Mary reached out just as quickly and smacked his hand.

"Mo-om!" he whined, pulling his hand back. "What was that for?"

"That was for remembering some manners."

"It's not like we're company," he said. "It's just family."

"Family is no excuse to have bad manners," she replied, smiling at Keira as she handed her the salad bowl.

They passed the dishes around and the growing boys got their food, the table quieting as everyone began to dig into the delicious, rich pie. Rosalee savored the food as well as having her family around her. She loved the Sunday night tradition. And maybe Elizabeth had forgotten about their conversation earlier.

"Mom was telling us earlier how she ran into an old friend a few nights ago," Elizabeth said into the silence. Her tone was conversational, but Rosalee felt like a teenager whose parents were trying to sniff out an illicit boyfriend.

"That's right," Rosalee agreed. "I was out to dinner with some co-workers, and my old friend George Bowen was at the restaurant with his daughter. Turns out he's moved to town. It was such a surprise!" she said, "I haven't seen him or talked to him in…oh…over 40 years now."

"How fun!" Mary said. "Was this a friend from Carlton?"

"Kind of," Rosalee said. "His aunt and uncle lived in Carlton—the Millers," she said to Elizabeth. "You probably met them when you were little visiting Granny. Anyway, he lived in Kansas City, but he came to Carlton one summer to work with his uncle before going off to college. We…hit it off," she finished. "But neither of us was good at keeping in touch. He went off to college and I started senior year." She trailed off and took another bite of food.

Mary started telling a story of an old high school classmate she'd run into at the grocery store, and Rosalee was grateful. She glanced over at Elizabeth as Mary's story steered the conversation toward other reminisces of awkward encounters with old friends and exes. Elizabeth seemed to have let Rosalee's story go for the time being. Rosalee found herself slightly irritated at her daughter's sometimes-aggressive curiosity. Did she really have to know absolutely everything about everything? Granted, Rosalee had been the one to bring it up initially, but still. Any normal person would have just taken it at face value, she thought. Not acted like Woodward and Bernstein investigating Watergate. *You know it wouldn't bother you so much if George were really just an old friend*, a little voice inside her head commented.

She told the little voice in her head to just shut up already.

Rosalee managed to mostly relax and forget about her chance encounter with an "old friend" for the rest of the evening over more coffee—decaf after dinner—and a few games of rummy with her grandkids. But back at home, the restlessness started coming over her again as she went through her normal evening routine. She walked and brushed the dog. She took her shower and painted her toenails. She tried watching television but ended up flipping channels. She even tried calling Betty, thinking that she might want to have a little conversation with her oldest friend about the appropriatness of handing out her phone number. But Betty wasn't home. With a deep sigh, she leaned back on the couch and stared at the ceiling.

chapter 8

July 1973

I'd just gotten home from babysitting, and was flipping through a magazine, lying on the floor in front of a fan, trying to cool off from a few hours of playing outside. I heard a knock on the door and contemplated just ignoring it, figuring it was the mailman with a package or a salesman or Jehovah's Witness. But, I got up anyway. Mama would be horrified if I was home and didn't answer the door.

I was glad I did.

"George!" I said, a smile forming on my face. "What's up? Why aren't you at work?"

He leaned against the door jamb, and his smile showed off his dimple. "Uncle Jim kept talking about the great swimming hole around here today, and I told him it was cruel and unusual punishment to keep talking about it on such a hot day and not letting a guy experience it for himself. It was a persuasive argument."

I smiled back. "You are pretty persuasive."

He reached out and lightly took my hand. "So I'm betting you know some good places to swim," he said. "You want to show a guy around, or do I need to use my persuasive powers on you, too?"

Not likely, I thought. But I tried to play it a little cool.

"Nothing to do right now," I said, only slightly distracted by his hand still holding mine. "And you're right about it being crazy hot."

"Well, then," he said, still smiling. "I've got shorts in the car. How much time do you need?"

I grinned, squeezed his hand, and started backing up. "You know where the downstairs bathroom is. I'll be five minutes," I said. "And I've got a cold coke in the fridge I was saving for later. First one to the car gets it."

The words were barely out of my mouth and I was running up the stairs. I heard George laugh and his feet thunder down the porch steps. I couldn't keep the grin off my face. Running into my room, I threw open the top drawer of my dresser and unearthed my swimsuit, a plain, dark blue bikini that Betty had talked me into getting on sale at the department store last time we went into Springfield. I ripped off my clothes and tugged on the suit, thankful that the top was a halter style and I didn't have to mess with tying fussy strings. I pulled on the cut-off shorts I'd just taken off and ran across the hall into the bathroom, grabbing a towel. My sunglasses were in my bag, sitting down by the front door from babysitting. I raced down the stairs, trying to think if I needed anything else. Bottle opener. Yes, one was in my bag.

I got to the bottom of the stairs just as George was walking out of the kitchen with the coke in his hands.

"Confident, are we?" I asked.

He smirked and glanced between me and the front door. I

lunged for my bag and my keys and George lunged for me, his arm wrapping around my waist and swinging me away from the door. I squealed.

"No fair!" I gasped. "I've got to lock the front door!"

We were both laughing hard as he set me down on the front porch, his arm still firmly around my waist.

"This truce only lasts long enough for you to lock the door."

I was still laughing as I fumbled with the key, but eventually we heard the deadbolt click into place. The skin on my waist suddenly felt a rush of hot air, and I turned, leaping off the porch after George. I was seconds behind him, and threw myself into his side, and knocking him off balance just enough to make my lunge for his car count. My fingers brushed the hot metal and I turned, triumphant, to find George standing very close, his face still creased in a smile and his eyes crinkled from laughter. We were both sweaty and breathing hard.

"You, Rosalee, are one of a kind," he said. He held up the bottle of Coke between us, then rested the cold glass against my neck. I shivered.

"I have to say, I kind of figured this was mine. But you earned it," he said.

"You've met my brothers, right?" I said. "They are their own full-contact sport." I reached up and wrapped my hand around the bottle, my fingers overlapping slightly with his.

"If you're nice, I'll share," I said.

"I'm always nice," he replied. He let go of the bottle and reached around me, unlocking the passenger door of the car so I could get in. My body was trapped in the space between him and the car. His eyes never left my face as he turned the key. I found myself staring at his mouth. He winked, I blushed, and he was walking to the driver's side. I stood frozen for a second, then shook my head and climbed in. I fished around in my bag for my bottle opener before setting the bag on the floorboard. I opened my Coke as the engine roared to life.

"Which way?" George asked, looking at me with another smile, this one sweet and friendly.

"Left at the end of the driveway," I replied, taking a long drink. The pop was cold and fizzy and sweet and pretty darn delicious. I pulled it away from my lips and offered the bottle to George.

He raised an eyebrow. "Sure?"

"Yep. Take it. It hits the spot."

We were quiet on the drive, passing the coke back and forth while I gave him directions. In ten minutes we were on the bumpy gravel road that led to the spring. The trees along the road made shadowy patches on my bare legs and arms as it filtered through the trees that occasionally brushed along the side of the car. It was only two miles, but you had to take them slow. I didn't mind, though. We'd left the radio off, and I just enjoyed the peace—the sounds of the birds and squirrels, the crunch and hum of the car, the warm breeze blowing my hair.

By the time we'd gone the two miles and pulled into the clearing, it felt like we'd entered into the remotest pocket of the world. George parked the car and turned it off. We gazed for a moment at the spring-fed pool. The grass sloped slightly down to the water on our side. To the right, some huge rocks under a big oak tree made a perfect diving board and rope swing platform. Trees and undergrowth crowded around the water, except for the narrow stream that rushed off toward our left. I loved this place.

"Does it feel as great as it looks?" George asked, turning toward me.

"Better."

We opened our doors and walked toward the water. I kicked off my sandals and set down my bag. George shoved off his own shoes and pulled his t-shirt off over his head. I have to admit I took advantage of the few seconds in which his face was covered by the shirt to admire his lean muscles. I turned away, and reached down to slip off my shorts, although I hesitated, aware of George right next to me and suddenly feeling shy.

Don't be silly, I scolded myself. *You go swimming with boys all the time.* I quickly dropped my shorts, pulled off my t-shirt, and ran toward the big jumping rock. I could hear George laughing behind me, but I didn't slow down or turn around. I jumped up on the rock and, without slowing down, ran off the edge, tucking my knees up to my chest and closing my eyes just before hitting the deliciously cool water. I let myself sink, enjoying the refreshing water, the peacefulness, the weightlessness—before kicking my legs and reaching my hands toward the surface. I broke through the water, tilting my face up slightly so the water would push my hair way from my face.

When I opened my eyes, I glanced around for George and found him standing on top of the rock, grinning at me.

"Well, what are you waiting for," I said as I treaded water.

"Didn't want to accidentally land on top of you," he replied as he grabbed the rope. He walked backward until there was no more slack in the rope, then bounded across the rock. As his feet left the ground, he let out a whoop, sailing almost all the way across the creek. He hung on to the rope as it hit its peak.

Then just as he started to swing back toward the rock, he let go. I laughed at his gigantic splash, and instinctively turned my head away from the spray. A moment later, George's head popped up so close to my own that I jumped, startled at how quickly he'd swum through the water.

"Boo," he said.

I laughed and smacked his shoulder. "Smart aleck."

He grinned. Surrounded by the blue sky and blue water, his eyes were brilliant, deep and mesmerizing. His shaggy hair was plastered to his forehead, dripping water down his cheeks. A few pieces of hair clung to his cheekbone. I wanted to reach out and push the hair off his face. The thought made my insides flutter. I wasn't experienced with boys at all, but I knew that a gesture like that would be a statement of some kind, a silent acknowledgement that maybe I was open to something more than friendship. But I thought maybe I was okay with saying that.

My fingers softly—but with no hesitation—skimmed the top of George's cheekbone, carrying the wet hair off his face. I let my fingers run through his hair, my hand coming to rest on his shoulder for a moment before slipping off into the water again.

Uncertainty hit me belatedly, and I opened my mouth to fill the silence with something funny. But before any words emerged, George's rough hand slid around my bare waist, the other hand cupping the back of my head, tangling in my own wet hair. And then he kissed me.

My insides felt like I had just gone down the first drop of a roller coaster, and my skin sizzled. His lips were soft but firm, asking questions that my own mouth answered enthusiastically. I stopped thinking and became a mass of sensations. The gentle pressure of George's hands…the feel of hot skin and cold water and sunshine on my back…the cinnamon taste of his mouth. I wrapped my arms around his neck and his hand on my waist became an arm wrapped around me, our bodies pressing into each other.

When George eventually pulled back, I opened my eyes to see his blue ones still inches away from me, their corners crinkled slightly in a smile. I moved my arms and tried to pull away, the rational part of my brain slowly waking up and wondering what in the world had just happened, but George's arm remained firmly wrapped around my waist.

"Well," he said.

"Well," I replied.

As I searched for something not-stupid to say, George's head suddenly dipped slightly, and the arm not wrapped around me snaked behind my knees. I yelped as he scooped me up, then squealed as I found myself launched out of the water. I landed in the water with a splash and emerged laughing.

"Oh, it's on now."

chapter 9

October 2018

Rosalee wheeled an empty book cart back to the children's desk and glanced at the Dr. Seuss wall clock as she parked it against the wall. One more hour. She glanced at the four other packed carts waiting to be shelved and turned to Caroline.

"I think I'll just take care of another cart here unless you have something else you need me to do," she said.

Caroline also glanced at the clock, then at the book carts. "No," she said. "Go ahead with those books. I'd say that's a fairly pressing situation."

Rosalee smiled and headed out into the stacks. The nice thing about shelving books was that it felt like time to herself. She could let her mind wander or work out some issue. The bad part about shelving books was that it was time to herself. She was thinking more and more that sometimes too much time in her own head was not necessarily a good thing. Tonight, of course, she was thinking about George. It'd been a week now since she'd seen him. She'd passed the point of waiting anxiously for the phone to ring and had managed to stop thinking about him every waking minute. Only when she wasn't paying attention to anything else, like shelving books, she wondered what he had been doing for the past 40 years. Not work—he mentioned that—but what he'd been doing. What was his family like? What were his hobbies? Did he still like to make furniture and build things?

Rosalee shook her head. Okay, she told herself, it's time to think about something else. Like your garden. Or the neighbors. Yes, that sounded good. She and Celia had come up with the idea of having a block party. The weather was perfect, and most of the neighbors were already on wave-and-say-hi-when-you-pass terms, if not closer. They'd decided to get together for lunch tomorrow to plan the details.

Rosalee started running through questions in her head: did they set up tables and food in the street or in someone's front lawn? How would they let people know? Did they want to make it potluck? Or maybe provide the meat and have everyone else bring sides? They'd need more than one grill if they did a cookout. Or they could do a chili cook-off kind of thing. Should they set up games? What about music? There was a lot to think about, but she was pretty sure the whole idea would go over well with everyone on the street. She had a feeling that once they had the frame of an idea and the word got out, the rest would take care of itself. She smiled to herself. It was going to be fun.

She finished the cart with five minutes to spare and spent those last few minutes chatting with Caroline and straightening up the little-people tables and chairs and puzzles. Caroline was planning a trip to Ireland with her husband soon, and she was brimming with excitement.

"I've never been anywhere outside of the country," she confessed. "Bill wanted to just take care of everything on our own, but I thought a tour would be nice for our first trip like this, don't you think?"

Rosalee nodded. "I've traveled both ways," she said. "And there are benefits to both. If you want to not have to think about things too much, a tour is an excellent idea, especially for your first trip to a foreign country. Once you get a feel for international travel, then you can try it on your own if you want. Or not!" she said with a laugh. "Some people love tours and wouldn't travel any other way."

"You sound experienced," Caroline said.

"Well," Rosalee said, pausing in her puttering, "I guess compared to some. My husband and I went to Ireland on our honeymoon. That was a tour. And then after our kids were born, my husband surprised me for our anniversary one year with a trip to Great Britain. That was on our own. So compared to some, two trips is a lot of experience, but there are a lot of places I still want to go." A small, sad smile touched her mouth. Until she'd said it out loud, she'd forgotten how true that was. She remembered the young girl, eating pie and drinking coffee and talking so enthusiastically to a handsome boy about wanting to see the world. It had been the first time she'd really told anybody about that dream. Of course, later she'd talked about it with Tommy—even before he'd managed to talk her into a date. Back when they were just friends and Tommy was just patiently waiting for her to get over George.

"I think you just went on another trip around the world," Caroline said.

Rosalee laughed, her cheeks reddening. "I'm sorry," she said. "My mind has just been wandering lately. It's jumping between past, present, and future all the time. I can't keep up."

Caroline raised her eyebrows. "And I'm guessing running into that extremely handsome man at the restaurant the other night has something to do with it."

"Partly," Rosalee admitted, her face flushing a little deeper. "Although I think it really started when I took pie to the neighbors."

The two began walking toward the front door, waving goodbye to the two co-workers locking the doors. They waved goodbye and climbed into their cars. Rosalee smiled again as she checked her mirrors and backed out of the parking space. *You know*, Rosalee thought as she started driving home, *it's nice to be making friends again.* She loved Betty to the moon and back, but phone conversations—no matter how lengthy—just couldn't replace a flesh and blood person to talk to and do things with.

The next day Rosalee decided to take Billy on a long walk in the morning before she met Celia to talk about the block party. She wasn't in a hurry, so she let Billy stop as often as he wanted to sniff at fence posts and mailboxes and car tires. She breathed deeply of the fall air, crisp and rich and damp. She could tell someone had a fire going that morning, although she thought it might end up too warm for a fire by the afternoon. When she got back to her house and dropped Billy off, she caught a glance of herself in the hall mirror. Her cheeks and lips were rosy from the walk and the wind, and her hair was windblown. She ran her fingers through the chin-length brown and gray strands—more gray than brown these days, to be honest—but decided it wasn't that bad. She smiled a little to herself. Elizabeth would be shocked at her casual attitude, but honestly, Rosalee thought casual and windblown was not the worst look in the world, especially when one was simply going to spend time with a friend and neighbor.

A few minutes later, she knocked on the Blairs' door. She heard thundering footsteps and smiled at Tripp as he opened the door.

"Hey, Mrs. McDonnell," he said. "Mom!" he shouted, turning away from the door. "Mrs. McDonnell's here!"

He ran back to whatever had been occupying him before, leaving the front door open. Rosalee took it as an invitation and stepped inside, closing the door behind her. She followed the sounds of baby chatter and clanging pots to the sunny kitchen and met Celia in the hallway.

"Oh, good!" she said, giving Rosalee a quick hug. "I figured Tripp just left you standing there, and I was hoping you'd come on in. I just made coffee."

They chatted as they filled their mugs and doctored the rich, dark coffee. Celia talked about all of Aislinn's new tricks and the words she was starting to say. Rosalee talked about her grandkids and commented on the fall flowers in the neighbors' yards. They took their coffee and Aislinn and moved into the living room. Celia deposited Aislinn on the floor next to two baskets full of toys and went back to the hallway to take a quick peek at Tripp. Rosalee settled into one of the two soft and cushiony green armchairs. The chairs were positioned on either side of a big picture window, with a low, dark wood table between them. Sunlight streamed through the white sheer drapes and made a soft pool of light on the turquoise-and-blue swirled rug that Aislinn sat playing on. The little girl's head was buried deep in the basket of toys, her hair a fluffy brown halo in the sunshine.

Celia returned and sank into the matching chair.

"All quiet on the Western front?" Rosalee asked, taking a sip of coffee.

Celia laughed and tucked her legs up underneath her and cradled her cup of coffee. "Normally he'd be in school, but this morning he complained of a stomachache and I kept him home. Of course, now he's feeling fine and obsessed with his Legos. Anyway, let's talk block party. I had originally thought maybe having a few grills going and just doing a cookout kind of thing. Have everyone bring meat and a side or dessert. We could make a bunch of hot cider and hot chocolate and maybe some iced tea for people who don't want hot drinks. What do you think?"

"I love the idea," Rosalee said. "Oh! Where's my mind. Hang on a second." She set the white ceramic mug on the table and stood up, going quickly to the front door where she'd left her purse. She dug around for a moment, then returned to the living room with a small Moleskin notebook and pen in hand, reading glasses perched on top of her head. "I have to write everything down, and even then it doesn't always work," she smiled as Celia laughed. "Now. Who are you thinking of for manning the grills? I'm guessing we'd need at least two." She opened up the black notebook, slid her reading glasses down from the top of her head, and started writing.

"Well, Levi said he'd man one, and I'm pretty sure we could get Chuck from across the street and Mr. Wilson. The two of them are always grilling something."

It seemed like the best plan. They ironed out drink details and pulled out Celia's calendar to pick a date. Celia said she'd talk to the neighborhood association to make sure they didn't need to do anything official. Rosalee said she could get her granddaughter to help her make flyers when she came over on Friday night.

"Tripp will love passing flyers out," Celia said with a laugh. "That boy is so social most of the time."

"What about tables?"

Celia thought the neighborhood association had folding tables in the clubhouse, and Rosalee said she had tablecloths they could put out.

"Just to be festive," she said.

Thinking of the clubhouse gave them the idea that it would be good to have a bad weather plan, so Celia said she'd reserve the clubhouse for that day as well, and they could put the alternate location on the flyer.

"This is going to be so much fun!" Celia said. She leaned over toward Rosalee and lifted her coffee cup. "Here's to what is sure to be the first annual Elm Street Fall Block Party!" Rosalee laughed and clinked her mug against Celia's. "I'll drink to that."

When Rosalee walked in her own front door later, her phone was ringing. She shoved the front door closed, not taking the time to lock it, and dropped her purse and keys on the hall table as she walked quickly to the kitchen.

"Hello?" she said, slightly breathless from her haste.

"Mother, you really need to turn your cell phone on when you're out. I've been trying to call you for an hour."

"Hello, Elizabeth," Rosalee said. "So wonderful to hear your voice."

Rosalee imagined she could hear Elizabeth rolling her eyes. As expected, Elizabeth ignored her comment.

"I was wondering if you're still planning on coming to Keira's volleyball game tonight?"

"Of course," Rosalee said. "Seven o'clock, right?" As their conversation began, Billy wound himself around her legs, and she reached down to scratch his ears.

"Yes, at seven. Jonathan wondered if you wanted us to come pick you up? We'll probably grab some burgers on the way, but we can get you after that if you don't want to eat."

"Burgers sound great," Rosalee said. She sat down in one of the kitchen chairs and Billy rested his head against her knee as she continued to pet him. "What time?"

"We'll come by around 5:30. See you then."

"Bye, sweetheart," Rosalee replied before hanging up. She had barely set the cordless phone down on the kitchen table when it rang again. Smiling, she prepared to give Elizabeth a hard time for being the one to forget something.

"Hello?"

"Rosalee?"

The smile slid off of Rosalee's face and her hand stilled on Billy's head. The male voice on the other end of her phone was definitely not Elizabeth, or Charles, or Jonathan, or any of her grandkids. It wasn't immediately recognizable, but familiar like the memory of a memory.

"Yes."

"Hi, it's George. Sorry it's taken me a while to call. It's been a while since I moved anywhere, and I'd forgotten how much work goes along with it."

"I can imagine," Rosalee said, thankful for the cultural norm of opening conversations with small talk. Her mouth could work properly while her brain caught up. "It's been so long since I made a move, I don't think I'd even know where to start."

"Well, for one thing," George said, "hire movers. Worth every penny."

Rosalee laughed. "Noted," she said. She resumed stroking

Billy's head and leaned back in the kitchen chair as George told her about all the lines he'd had to stand in that week, and how many times he'd been put on hold calling city or county offices. *What were you worried about?* She asked herself. *This is nice. Just catching up with an old friend.* She smiled as George talked, thinking that he could still make the most boring things entertaining.

"So, a chance meeting at a noisy restaurant isn't ideal for catching up," George said after exhausting his moving stories. "And while I can clearly blather on and on over the phone, I want to hear about you, too. Have some real conversation. I was thinking it'd be great to meet sometime soon for a cup of coffee."

"That sounds nice," Rosalee said. The harmless phone conversation had eased her nerves considerably, and she realized that having coffee with George really did sound like a great idea at that moment. "How about this weekend sometime? There's a great coffee place downtown by the courthouse. Ida's."

"I've seen it," George said. "Sounds perfect. How about Saturday morning around 10?"

"It's a...plan." She caught herself before saying "date." She felt at ease, to be sure, but there was no sense on saying such a loaded word as that. Better to keep things safe and relaxed.

"See you then."

They finished their goodbyes and hung up.

Rosalee looked down at Billy's goofy grin and big brown eyes. "Well, buddy," she said. "That was much less painful than I anticipated."

chapter *10*

August 1973

The hot, early August sun had turned me into a lizard baking on a river rock. The trees lining the creek whispered to each other and to the slowly moving water. I felt like I had become one with the patchwork quilt beneath me and the grass beneath that. George and I had come out to the creek for a picnic, and had been talking about a new album he had just bought. The summer sun had lulled us into quiet. My hand lay in his; his thumb gently and lazily rubbed a circle on my palm.

A shadow covered my face, and a moment later George's lips pressed against mine. I smiled against his mouth, accepting and returning his cherry-coke-flavored kiss. I'd been right that day in the drug store—George Bowen could most definitely kiss my socks off. And, to be perfectly honest, if I let my guard down, he could probably kiss some other articles of clothing off my body without even trying hard.

George's warm, work-roughened hand slid just underneath my t-shirt. My skin tingled as his hand slowly worked its way up, his kiss deepening. It took every ounce of willpower I had to pull my lips away from his and sit up on the quilt.

"Baby, what's the matter," George asked. His shaggy end-of-summer hair was mussed, the deep blue of his eyes just a thin ring around his pupils. His long, tan fingers brushed my own messy hair out of my face. Why did he have to be so gorgeous? I pulled my knees up against my chest and sighed.

"We've talked about this," I said. "I'm still an old-fashioned girl." I said it lightly, desperately trying for a playful tone. "None of that free love stuff around here."

George smiled and ran a finger down my arm. I shivered. "I know, Baby," he said. "And I respect that." He leaned in and kissed me again. "You're just so yummy," he murmured against my mouth. "We don't have to…you know…do everything."

"I'm not sure you get the concept of 'old-fashioned,'" I said as his lips moved along my jaw. "And stop trying to distract me."

He pulled back just enough to grin at me. "But it's fun. And you like being distracted."

"Exactly." I scooted away a few inches, trying to catch my breath. "Saying no is hard, and I get tired of having to do it all the time. You say you respect my feelings, but it doesn't feel like it."

George's smile faded into seriousness. "Rosalee, I care about you. You're smart and funny and thoughtful…and smoking hot." I blushed. "I'm headed back to Columbia soon, and I want to be with you while I still have a chance." He rested his palm against my face. "I want to make the most of every last minute I spend here with you."

"But that's just it," I said, my eyes burning. "You're leaving. Seizing the moment and giving in to our feelings sounds romantic and all, but I'm just not there, and I don't know if I ever will be." I covered his hand with my own and squeezed it gently. "I've been as honest with you this summer as I know how to be. You've had more of me—the real me, the inside me—than anyone else ever. But that's all I can give right now."

I waited, watching George process my words, refusing to flinch or look away from his eyes. I was aware of the smell of honeysuckle, and the unmistakable sound of Mr. White's old pickup rumble down the road. The sun, which moments ago felt comforting and lovely, suddenly felt unbearably hot, and my skin prickled and itched.

"Rosalee," he said, moving his hand from my face to rest at my waist. "I can't give you some kind of commitment. I'm still in school…I'm still figuring out my life. I care about you, but I'm smart enough not to jump into something while neither of us are ready."

"And that's why I never asked you for a commitment," I said, pulling away from his touch. "And that's why I can't be with you the way you want. You just said it. There's no guarantee after next week. I would never ask you for something you can't give. All I'm asking is for you to give me that same courtesy."

I stood up, seconds away from tears, confused, hurt, and furious at myself. I'd told myself I'd be cool, be grown-up. Not let my emotions get the better of me. I took a deep breath as George stood up to face me.

"So is this it?" George asked. His face was unreadable, which shook me even more, because normally I had no trouble picking up on George's thoughts.

"It doesn't have to be," I managed. I thought about what Jane Austen's Elizabeth Bennet would say and then just imagined I was her. "But if this entire summer has been one long seduction for you, if all you're after at this point is sex, then yeah, I guess this is it."

I summoned every ounce of adopted confidence I could and just looked at him. Daring him to admit it, but crying out with every molecule for him to act like we really had been friends. Been more than friends.

I swear I could hear George's wristwatch ticking. It was a long, long 60 seconds.

He let out deep sigh, his face and body relaxing and melting into a sad, but more George-like expression.

"No, Rose," he said, quietly. "This summer has not been just one long seduction." His mouth quirked. "Not gonna lie...I was hoping it'd be in the cards, but,"—he held up his hand—"I realize it's not. So. Let's just enjoy the next week, okay? No pressure."

I raised an eyebrow, and he gave me a full smile this time.

"I promise," he said, stepping toward me. "You know what I like most about you?" he said, grabbing my hands. "The way you don't apologize for who you are. And the way you challenge me to be a better person without even saying anything, just by being you."

He leaned forward and pressed his lips against mine. "You, Rose, are the most confident woman I know."

My heart was melting and singing and trembling all at once. "I'm not confident," I protested. "I'm the least confident person I know."

George shook his head, smiled, and leaned his forehead against mine. "Nope," he said. "You are. One day you'll realize it."

chapter *11*

October 2018

Rosalee sat in her car, her hands still clutching the steering wheel despite having been parked in front of Ida's for at least five minutes. She'd decided to get to the café early for her…meeting? Get together? It felt like a date…with George. She thought it would help her to calm the nerves that had returned since their phone conversation. So much for that idea.

Stop acting like a child, she told herself. *You are a grown woman. One who has been married, had children, lived a full life—lives a full life,* she corrected her mental self, not wanting to sound like she had one foot in the grave already. *Now put on your big-girl pants and get out of the car.*

She took a deep breath and pulled her keys out of the ignition, tossing them in her handbag. A small bell jangled as she stepped inside Ida's. Rosalee paused just inside the door and glanced around. Although it was comfortably full, her favorite spot—two squishy striped chairs by a window—was empty. Jessica told her once that this prime spot was often empty when you least expected it because it wasn't near a power outlet, and so many people came into Ida's to get on their laptops.

Rosalee glanced toward the coffee counter, but then walked toward the chairs, deciding to claim her space before George got there. Plus, she figured it made more sense to order once he was there. She sat in the chair facing the door and pulled out the book Caroline had suggested she bring. It was a good suggestion. By the time she sensed someone sit in the chair opposite her, she'd basically forgotten why she was at the café.

"George!" she exclaimed as she glanced up from her book. She smiled, set her book on the table next to her chair, and stood up. They hugged before she had time to think about whether or not that was the right greeting, and it felt good, so she decided it must have been. "It's so good to see you!" And it was. She laughed a little to herself, realizing she'd been picturing the old George all week—not the present-day George whom she'd run into at the pizza restaurant. He had the same gorgeous blue eyes and easy smile, but the confidence seemed more earned in present-day George. It was more of "I'm comfortable with myself" and less "I know I'm pretty awesome."

"It's good to see you too, Rosalee," George said, eyes crinkling. "Have you ordered yet?"

"No, I was waiting," she said.

"Let me know what you want," George said. "You save our seats."

She ordered a cappuccino and chocolate biscotti, attempted to give him some money for it, then graciously smiled thanks before sitting back in her seat. She watched him walk to the counter, and watched at least two of the other female customers watch him as well. She smiled, remembering the feeling of being on display but invisible, since it wasn't really her on display after all. From the angle of her chair, she could see George's profile, and watched him joke with the barista. Not flirting, she decided, which was for the best since the barista was at least 30 years younger than George.

He turned and looked her direction, smiling when their eyes met. Rosalee blushed slightly. George settled into the chair opposite her.

They chatted about George's new condo while they waited for their drinks. As they sipped their drinks—cappuccino for her and what looked like black coffee for him—they had what Rosalee felt was "first-date" conversation. They talked about George's move, his house, their kids and her grandkids. He asked about her work at the library and tutoring, she asked about what he'd been doing before retirement and how he was enjoying consulting. Rosalee happened to mention the block party she and Celia were working on.

"You should come!" she said. "I think it'll be fun. Next weekend. Just bring something to drink."

George said he'd love to come, and that in his Chicago neighborhood they'd had an annual block party for years.

"There were a handful of us who'd moved onto the street all within about two years of each other, and we all had kids, so we started doing it around back-to-school time," he said. "Most summer nights we'd end up on someone's front porch after dinnertime, kids running around playing and parents with a glass of wine in hand." He smiled. "It was fun. The September party was our goodbye to summer. As the years went on and more people moved in, it was less about the kids and more about just having fun and being neighbors."

"That sounds nice," Rosalee said. "We used to be much closer to our neighbors as well. Getting to know the Blairs has really made me miss that."

They'd finished their drinks and George reached to the end table and took her cup, asking if she wanted a refill.

"So," she said, wrapping her fingers around the refilled mug as he handed it to her. "I feel like we're on a first date, doing all the get -toknow-you stuff. But it feels strange."

George met her eyes. "It does," he agreed. "But I wasn't sure where else to start. It's been such a long time. And we didn't part on the...best of terms."

She appreciated his directness, and the fact that he wasn't trying to pretend their history was all fun and laughter. But she also appreciated that he wasn't being overly dramatic either. Maybe a cautious and gentle approach was best.

"It's true," she said, "but I think we can skip to the 'tell-me-what-I-missed-in-your-life' stage, don't you?"

George smiled, but she could see his fingers drumming the edge of his mug. "Agreed," he said. "You go first. Give me the timeline and we can fill in the details later."

Rosalee crossed her legs and clasped her hands around her knee. Her heart warmed pleasantly at the sound of "later."

"Well. I married Tommy McDonnell in 1975, moved here in 1984. Had two kids. Kids grew up, went to college, got married, had kids. Both live here. Tommy got cancer in 2000, then fought it off and on until he died in 2015. I work part time at the public library, have the best neighbors, and spend a lot of time with the grandkids. And I have a dog named Billy."

"That was...concise." George's mouth twitched.

Rosalee smiled. "Isn't that what you asked for? Now your turn."

George took a sip of his coffee. "Okay," he said. "Married Jeanette in 1974, moved to California. Moved to Chicago in 1982 to work for a bank. Worked for that company for 10 years until they got bought out, then started working as an accountant for a big hospital system. Jeanette died from a heart attack in 1990. I have one daughter, no grandkids."

"You know, when you just lay out the facts like this, we both sound pretty boring," Rosalee said lightly.

"Ah, but the devil's in the details."

Isn't that the truth, Rosalee thought to herself. She knew she had opened the door to the past, but it was still a bit jarring to hear it. 1974. Jeanette. Daughter. George's fingers were still tapping an unknown rhythm on his mug, and while Rosalee didn't think anyone else in the café would be able to see past his casual and friendly smile, she could see the wariness in his eyes. She knew that the next step in their conversation—and in the "later"—was hers.

"Then something tells me we may need more than one coffee date," Rosalee said with her mouth. With her eyes she said, *It's been a long time and life's too short for grudges anyway. I forgave you a long time ago.*

Thank you, George's eyes replied.

His fingers stilled and his mouth switched from friendly to flirty—and darn it if her insides didn't jump. "Music to my ears," he said. He glanced at his watch. "If you've got the time, I've got another hour before I have to leave for an appointment. Start at 'married Tommy McDonnell' part. The name sounds familiar, but I can't picture him. I want to hear that story."

chapter *12*

November 1973

I flipped through my mom's *Better Homes and Gardens* magazine, glancing up at our television as my brothers, Dad, and George all let out an exclamation. One of the red-and-gold players was waving their arms at the ref, gesturing to the other team. The ref stared straight ahead, signaling a penalty and automatic first down. The player stomped off.

"That was a sh—" George cut his word short, glancing at my brothers and dad—"terrible call," he finished. My dad agreed, focused on the game, either oblivious to or choosing to ignore George's almost curse word. I'd never said anything about watching his language, but over the course of the summer, George had eaten several dinners and watched some intense Little League games with my family, and he was pretty observant. He glanced over at me and winked. My face flushed, and I winked back. I'd been so surprised when he'd called and asked about coming to visit this weekend. We'd talked on the phone a few times since he'd headed back to college, but after our last conversation before he left, I'd honestly expected him to disappear. I'd almost dropped the phone when he'd called the week before.

For a week after George went back to school for the fall semester, I'd held my breath, hoping he'd call or write. The second week I'd moped, lying on my bed listening to sad music and thinking back over every one of our conversations, wondering if I could have done something different to keep him interested…well, aside from sex. But I had a feeling that wasn't exactly the thing to keep him interested either. The third week I'd resigned myself to the summer having been a lovely moment in time, a blip in my personal history, and a very special memory. Of course, then he'd called. It was a short, casual conversation, mostly revolving around a book he'd read he said he thought I'd like. After that, I hadn't really expected much, but last week he'd called again wondering if I was busy this weekend and saying he thought he'd come down for a visit. I was confused and excited but determined to just enjoy it and try not to get my hopes up.

"Whaddya think of the Chiefs' chances this year?" my brother Jimmy asked George. "Kevin's dad says they're going to go all the way."

My dad grunted. "Les always says that," Dad said. "He's an optimist, and sometimes an idiot. But this year he might be right."

"I don't know Kevin's dad," George said, "but I agree with your dad," he said to Jimmy. "I'm cautiously optimistic."

I watched the game for a few minutes, then went back to my magazine. I was sitting about as close to George as possible in my family's living room. Fortunately our couch sagged a little, so it looked natural. By the time I finished the *Better Homes and Gardens*, it was half time. George reached over and squeezed me knee as I set the magazine back on the coffee table. "Want to go for a walk during half time?" he asked.

I raised my eyebrows.

"Just a short one," he responded with a grin. "Maybe down to the stop sign and back? It's such a beautiful day."

"You don't have to ask me twice," I said, standing up and holding out my hand.

"Take notes," he said to my brothers as the announcer began talking. I laughed and we walked out the door.

It was a beautiful early fall day. The leaves had just started turning, and it was cool enough for jeans and a flannel shirt but warm enough to go without a jacket. The sky was a clear, deep blue, and the air smelled like fall. I took a deep breath and smiled as we walked toward the road. George squeezed my hand but didn't say anything.

"How are your classes?" I asked after a while.

George shrugged. "They're okay. Shakespeare, Western Civ, World Religions, Geology, and Intro to Accounting."

"Accounting? Do I detect a possible major?"

"We'll see how the semester goes, but so far it's looking good. My advisor said I shouldn't commit one hundred percent until I take Accounting II, but right now that's the plan."

"That's great! Does it feel nice to feel like you have a direction?"

He nodded. "Makes college feel like it has a point, you know?"

I hip checked him as we rounded the stop sign and headed back toward my house. "And what about your social life?" I teased. "What's happening outside of class? I know that's really why you go to college."

He returned the friendly bump but wrapped his arm around my shoulders at the same time. We stumbled slightly on the road before falling into step with each other.

"I'm having a good time," he said. "I'm having a good time with you, too."

I snaked my own arm around his waist, not saying anything as I tried to come up with a good way to convey Hey, I know you never promised anything to me and I understand if you're dating and that's okay. Because I really wanted to find out if he was dating anyone…because, of course, I hoped he wasn't. But I also didn't want to seem like the small-town high school girl that I was.

"Anyone special?" Curiosity won.

He smiled. "No," he said. "No second dates."

I appreciated the implication—that there were some first dates. He hadn't promised me anything, after all.

"What about you?" he asked. "Got any fish on the line?"

I rolled my eyes. "You spent a summer in this town. We've all known each other since elementary school, and if it hasn't happened yet, it's not happening."

He laughed. "At least it's your senior year. Only a few more months and you can shake the dust off your feet."

I shrugged. "Yeah, we'll see."

"What about college?" George asked. "Travel?"

"I've got to make it through a year of working and saving first," I said. "And then we'll see." What I didn't say was that it got pretty discouraging listening to people talking about their post-graduation plans. Everyone who was staying had no plans on ever leaving. And everyone who was going was going right away. Shaking the dust off, as George put it. I worried about having the discipline to save the money I earned and keep my goals from fading in the day-to-day light.

I reclaimed my spot on the couch by George when we got

back to the house, and I read a mystery novel from the library while the rest of the family watched the game. George stayed for supper, then we went for a drive. My mother gave me a meaningful look as I put on my jacket.

Make sure you keep driving young lady, her look said. *No parking and…you know.*

I rolled my eyes and responded with my own look. *Mother,* my look said. *Trust me.*

It's not you I'm worried about, her look replied with a raised eyebrow. *I know about college boys.*

I rolled my eyes again and gave her a kiss on the cheek before heading out the door.

And we really did just go for a drive. George told me funny stories about his roommates, like the time Dave had accidentally double booked himself with two different girls.

"He thought that he'd set up a date with Kathy on Friday night and Stevie on Saturday. But it turns out he'd actually told Stevie Friday too."

"What happened?"

"This is the best part, or worst, depending on your perspective. He'd asked them both out to the same restaurant…"

"No!"

"…so they all three show up at the same time. He tried to talk his way out of it, but Kathy and Stevie—who turned out to be sorority sisters—ended up ditching Dave and going out to dinner with each other."

I laughed. "Good for them!"

I told him about the freshman who had hijacked the school loudspeaker to ask Betty to the fall dance.

"Doesn't she have a boyfriend?" George asked.

"Yes! And I would say he embarrassed himself for nothing, but now all the freshman and sophomore girls think he's so romantic. Fast track to popularity."

George grinned. "I'd say that kid's pretty smart."

After we'd covered all the nearby back roads, George turned back onto my street and drove up to my house.

"Thanks," I said. "This has been a fun day."

"Yeah, it has," George said. He smiled and my heart hitched. He glanced up at the house and noted that all the downstairs lights were off, then leaned toward me.

I met him across the gearshift. It was the kiss I'd been dreaming about through every boring lecture at school and every sad song on the radio. His hand cupped the back of my head, and I leaned into him.

After a few delicious minutes had passed, George pulled away slightly, his lips still inches from my face.

"You should come visit," he said. "I have some friends—girls—you could stay with in the dorm. They'd even let your mom call." He grinned and I laughed.

"Maybe," I said, resting my forehead against his. "My friend Karen is looking at colleges, and she has been talking about heading up to MU for a visit. My parents may be more amenable if I hitch a ride with her. Would that be okay?"

"I just miss you," he said. "Bring whoever you want. Even your brothers, as long as you can come."

"I am NOT bringing Jimmy and Lloyd!"

We both laughed again, and he pressed his lips to mine one more time before getting out to walk me to the door.

chapter *13*

October 2018

Rosalee pulled two cherry pies out of the oven and added them to the row of fruit pies taking up every available space on her dining room table. Those were the last two. She turned off the oven and glanced at her clock. She had about 20 minutes until it was time to start setting up the tables outside. She took off her checked apron and called Billy, sending him out into the backyard. Although Billy was an extremely well-behaved dog, she thought the excitement of the block party would be a little much for him, and planned to leave him in the house for a while.

She smiled as she watched him running circles in the backyard, chasing a bird or a squirrel or maybe just his own shadow. It was a beautiful day. Rosalee thought it couldn't have been more perfect if she and Celia had ordered it from a catalog. The sky was a cloudless, deep October blue. The weather was cool enough for a sweater, but the sun was warm. A wet summer meant the leaves were in full show-off mode, and every now and then a gentle breeze would send a handful cascading to the ground, filling the air with the pungent scent of crushed autumn leaves.

Rosalee left Billy outside for a few more minutes and went

into her bathroom to touch up her makeup. Another swipe of mascara and some of that new cinnamon-colored lipstick that Jessica had helped her pick out. She normally wouldn't go to too much trouble for the neighbors—they'd seen her sweating and grubby doing yard work in the middle of summer, after all—but she had impulsively invited George to come to the block party after their coffee date the other day.

Her phone rang as she capped the tube of lipstick. She picked up the extension in her bedroom.

"Hello?"

"Mom, it's Elizabeth. I'll be there to pick you up in 10 minutes."

"Did we have something planned that I forgot about?" Rosalee asked.

"No, I'm just out doing some shopping, and thought you might want to go grab something to eat."

Rosalee rolled her eyes but smiled. "Sweetheart, that is so thoughtful, but I'm busy today."

"Busy? Doing what?"

None of your business, Rosalee thought.

"We're having a block party."

"A what?!"

"A block party. You know, all the neighbors get together potluck style and socialize out in our front yards. Levi and Mr. Roberts are grilling."

"Mother, I just...I have no response to this. I'm very surprised."

"You're welcome to stop by if you'd like," Rosalee said, "and I appreciate the shopping offer. But I do need to get going. I'm helping Celia get everything set up."

Elizabeth sighed so loudly Rosalee was sure the neighbors

could hear her even through the phone and walls. "You are a mystery to me these days, Mother. I suppose we'll still see you for dinner Sunday?"

"Of course," Rosalee said. "Don't be ridiculous. Have fun shopping."

Rosalee shook her head as she hung up the phone. Elizabeth could be so dramatic sometimes.

An hour later the party was in full swing. Folding tables set up under the big oak trees in the Roberts' front yard practically sagged under the food. Delicious-smelling smoke wafted from two gas grills as Levi and Mr. Roberts kept people's plates full of burgers, hot dogs, and sausages. Children ran or rode bikes and scooters. The neighborhood association had gotten permission from the police department to block off the street for the afternoon, so the kids were free to make the street their own. Rosalee glanced around and smiled at the groupings of lawn chairs scattered in the general area of the food and drinks, neighbors chatting and eating and laughing, getting to know each other better or meeting for the first time.

Celia stepped up beside her and held up a plastic cup.

"Well, friend," she said, tapping her cup to Rosalee's. "I'd say this is a success."

"Indeed," Rosalee agreed. "Such a fun afternoon."

"Speaking of fun," Celia gestured to a figure walking down the street toward the crowd. "I think all the neighbors are accounted for. This must be your date."

"Old friend," Rosalee corrected. But she reached up to smooth her hair and checked to make sure she didn't have any stray crumbs on her mouth.

Celia smiled at her. "You look fantastic," she said. "Relaxed and happy and gorgeous. Now introduce me."

Rosalee reached over and squeezed Celia's hand, then the two walked toward George. Rosalee's heart jolted as they came closer. He was wearing jeans and a blue flannel shirt, the sleeves rolled up slightly, making Rosalee think about the day they met. He looked just as good now as he had then. She wondered if he'd dressed this way on purpose, but decided men didn't remember those kind of details.

"You picked the perfect day for a block party," George said as he walked up to them. "I'm glad you could make it," she said with a smile and a hug. They stepped apart, and Rosalee hoped her pink cheeks could be attributed to the fresh air. "George, I'd like you to meet my friend and neighbor Celia Blair."

"It's a pleasure," George said, shaking Celia's hand.

"Likewise," she said. "I've heard a lot about you."

"Not that much," Rosalee quickly interjected in response to George's sideways grin and raised eyebrow.

Celia laughed and squeezed Rosalee's arm. "I hope you'll stick around for a while, George. I'd love to stay and hear juicy stories about Rosalee's young and wild youth, but I've got to go make sure my own young and wild youth are staying out of trouble."

"I like her," George said as they watched Celia make her way toward the playing children.

"Me, too," Rosalee said. "They've been wonderful neighbors, and I'm really glad we've become friends."

The two stood for a moment just taking in the sounds of laughter and conversation, soaking in the sun and scent of charred meat.

"Where are my manners?" Rosalee said, shaking herself out

of her reverie. "Come and grab something to eat. Everything is delicious."

"Did you try it all?" George asked as they walked toward the tables.

"Of course," she said with a smile. "Hostess duty, after all."

"Mmm."

Rosalee smacked George's arm lightly and he laughed. They fell into small talk as he filled up a plate, and Rosalee got them both cups of spiced cider. There weren't any free lawn chairs, so she led him to the wide front steps on her front porch. Was Rosalee secretly happy to have George all to herself? Yes. And they were close enough to the action—two small groups of people were sitting on her front lawn chatting—to not look like they were being antisocial.

"So, last time we talked," George said around a bite of cheeseburger, "we were debating the joys of teenage daughters."

Rosalee rolled my eyes. "So much drama," I said. "The day we dropped her off at college, I swear Tommy and I drank a whole bottle of Champagne."

George laughed. "Fortunately, by the time Kristen got to college, the drama had mostly disappeared. Which is good since she went to the University of Chicago and lived at home. I might have gone out of my mind otherwise."

"Did the drama go when she lost her mother?" Rosalee asked.

"Sort of. She was 16, so for a little while things were a lot worse. Both of us grieving. Her blaming me. Me blaming me. Even though it was a heart attack—no one's fault. After several weeks of basically being useless, my boss forced me to go to counseling, and the counselor…strongly encouraged me to bring

Kristen. It took some bribing, I'm not going to lie, but it got her there. And after a while it started to help."

Rosalee expressed surprise that his boss would take such an interest in an employee's mental health. "You see that more these days, but that seems pretty unusual for that time."

"Oh, you're a hundred precent right. I was shocked that he'd bring it up, but he'd lost his own wife suddenly a few years before so I think he was more sensitive to it that most. And I really was useless at work. I'd just sit and stare off into space for hours. I couldn't get any work done."

Rosalee sympathised, remembering the time just after Tommy had died, the days when she couldn't get out of bed, and nights when she couldn't sleep. She'd spend all night sitting on her back porch and staring at the sky. She couldn't imagine doing all that with a 16-year-old at home.

Rosalee wasn't sure how long they sat there talking. George told stories about living in Chicago, a city he clearly loved. She told him ridiculous camping stories—because every camping trip the McDonnell family had taken involved some kind of minor disaster. There was the time Charles singed off his eyebrows building a fire, or the time they'd gone out for a hike and lost 10 year old Elizabeth. They'd gone so far as to get the park ranger, who then promptly found Elizabeth back at the campsight laying in a hammock fast asleep.

"It was the one place we didn't think to look," Rosalee said as George laughed.

George asked about how it was when Tommy first got sick, and for the first time in a long time, Rosalee was able to talk about how hard it was—really, really hard—without feeling guilty or ashamed or exhausted all over again.

"I never minded taking care of him," she said. Rosalee and George were facing each other, backs resting against the stone columns of the porch. She gazed just over his shoulder, watching two dogs chase each other in circles around a big oak tree. "In sickness and in health, you know? And I loved him. I wanted to take care of him. I just…got tired. And after a while, the illness changed Tommy. He wasn't himself for quite a while. And that made it harder. Almost like caring for a stranger instead of my husband, you know?"

George had always been a good listener, watching a person talk as if he had all the time in the world. As if what you were saying was the most important thing he'd heard all day. Really hearing you. But now, as Rosalee glanced at him, she saw a new depth to his gaze, an empathy keeping company with his interest. She saw a man who genuinely cared, and she felt as if he *did* know. For the first time in a long time, Rosalee felt truly *seen* and understood. It was disconcerting, like finding an old shirt in the closet only to pleasantly discover it actually still fit.

"I think everyone's starting to clean up," Rosalee said, rising slowly her feet. "I should go help. I didn't realize how long we'd been sitting here!"

"Let me help," George said, picking up his empty plate and cup as he stood.

She tried to wave him away, but he just ignored her and started wrapping and lifting and carrying and basically just doing whatever Celia directed him to do. As Rosalee walked by Celia with arms full of empty pie plates, Celia winked and mouthed the words I love him.

And once upon a time, so did I, Rosalee thought to herself as she carried the dirty dishes into her house. *And, heaven help me, I think I could again.*

She squashed the thought quickly and finished helping with cleanup and saying goodbye to neighbors, all of whom said, "We should do this every year!" Rosalee sincerely hoped they would. It hadn't been too much work to organize, and, on the day of, everyone chipped in to help.

When the last bag of trash had made it into someone's bin, Rosalee walked over to Celia and Levi sitting on their front porch, watching Tripp ride his bike up and down the driveway and Aislinn toddle around the front yard. Rosalee reached down and gave them each a hug.

"Success!" she said. "What a great afternoon."

"Agreed," Celia said with a smile. "And the kids played so hard, I'm pretty sure they're going to sleep like rocks tonight."

"Speaking of," Levi stood up and walked over to pick up Aislinn. "This one might need a little nap to make it to bed time."

Aislinn grinned at him as if saying, "Fat chance, Dad." But Rosalee was confident Levi's will was stronger.

As they walked by and into the house, Levi stopped to give Rosalee a kiss on the cheek. "It was a great party," he said, then dropped his voice to a whisper, "and I really like your friend." He smiled and waved a hand to George, who, Rosalee realized, had walked up behind her.

"I should take off," George said after Levi and Aislinn had gone inside.

"Well, it was lovely to meet you," Celia said, giving George a hug. "I hope you'll come around again sometime."

George glanced at Rosalee with a small smile. "I hope so too," he said.

"I'll walk you to your car," Rosalee said and waved goodbye to Celia and Tripp. Rosalee and George were quiet as they walked down the street. Rosalee was tempted to reach out and grab George's hand but squashed the impulse. Not yet. No sense in getting carried away.

"Well," Rosalee said as they reached the corner, "I'm really glad you came."

"Me, too," George said. "And I'm glad you're glad." They both laughed. "Can I call you soon?" George asked.

"I'd like that," Rosalee said, ignoring the butterflies in her stomach.

"Good." George leaned down and Rosalee's breath caught in her throat. He kissed her cheek, then straightened, his eyes crinkled from his smile. "I'll talk to you soon."

He got in his car and drove off, Rosalee managing a wave and fighting the temptation to hold her hand to her cheek like a teenage girl. She turned toward her house, but before she got more than three steps down the street, she noticed a silver Honda that she recognized idling on the curb. A car that must have turned on the street as she stood saying goodbye to George. A car whose occupant was no doubt on the brink of exploding from curiosity. Rosalee walked up to the driver's side window and it rolled down.

"Hello dear," she said. "Did you have a successful shopping trip?"

"Mother," Elizabeth said. "I hope you have coffee at your house, because I think we need a nice, long conversation."

"Of course," Rosalee replied. "I'll meet you down there." *But don't get your hopes up,* she thought. *You're not getting the long version of the story. Not yet, anyway.*

chapter *14*

November 1973

As I'd expected, my parents were reluctant to let me go see George at the university, but once I convinced them that I wouldn't be there alone and that I had plenty of money saved up to make the trip, they told me to go ahead. I was unbelievably nervous. It was one thing to see George in the comfort of Carlton, another to see him on a university campus. He was going to be in his element, and I was going to feel like a fish out of water. Betty came over a few days before we left to supposedly help me pack, but really to try and calm me down.

"Don't worry," she said. "Number one, he asked you to come visit. Number two, you are gorgeous and smart and funny."

"And a country bumpkin." I was laying face down on my bed—a touch dramatically, I have to admit—wallowing in my worry and insecurity.

"Stop that!" she said, smacking my butt, and not gently. "Ow!" I said, but she ignored me.

"Do you think there are no people from the country who go to college? It's not the 40s, you know! Just because you know everyone's family tree and still hang up your clothes to dry on a clothesline doesn't mean you're stupid or not worth a person's time." It was possibly the most profound thing Betty had ever said to me, and I tried to take it to heart.

"I know, I know," I said, rolling over to my back. "You're right. I'm just…nervous."

"Get up, silly," she stood up and pulled me to my feet. "Let's pack. I can't come with you to hold your hand, but I can at least make sure you're going to look good. And looking good is the first step to confidence."

I laughed but figured there was some wisdom in that. It took the better part of the afternoon, but between the two of us and a couple of Vogue magazines, we managed to get my overnight bag stuffed full of (hopefully) everything I would need.

I'm bringing too much," I said with a grunt as I shoved the bag closed.

"No way," Betty said. "This way you have options. You don't know what the campus style is, so you need to be ready to adapt. Plus, he hasn't told you what all you're doing, so you need to be prepared for anything."

Again, I couldn't really argue with her. I'd managed to talk her down from some extravagant additions (I was quite confident I would not need a semi-formal dress and high heels), and to limit the potential outfits to things I would actually wear in normal circumstances. Betty kept telling me to just be myself, and I'd accomplish that easier if I felt like myself.

"I've gotta jet," she said, hanging up the last of the discarded shirts. "Have a blast and don't be a prude."

I laughed as she gave me a quick hug and ran down the stairs. I heard her call goodbye to my mom, and then the screen door slammed closed. I sat down on my bed and stared at the overnight bag, full of so much more than clothes and an extra pair of shoes. What was I even doing? I was a high school senior in a small town, getting ready to graduate and go to work, probably in the same small town. I could save a lot of money living at home, after all. George was in college, getting a degree, and not even planning to stick around Missouri. All I could hear in my head were the voices that kept talking about making a plan for the future.

In my quietest, most private moments, when I let myself listen to the deepest secrets of my heart, I thought that a future with George sounded pretty great. Travel the world together, get a house, raise a family. But I knew that George wasn't thinking any further than the next semester and getting a degree. I knew we had fun together, and I believed him when he said he cared for me, but I also believed that he wasn't in a long-term frame of mind. Long term was for "old" people. We were young, free. But young and free could also be nerve-wracking and stressful.

I could call Karen and tell her I wasn't going with her after all. I could call George and tell him I'd come down with some bug and wasn't feeling well enough to make the trip. I could take a step back and let the summer fling slip into the scrapbook of my mind, a beautiful "remember when." I could wipe away a few tears now but save myself a possibly deeper heartache later.

I sighed and flopped back on my bed again. That wasn't what I wanted, and I knew it. It was comforting to think about, but my life was safe enough as it was. Don't get me wrong, I don't think I'd ever be considered a big risk taker, but if spending the summer with George had taught me one thing, it was that sometimes a small risk was worth it. Sure, things had ended on a sour note, but that hadn't taken away the weeks of sweetness. And he'd come to visit and asked me to come see him. Who knows what would happen in the future, but I knew one thing for sure—if I tried to only live my life by what I could see planned out, I probably end up happy, but I'd surely end up with some regrets.

Karen and I left early the next morning. It was only a four-hour drive from Carlton, but Karen wanted to attend a couple of classes in the science department. Since it was a college visit, we'd been able to get excused absences from school.

"Honestly," Karen said as we drove out of town. "Even if the weekend is completely terrible, it would almost be worth it just to skip a day of school."

It was the perfect day for a drive. Blue skies, sunshine, crisp November air. We rolled the windows down, blasting the radio and singing along. Even though we were wearing scarves and thick sweaters, it got cold after a while, so that didn't last the whole trip. I read a little bit of the copy of *Persuasion* that I'd brought along with me, and we stopped once for snacks, gas, bathroom break, and a driver switch. Karen was working on geometry homework, so I mostly just watched the farms and towns and cows roll by, and thought about my future. And George, of course.

"Are you thinking about going to MU?" Karen said at one point. "I thought I heard you say once that you weren't going to college right away?"

"You heard right," I said. "I'm going up to visit a friend."

She grinned. "A boy, am I right?"

I nodded, blushing a little. "George Bowen? He was in town visiting his aunt and uncle last summer."

"Oh, I remember," she said. "Totally gorgeous and totally attached to you. I don't think I saw either of you much on your own last summer."

I guess it made sense that everyone in our small town would have noticed the out-of-towner…and the person he spent the most time with.

"So…does he live on campus?"

"Yeah," I said. I knew what she was politely asking-but-not-asking. "I'm staying with his friend in one of the girls' dorms." I glanced over at her and grinned. "You know my mother would never let me go up there if she thought it would look 'improper.'"

Karen laughed, and we talked a little more about our respective plans for the weekend before she went back to her homework. My stomach twisted with nerves as the mile markers counted us down to Columbia, but I was thankfully distracted for a little while following Karen's directions. We pulled up in front of the residence hall I'd be staying at and the nervousness returned. I think I might have just sat in Karen's car all weekend, but she was opening her door and getting out to come around the driver's seat. I slid out and opened the back door, pulling out my purse and overnight bag.

"I'll just pick you up right here on Sunday," Karen said as I shut the door. "Ten o'clock? I don't want to get home late."

"Sounds great," I said. "Have a fun weekend."

"You, too." She winked at me before getting back in the car and pulled away from the curb. I watched her drive away, then turned around and stared at the brick building behind me. Well, nothing left to do but go inside. George had class until two, but his friend was done early on Fridays and had said she could meet

me. I glanced down at the slip of paper with her room number
on it: 452.

A few minutes later, I was knocking on a door with that
number surrounded by magazine cutouts of musicians and
musical instruments, and scraps of paper with quotes of song
lyrics. I guessed that George's friend, or her roommate, was really
into music. I recognized some of the song lyrics, so maybe that
meant we'd get along okay. Enough for the weekend, at least. I
knocked.

"It's open!"

I opened the door and took a few steps in.

"Rebecca?" I asked, peering around the room. I found the
source of the voice sitting on the bottom bunk bed, a guitar in
her lap and piles of paper surrounding her.

"Guilty," the girl smiled. She had long, straight, blond hair
with a thick fringe of bangs that highlighted her pale blue eyes.
"Sorry about not coming to the door. It's just…" she gestured
with one had to her nest "…a little easier."

"No worries," I said with my own smile.

Rebecca gestured across the small room with her head to a
battered old couch. A pillow and couple of blankets sat neatly at
one end.

"That's where you'll be crashing. My roommate's out of town
this weekend, but she's weird about people sleeping in her bed."

"No, this is great," I said, walking over to the sofa and setting
my things down on the floor next to it. "I just appreciate you
letting me crash."

"No sweat," she said. "When George told me we had the
same taste in music, it was a no-brainer."

I sat down on the sofa and we chatted for a while. Rebecca was a fan of modern singer-songwriters, but also a music major. Her primary instrument was the piano, but she was spending a lot of her energy focusing on learning classical guitar.

"I have this dream of creating some kind of folk-rock-classical fusion," she said. Her blue eyes sparkled as she leaned over her guitar as she talked. "I mean, the styles would go so well together, but I haven't quite managed anything good." She gestured at the piles around her. "That's what this mess is all about."

I asked a few questions about her music, and she even played a little bit of what she was working on for me. Slowly, I relaxed, caught up in the conversation about music and school. We somehow got to talking about our families—she was the third of five kids—and our hometowns. Rebecca had grown up in Kansas City, so she said moving to Columbia for school was almost like moving to a small town. Eventually I talked myself into asking her about George.

"I've really only known him a short time," I said, "and not in his own environment, you know? What's he really like?"

"He's great," she said with no hesitation. "He's a good friend, funny, loves his family, is nice to old people." I smiled at that. "And he's not a slacker, you know? So many of the guys around here are. Just smoking dope and not really caring about the future."

I was encouraged—so far, everything she'd said was consistent with the George I knew.

She'd stopped talking, but I could sense there was a little bit more. "I will say he's a bit of a player," she finally said. "Not that he's a jerk or anything. He never talks bad about the girls he goes out with, and he's gone out with a few of my friends. They always have nice things to say about him, even when things don't go any further than a couple of dates."

She strummed a few chords on her guitar. "I'm not trying to steer you away or anything, just thought it was good information to know."

I smiled. "Absolutely."

I changed the subject back to something less sensitive, and Rebecca was in the middle of a hilarious story about a girl down the hall when the alarm on her desk went off.

"Wow!" she said, reaching over to turn it off. "I had no idea what time it was. I've got to get ready for work."

"I'm so sorry!" I said. "You meant to be writing and I've been keeping you from it."

Rebecca waved her hand dismissively as she gathered up her papers and propped her guitar at the end of the bed.

"No worries," she said. "It'll keep. My roommate says I'm turning into a hermit anyway, so it was nice to have some company."

Once she was free of the piles, she stood up and rummaged through one of the desk drawers. Her had emerged holding a peace-sign key ring with a brass door key attached.

"To the room," she said. "Also, don't forget to go downstairs and sign in as a guest at the front desk. That way the RA doesn't kick you out if she sees you this weekend."

"Got it," I said, taking the key and pocketing it.

Rebecca grabbed her purse and a name badge, then waved as she hurried out the door. I glanced at the clock after she left. 1:30. I picked up my purse, double-checking that *Persuasion* was tucked inside. The idea of sitting in the dorm room—nice as it was—for a half hour made me antsy, so I thought I'd go downstairs, check in, then soak up a little sun on one of the benches in front of the dorm. A little reading away from the obvious clock would keep me from counting the minutes and getting nervous again. Hopefully.

I found a bench just to the right of the front doors of the dorm, shadowed by the brick building yet visible enough that George should see me when he walked up. I pulled out my book and took a deep breath, willing myself to relax. I made it through a couple of chapters when I felt someone sit down next to me on the bench. I smiled and turned, my eyes meeting the deep blue eyes I expected to see.

"Hey, gorgeous," George said, his mouth turned up in a cheeky grin. "You're exactly what I wanted to see on a Friday afternoon."

"Back at ya" I replied.

George reached out his arm and rested his hand against the back of my head. I accepted the invitation and leaned forward, pressing a kiss against his lips.

"Thanks for inviting me up," I said as I pulled back—but not too far.

"Thanks for coming," he replied softly.

We sat silent for a moment, simply smiling like a couple of idiots, until George pulled back and straightened.

"Well," he said. "Let's get this party started. Not literally. The literal party isn't until later. But I thought you might be in the mood to go get some coffee or ice cream?"

"Or?" I asked.

He laughed. "Lucky for you, my favorite milkshakes happen to come from the diner that serves my favorite coffee."

"Perfect." I stood up and held out my hand. "Let's go."

chapter *15*

November 2018

"I should probably go. Eyes are beginning to watch me from behind the windows."

"I'm not even there and I feel like I'm dropping you off after a date and trying to sneak a goodnight kiss without your parents seeing."

Rosalee laughed. "Yes," she agreed. "That's exactly how it feels."

Rosalee was parked outside Elizabeth's house for Sunday dinner. She'd just pulled up when her cell phone rang, George on the other end. She'd answered, as she'd been doing every day for the past two weeks since the block party. They'd met again for coffee, and he'd taken her out to lunch after a shift at the library. They'd also talked on the phone almost every day. Sometimes it was a five-minute call. *Just wanted to see how your day was going. I read a story in this magazine that made me think of you. Do you watch Downton Abbey? Did you see last night's episode?* Sometimes it was a leisurely conversation. They'd trade stories of the past 40 years, or talk about what books they'd been reading.

Elizabeth had been very curious when she'd stopped by after the block party and seen Rosalee saying goodbye to George.

Rosalee had managed to put her off, saying that he was an old friend who had recently moved to town. Elizabeth didn't quite buy it, and told her mother that she knew there was more to the story.

"You can't hide anything, Mother," she'd said. "Your face is an open book. And you know it will drive me crazy until I hear everything."

She'd added that maybe they could talk about it at dinner tomorrow. Rosalee had sighed, most certainly not ready for the whole-family scrutiny.

"Give me a couple of weeks," she asked, knowing that with Elizabeth, deferment was possible but denial was out of the question. As she'd said, Rosalee was an open book. "I'll give you the whole story then."

When Elizabeth had opened her mouth, a stubborn look on her face, Rosalee reached inside for her "mom" voice. The one she hadn't had to use in years.

"Elizabeth Anne," she'd snapped. "I am fully within my rights to just tell you to mind your own business. My friendships—and whatever stories that may go with them—do not concern you. But I love you, and I know you're curious, and I have nothing to hide, so, yes, I will satisfy your curiosity. But I've only just reconnected with George, and it's a long story. Give. Me. Two. Weeks."

Elizabeth's mouth snapped closed and she winced. "Of course," she said, "Of course, you're right. And look at me!" she'd said with a laugh. "Here I almost forgot the whole reason I stopped by in the first place."

She went to a pile of bags by the front door and pulled out some shoeboxes. "I know you probably would prefer shopping for these yourself, but I saw a few pair that just looked perfect and thought I'd bring them by to see if you liked any of them. I can return what you don't want them."

Rosalee smiled and gave Elizabeth a hug. "You are a very thoughtful daughter."

Now here she was, prepared for 20 questions. Or one big question. It had been two weeks, and Rosalee knew Elizabeth would be ready to pounce. That girl was so curious she should have worked for the CIA or NSA. She was happiest knowing everyone's business, and Rosalee knew the more you told her, the more you could keep to yourself. And besides, if she was starting to spend this much time with George, more members of the family would begin seeing him, and while she'd like to keep him all to herself for as long as possible, she also enjoyed all the time she got to spend with her family. *Time to put on your big-girl pants, Rosalee McDonnell,* she told herself.

"Call me tonight," George was saying. "I want to hear how it goes."

"I will," she said. "Talk to you later."

They hung up. Rosalee gathered her purse, stepped out of the car, and made her way to the front door.

Everyone else was already there, and the pre-dinner chaos was at normal levels, the boys running in and out of the house, screen door slamming in their wake despite various calls of "stop slamming the door!" The adults were gathered in the kitchen, drinks in hand, watching Elizabeth put the finishing touches on dinner and talking about the week's dramas. Keira was tucked up on a stool by the counter, munching on pre-dinner crudités and reading a fat paperback. She tilted the cover toward Rosalee as she walked over, and Rosalee grabbed a carrot stick and gave Keira a quick side hug.

Rosalee made the rounds in the kitchen, saying hello. She snagged the boys as they ran through, giving quick hugs to much protest. She joined in the chitchat and helped set the table, and before long they were all seated, passing delicious-smelling food around the table.

"So," Jonathan said once everyone had filled their plates. "Elizabeth said you've been seeing a lot of an old friend lately." He looked at Rosalee with a smile.

I see, she thought. *Getting Jonathan to do your snooping for you.*

"That's right," Rosalee replied. "George just moved to town a few weeks ago, and we hadn't seen each other in...oh, at least 40 years."

"Something about your 'old friend' being a man makes me think there's a story," Mary said, a mischievous glint in her eyes. "And I love a good mealtime story."

"First, I'd just like to say that I think everyone is acting like it's the craziest thing you've ever seen that I happen to have an old friend who happens to be a man," Rosalee said. "You all do realize that I lived a good chunk of my life before you all came along."

Everyone laughed. "I'll be honest, Mama Rose," Jonathan said. He must have sensed her irritation, because he hadn't called her that in ages. "It's just that you've been pretty predictable for a long time. It's more the change that's got us curious. Not bad change!" he emphasized, as Rosalee opened her mouth to protest. "Just change. You're going out...hosting parties...making your own plans. It's just different."

Rosalee nodded. "I can see your point," she said. I *wonder if they've been talking about this behind my back?* She thought to herself. "Honestly, it all started with my cute little neighbor boy, and his family's friendliness, that made me realize I'd gotten into a rut before I ever ran into George. But you want a better story," she said, "so here you go."

She told a condensed version, although she didn't tell them it was a condensed version. For one thing, no one had time—and teenage boys had no patience—for every detail. And, frankly, every detail was none of their business. So she told them the basics.

"I met George one summer while he was visiting our small town. We got very close, but George went back to college and I went back to my senior year of high school. We kept in touch all that year, visiting each other for weekends, talking on the phone, even writing letters. It was spring and we all looked forward to the school year ending. I was looking for work, and George was going to be starting a job in Kansas City.

"He started asking me if I'd think about looking for a job there, and while he said I could stay with his family, he was getting an apartment, and I could tell he wanted me to stay with him. And I wasn't comfortable with that. I asked him to give me until graduation to think about it and do some early looking at jobs. We'd agreed from the beginning that we wouldn't be exclusive unless we ended up in the same place again. The week before graduation George called me to tell me that his friend Jeanette was pregnant and the baby was his. They'd decided to get married. And that was that."

"Wow, Grandma," Keira said while the adults stared at Rosalee. "Who knew you had a tragic romance in your past."

Rosalee waved her hand at Keira. "It was a long time ago. And it was after that that I started spending time with your Grandpa, and look how that turned out. Not so tragic after all."

"I just can't believe after that you'd be interested in reconnecting," Elizabeth said. Rosalee shrugged and filled her fork with food again, ready to get on with dinner. "Like I said, it was a long time ago. Before we said our goodbyes, George and I were friends. We had fun together. Any hard feelings are definitely in the past. At my age, you don't treat friendships lightly."

Rosalee saw Mary and Charles exchange a glance that said they'd discuss things later, and she watched Elizabeth open her mouth to say something. But before she could, Rosalee turned to Austin and asked him if he was playing basketball again this winter. His enthusiastic response seemed to get the conversation back to family topics rather than let's-analyze-Rosalee's-life-choices topics. To be sure, once Austin wound down, Rosalee asked Jonathan when Corbin was coming home for winter break, and why Jessica hadn't been able to join them for dinner (she already knew Jessica was working—but she really just wanted to stop talking about herself and George for a while).

After dinner, Rosalee was run out of the kitchen cleanup, and settled in the family room with the kids. Austin and Chris pulled out a board game, while she and Keira and curled up on the couch, Keira with a book, and Rosalee with the cat.

"So, Grandma," Keira said, glancing toward the door. They could hear music and laughter coming from the kitchen. She leaned a little bit toward Rosalee. "So," she said again, her voice soft, "just between us, are you dating that guy, George? I mean... is that why you two have started hanging out again? Is his wife dead, too?"

The boys stopped their playing and sat up, not trying to hide their interest. She hesitated but decided the interest of her grandchildren seemed less like meddling and more friendly interest than that of their parents.

She leaned in herself. "Just between us," Roslaee repeated Keira's words in her own soft voice. "Not right now. We really are just friends. And yes, his wife is dead."

"But do you think you might want to date? Do you think he might want to?" Keira asked.

"To be honest, I'm not one hundred percent sure. But I think so. We're a little flirty with each other, and we are spending a lot of time together. But we haven't talked about anything, and I'm okay with that. No need to rush."

"Well, you might not want to take things too slow," Austin said. "No offense, Grandma, but you're not getting any younger. You haven't got all the time in the world."

"Austin!" Keira exclaimed. She threw a throw pillow at him. "So rude!"

Rosalee just laughed. "You have a point, darling," she said. "I'll keep that in mind."

chapter *16*

November 1973

If Karen noticed that I was quiet on the way home, she didn't say anything. I asked her about her weekend. She'd seemed to have had a great time. She told me about the classes she went to and some of the people she'd met and a party she went to.

"I cannot wait to be in college," Karen said. "I mean, this weekend just makes high school feel...a little juvenile." She laughed. "Listen to me. I sound like a pretentious idiot, don't I?"

I smiled. "No," I said. "You sound excited and like it's your senior year. I'm pretty over high school myself."

For a few minutes we were both quiet, just listening to the radio and the road noise.

"So how was your weekend?" Karen asked.

"It was nice," I said, eyes out the window. "We mostly just hung out. Went to a party on Friday night. Hiking on Saturday and a bonfire Saturday night."

"Sounds like fun!" Karen said.

"Mmm."

I kept my eyes looking out the window, watching the trees and farms roll by. I knew she was expecting a more enthusiasm, but I was feeling too much to muster much enthusiasm. I needed to sort through my thoughts before I spilled them.

It really was a nice weekend. A lot of fun, actually. Coffee and milk shakes had gotten rid of any residual awkwardness, and I had started to relax. He'd mentioned the party as we were paying our bill, and it had sounded like fun. I wanted to meet his friends and see George in own environment, not stuck in a small, nowhere town. He'd taken me back to the dorm to change, and I mentally thanked Betty for her help in getting outfits together ahead of time.

I felt pretty good even after we arrived at the party. George anchored me with a gentle hand on my back as we walked into the large, Victorian house and started saying hello to the people already there. Everyone was friendly and easy to talk to, and it was fun joining in conversations about music and books. The sometimes-heated political and current events discussions went mostly over my head, but it felt like a college thing.

As the evening went on things unraveled. The music got louder, the smoke—both tobacco and pot—got thicker, and by this point, almost everyone had been drinking for a few hours. It wasn't that anything terrible started happening, it's just that everyone got really, really relaxed. Girls got flirtier, and George was a prime target. They stood closer to George while we talked, pressing their bodies against him. A couple of girls tried going in for kisses, and one even said, "Oh, come on, George. I had a terrible week, I just need a good, friendly make-out session." At this point, I'd basically become invisible.

To be fair, George didn't encourage them. He was friendly and a little flirty but nothing to get upset about. He made it clear that he was with me and was as sweet as can be. But I was still unsettled. It was clear that George was popular…and pretty clear that friendly make-out sessions were at least an occasional occurrence.

It was late when we left, and I could sense that George was nervous as we walked back to the dorm. I simply asked what the plan was for tomorrow, and enthusiastically agreed when he suggested a hike.

"Just the two of us," he said, taking my hand. I squeezed his hand and smiled.

"Sounds perfect," I said.

"Some buddies of mine are also having a bonfire," he added. "But it's up to you."

On the one hand, a bonfire sounded fun. On the other, I was pretty sure it would be a repeat of the party. But if I really wanted a relationship with George, it wasn't going to happen in a vacuum.

"Of course we should go," I said. "I love bonfires. And it's another chance to spend time with your friends. Will it be some of the same people who were at the party?"

"A smaller crowd, but yeah, I think most everyone who will be at the fire was there tonight."

We chatted a bit more as we neared the dorm, stopping at the corner just outside the range of the lights by the front door. George wrapped his arms around me, and I slid my own arms around his waist.

"I'm glad you're here," he said softly.

"Me, too."

I met his lips with my own as he leaned down to kiss me. We took our time, savoring the touch and taste of each other, the feel of our lips and hands and bodies pressed together. His arms were wrapped around me, the only thing keeping me from melting into a puddle on the sidewalk.

Eventually George pulled back slightly and smiled. "See you tomorrow."

"Mmm," I managed. "Tomorrow."

I should have told Karen about the hike. It had been a glorious day, a beautiful trail, and George was the best company. I got back to the dorm that afternoon feeling fantastic, glowing, energized, and well on my way to being in love.

And then the bonfire. My good mood had made me optimistic that it would be different from the party, and, to be fair, it was. The atmosphere was laid back, the people very friendly. There was less drinking, and I only saw one couple smoking. George seemed more relaxed, too, and while at first that was a good thing, as the evening went on, I began to feel more like an outsider. The smaller crowd was clearly closer. There were more inside jokes, and the conversation tended to be about shared experiences and references that I wasn't a part of. The girls still flirted, and while he was never inappropriate, George definitely flirted back more than he had at the party. I could see what Jennifer meant. George was the kind of guy who just liked women. Not in a gross way, but he made all the girls feel special. I caught a few allusions to past relationships and I worked hard to hide my discomfort. It was hard not to seem like the small-town girl having an adventure, and I was relieved when the night finally wound down.

Another bone-melting goodnight kiss almost made me forget my discomfort, but that night I couldn't quite shake it. When George said he'd try to come down to Carlton sometime before spring break, I smiled and said that would be great, but inside I wasn't counting on it. And not because of anything George had said, or done. It was just a feeling.

We'd made no promises to each other. Even though George had been the perfect gentleman all weekend, I remembered his desire for a more physical relationship. I believed George genuinely cared about me, but I also knew that realistically we were just friends. Kissing friends. Maybe-in-the-same-city-we-could-be-more-than friends. But I had no ties to him. And out of sight was often out of mind.

So I didn't quite know what to tell Karen. I could gush about the fun we'd had, the amazing kissing, the way George had acted happy to be with me and made a point to introduce me to his friends. But there was a nagging feeling inside me that my heart was about to be broken.

chapter *17*

November 2018

"So, I hear that I missed an exciting Sunday dinner this week," Jessica said. They were standing in Rosalee's kitchen getting snacks ready for their Friday night girls' night. Jessica was arranging movie candy into Rosalee's cut-glass dessert bowls—a childhood tradition she refused to give up—and Rosalee was manning the stainless steel pan on the stove full of clattering popcorn kernels.

Rosalee rolled her eyes. "Your mother is a little...dramatic at times."

"Don't I know it."

"I'm honestly not sure why it became such a big deal." The clattering had slowed, so Rosalee pulled the pan off the stove, dumped the contents into her big blue bowl, and poured melted garlic butter over the top.

Jessica shrugged as she arranged the dishes on a blue enamel serving tray. "You've been different lately, Gram. Making friends with the neighbors, being social at work. It's awesome! But different stands out. And you know how Mom is with different. I think your friend is just something for her to latch on to in order to process through her emotions."

Rosalee raised an eyebrow at Jessica, who grinned. "Psych 101."

Rosalee laughed, and the two made their way into the living room, where a romantic comedy was waiting in the DVD player. They set the snacks on the coffee table, went back to the kitchen for the drinks they forgot, then settled in with pillows, blankets, and the remote.

"So, are we going to get to meet him sometime?" Jessica asked as the previews began playing.

"He's just a friend!" Rosalee protested.

Jessica smiled. "We'll see," she said.

Rosalee's telephone was ringing when she and Billy walked in the door after a long walk Saturday morning. She let go of Billy's leash without unclipping it and reached for the receiver.

"Hello," she said, expecting to hear Elizabeth calling to make sure she was coming to the football game, or to see if she wanted to get food after.

"Hey, you."

"Hi," she said. "You just caught me coming back from a walk." She hoped George would now attribute her slight breathlessness to exercise. Which it was. Mostly.

"Beautiful day for it," he said. "What else do you have planned for your day?"

"Grandkid soccer game," she said, leaning over to unclip Billy's leash, then giving him a scratch behind his ears and a treat from the jar on the counter. "What about you?"

"Well, I was hoping to talk someone into a picnic in the park, but it looks like that'll have to happen another day."

Rosalee smiled, then surprised herself. "Do you want to come to a soccer game?" She asked. "Not quite a picnic in the park, but close."

"I'd love to," George said, almost before she'd finished talking.

"I think I should warn you that this is going to be one of those feels-like-high-school times," Rosalee said. "My family is... very interested in our friendship. And our history. Which I was forced to tell them."

"Forced, hmm." Rosalee heard the smile in his voice, and was glad.

"Wait until you meet my daughter. You'll understand."

"I'm not scared," he said. "I say bring it on."

Rosalee laughed and they decided to ride together. They agreed on a time for him to pick her up, then said goodbye. Rosalee spent the rest of the morning and early afternoon puttering around the house, doing a little cleaning and straightening. At lunch, she picked up a book that Caroline had recommended, and got so lost in it that she only had 10 minutes to get ready for the afternoon game. Rosalee quickly let Billy out into the backyard, freshened her makeup, and grabbed her green tote bag off of the hook by the door. Wallet, phone, two water bottles, lipstick. She'd just finished double-checking that the lights were turned off and letting Billy back in when the doorbell rang. Billy and Rosalee together went to open it, and she smiled at George.

"Good timing," Rosalee said as he bent down to give Billy a good head scratch. "I'm just ready. Let me get Billy a treat to soften the blow that you're not staying."

"Do you ever take him out with you?" George asked, following her into the kitchen.

"Now and then," Rosalee said as she pulled a dog biscuit out of the jar on the counter. "But we went on a walk this morning, so I don't feel too bad leaving him today. He's probably pretty tired anyway. Old dogs, you know."

Rosalee told Billy goodbye, then grabbed her bag, keys, and sunglasses as she followed George out the door. They chatted about little things as they drove to the park. Once there, Rosalee directed George toward the back of the parking lot, near the fields that she knew Austin played. He pulled into a spot and shut the car off, but neither of them got out right away.

"Is your family out there yet?" George asked.

She glanced at him and noticed his fingers quietly drumming a rhythm on the steering wheel. Rosalee smiled a little. Somehow George's nervousness—which he was trying to hide—made her feel more relaxed.

"Looks like everyone," she said cheerfully. "You ready, cowboy?"

He grinned at her, and Rosalee felt 16 again. "Let's go."

Rosalee and George got out of the car and began walking toward the collection of lawn chairs and backpacks and coolers on one side of the field. The air smelled like dirt and crushed leaves and charcoal. The players warmed up on the field, while parents and siblings chatted. Rosalee led George toward a familiar circle of chairs. Elizabeth and Mary sat talking, while Charles and Jonathan stood slightly apart tossing a football. Keira and Chris sat on a blanket playing what looked like a card game. Rosalee noticed one familiar face that she hadn't seen in a while.

"Corbin's home!" She said.

Rosalee waved at her oldest grandchild—well, tied with Jessica, but Corbin had been born one minute earlier—who stepped away from his conversation to come meet us.

"Gram!" he said, wrapping her in a bear hug. "I missed you."

"I've missed you too, college boy," she said returning the hug. "How are things?"

"Great," he said. "Except all my play time gets interrupted by class and homework." He winked, then turned to George.

"Hi, I'm Corbin," he said, extending a hand. "You must be George."

"Guilty," George said with a smile. "And I have to say, it sounds like college hasn't changed much in the past 40 years."

Corbin laughed, and the three of us turned and started walking toward the rest of the family. Rosalee asked Corbin more questions about classes and his girlfriend. They angled toward Elizabeth and Mary first, and Rosalee made introductions. Elizabeth and Mary stood and greeted George with hugs.

"It's so nice to meet you," Mary said with a warm smile.

"It's great to meet you, too," George said. He flashed his own charming smile. We all sat down. "So," George continued. "What's the story here?" He asked nodding out toward the field. "Who are we playing and what are our chances?"

Mary started talking about the team and the game, and soon Jonathan and Charles joined us. After a few minutes, talk had shifted slightly. Elizabeth was telling Rosalee a work story, Mary and Keira were talking books, and the men were all talking college football. The group heard the referee's whistle blow and the game started. Conversation slowed down, although it didn't stop completely. After several minutes of watching the game—mostly doing the grandma thing and watching Austin, Rosalee glanced around the knot of fans and felt a deep contentment. Everything just seemed right: the weather, the game, family together, and the tall man sitting next to her. She reached over and squeezed his hand. He turned toward her with a smile.

"Want a pop?" she asked. "Or some water?"

"Sure," he replied. "Some water, thanks."

She slipped her hand out of his and grabbed two bottles out of the cooler at the edge of the plaid blanket on the ground.

"Thanks," he said when she handed him the damp bottle.

"You're welcome," she replied, sitting back in the chair next to him. Rosalee set her own bottle to the side for later. George uncapped his bottle and took a drink. Holding it in his left hand, he reached over with his right and took her hand in his. He looked at her, his eyes asking, *Is this okay?* She smiled, and her eyes said, *Yes.*

Rosalee saw Elizabeth glance at the two of them and saw her mouth tighten slightly when she saw them holding hands. Her first instinct was to pull away, but instead she just took a deep breath and reminded herself that she was a grownup, she was not doing anything wrong, and Elizabeth could just relax. Elizabeth opened her mouth, and Rosalee braced myself for some kind of disparaging remark, but Elizabeth was still on her best behavior.

"So, Mom says you just moved to Riverton," she said to George. "What do you think so far?"

"I love it," he said. "Big enough to have everything you need and lots to do, but small enough to still be relaxed and laid back. It's been a good antidote to Chicago."

"I would love living in Chicago," Corbin chimed in, pulling his eyes briefly away from the game. "That's where I plan on looking for a job once I graduate."

"That's the first I'm hearing of that," Elizabeth said. "How long have you been planning this, anyway?"

"Chicago is a great city," George jumped in. "I definitely don't regret having lived there. It's easy to find your niche, and most neighborhoods I've seen are so community minded, that you sometimes forget you're living in such a large city. It's big and vibrant, but not pretentious. It's not a 'survival of the fittest' city by any means. Personally, I was just…ready for a change, that's all."

George's interjection seemed to derail Elizabeth's impending 20 questions—which was his intent, Rosalee was sure—and Corbin began asking George questions about different neighborhoods, museums and colleges, sports teams, and pizza. She listened to their conversation, a picture of the city springing to life in her mind as they talked. Despite her youthful desires, Rosalee hadn't traveled nearly as much as she would have liked to over the years. She'd always dreamed of places more far flung than a nearby Midwestern city, but as George and Corbin talked, Chicago moved onto her mental list of places to visit.

The second half of the game got pretty exciting—and everyone was watching closely and cheering loudly. Austin's team won in the last few minutes, and everyone was feeling very celebratory afterword. They often went out for a meal or to get ice cream after family sports games, and today it was a sure thing. Austin picked pizza, to nobody's surprise, so everyone packed their cars and headed to his favorite place.

"This is fun," George said after they'd gotten into his car.

Rosalee smiled. "Yes, they all seem to be on good behavior."

George laughed. "You're too hard on them."

"We'll see."

It turned out neither of them was exactly right or wrong. The questions started getting a little more personal at dinner, but nothing one could construe as nosy or out of line. Everyone seemed to have a good time and Austin remained the star of the night. Rosalee had to laugh later that evening on the telephone with Caroline, though.

"The whole day was so surreal," she said. She was wrapped up in an old blanket and sitting on her back porch swing, watching Billy sniff the whole yard. "It was seriously like being in high school all over again. I half expected Charles or Jonathan to say, 'What are your intentions, young man?' No, that's not true. I half expected *Elizabeth* to say that."

Caroline laughed. "Well, we all want to feel young again, right?" she said.

Rosalee laughed as well, and they chatted for a few more minutes about her weekend, then hung up the phone. She moved inside and sat on the couch for a while, rubbing the top of Billy's head and resting her own on a couch cushion. She thought about the day, about the past few weeks, even the past few months. Her eyes found the framed wedding photograph hanging on the wall.

"Almost like old times, Tommy," she said to the picture of two smiling kids. "Back when I wasn't old and boring."

It reminded her of a conversation they'd had once when both the kids were small. Tommy had found her sitting at the kitchen table, a cold cup of coffee in front of her and a distant expression on her face.

"Where'd you go, Rose?" he'd asked, running his hand softly down my hair as he sat down in the chair next to me.

"Peru," I'd replied.

His eyebrows rose.

I smiled. "I've been reading a book about Peru. And it reminded me that I always wanted to go there."

Tommy picked up my hand and kissed the palm, then rested it against his cheek. "I'm sorry," he said. "I'm sorry I haven't been about to take you to all the places you've wanted to go."

"I'm not." I replied with no hesitation. "I love you. I love our family. I'm so happy I married you."

He kissed my hand again. "But?"

I sighed and stared at the window, the light reflecting our kitchen and hiding the outside. "Are we boring, Tommy?" I said finally.

"Maybe," he admitted. "Or maybe not boring, just…in a season of sameness."

I smiled. "I like that. A season of sameness. Very accurate, because most days I feel like my life is a merry-go-round."

"I think that'll change," Tommy said. "The kids will get older. They'll start doing different things. They'll have more freedom, which means we have more freedom."

"But in the meantime…" I clunked my head down on the table and snored loudly.

Tommy laughed. "Rose, you are the least boring person I know, even if you spend your days in an endless loop of cutting up food and wiping bottoms. You're reading books about Peru! We're having existential conversations over cold coffee!"

I laughed and pulled him in for a hug and a long kiss. "I love you, Tommy McDonnell."

Rosalee came back to her dim living room and snoring dog with a small sigh. She missed Tommy. Even though it was strange to miss him now, when a lot of the interesting things happening in her life wouldn't be happening if he were still around.

Gently, she roused Billy for his last trip to the backyard, deciding her brain was just too tired to ponder the contradictions in her feelings at the moment.

chapter *18*

March 1974

It was getting very difficult to pay attention in any of my classes at school. If it wasn't senioritis, it was my preoccupation with thinking about my most recent phone conversation or letter from George. And if it wasn't George, it was worrying about finding a job after graduation more substantial than occasional babysitting. And if it wasn't job searching, it was thinking about George's latest idea.

"You know, you're probably going to have to look outside of Carlton anyway," George was saying over the phone. "And you won't have any trouble finding a job in Kansas City."

"I'm sure you're right," I said. I was sitting at the kitchen table, feet tucked up under me, my hands fiddling with the telephone cord and my eyes scanning the house and yard to make sure no one in my family was about to walk within earshot. "That's just a big move," I said. "I was thinking more like Springfield or Columbia."

"But Kansas City has the bonus of one very important soon-to-be resident," George said, his voice teasing. He had just gotten offered a job in Kansas City a few weeks before.

I laughed. "I know. And that is a very appealing factor. But I know it will be more expensive."

"I told you, you can stay with my parents for a while, they won't mind. My mom would be happy to have someone in the house besides my dad for a change."

I appreciated George's offer on behalf of his parents… especially since he'd first mentioned us getting an apartment together—two bedroom, he'd been quick to specify. I'd had to apologize for my laughter. There is no way that would work out, I'd told him very plainly. For one thing, my parents would have a heart attack, and lock me in the attic like a crazy aunt. For another, I could only imagine how long George would be content to stay just roomies…and it wasn't that long.

"Don't you trust me?" he'd been offended.

"Of course I do," I sighed. "It just seems like it would be unnecessarily difficult and stressful. I'd love to live in the same city, just not in the same house."

Despite George's best efforts at securing a commitment from me, I asked him to let me do a little looking at what kinds of jobs were out there in Kansas City, and to just take a few weeks to think. I knew we both had midterms coming up anyway.

"Let's talk again in a few weeks," I'd said. "I just feel rushed, and I want to be sure." I could tell George wasn't thrilled, but he'd agreed.

I hadn't mentioned anything to my parents yet. I knew I'd need a plan—well researched, thought out, with the ability to counter any argument. If I decided to go for it, I'd also need to be prepared to play my "I'm-an-adult-now" card, which also meant I'd need to be pretty confident in my ability to support myself, since such a move might mean burning the bridge back home for a little while. I didn't want to burn any bridges. I loved my family. It was one of the reasons I was hesitating about this plan, but I didn't think the very independent George would really understand.

Our public library carried copies of the *Kansas City Star*, so I'd head there after school most days to study and look through the classifieds just to get an idea of what kind of jobs were out there that I qualified for. There seemed to be quite a few: several nanny jobs, secretarial jobs, and retail customer service that didn't seem to require any prior experience.

In between studying for midterms, I made up a formal pros and cons list. I wrote out a list of some possible arguments I thought my parents would make and countered them as best I could. I took my tests, wrote a few papers, and somewhere in there decided to take the plunge.

It'd been a few weeks since I'd talked to George or gotten a letter. I had babysat enough in those few weeks to pay my parents for a long distance call, so I picked up the phone on a Sunday afternoon, knowing it was the time he was most likely to be in his dorm room.

"Hello."

"Hey, Dave," I said to George's roommate. "It's Rosalee. Is George there?"

"Hi, Rosalee, how's it going?" Dave was friendly, and sometimes I had to try and hurry him along when he answered the phone. I wasn't paying long distance to talk to him, after all.

"Pretty good," I said. "Midterms are over. How about you?"

"No rest for the wicked," he said. I could hear the smile in his voice. "But you didn't call to talk to me," he continued. "George is right here, hold on."

"Hey."

"Hey yourself," I said. "How are you?"

"All right."

I paused, waiting for more. The moment stretched.

"So, I guess I've emerged from my rabbit hole," I said. "Sorry to be so distant there for a while."

"It's cool," George said. "I understand."

Another moment.

"I'm planning to talk to my parents tonight," I finally said, since small talk clearly wasn't happening.

"Really?" Finally, a little color in his voice. "What about?"

I smiled. "I want to move to Kansas City," I said. "I've been looking through classified ads and there's plenty of opportunities. More than here, that's for sure. I've got my reasoning and arguments and pros all laid out. My parents won't be able to resist my logic."

He laughed, and my neck muscles relaxed a little.

"I love it when you get logical," he teased.

"Hey, it comes in handy," I said with a laugh. "Seriously though, I know you think it's silly to be this extreme, since technically I'm going to be old enough to move out anyway, but I like my family. I don't want any strained relationships if I can avoid it."

"I understand," he said. "I can have my folks write to them if you'd like."

"That would be great," I said. "Actually, I'll probably talk to them tomorrow night. Walker has a ball game tonight. A letter coming after would be helpful, I think."

"I'll ask them tonight when they call," George said.

We chatted for a few more minutes, mostly George telling funny stories about his friends. It was nice now that I could put faces to most of the names. I told him about a couple of pranks some likely bored seniors had pulled at the school. Finally George admitted he had a ton of studying, so we said our goodbyes.

"This is really, really good news," George said. "I've missed you."

"Me, too," I said.

At supper the next night, I asked my parents if I could talk to them about something. "I have an idea of what I'd like to do once the school year is over," I said.

My parents exchanged a slightly apprehensive look, and my mom said, "I wasn't aware there was that much to discuss," she said. "You already know you'll need to find work."

I smiled, "I know. It's more like an idea for a job. Let's just talk about it later, okay?" I said, glancing at my brothers.

My dad changed the subject, and everything was normal. I didn't start getting butterflies in my stomach until I was doing dishes.

I was putting the last plate away when my parents walked into the kitchen. My mom put on a pot of coffee, and they sat at the table.

"The boys are watching TV," my mom explained. "Now's probably your best chance."

"Oh," I said. I sat down at the table across from my dad while my mom got out coffee mugs and a tin of cookies. I laced my fingers together on the tabletop, and stared at them as I started talking.

"I've been trying to figure out what kind of job I'd get here in Carlton, and started thinking that maybe looking a little further away might be nice. There would be more options, and I'd get the chance to move away for a bit, like if I was going to college."

"Are you thinking Springfield?" my dad said. "It's not a bad idea."

"Yes, but the benefit of staying home is saving money that you don't have to spend on room and board somewhere," my mom interjected.

"Not Springfield," I said, still looking at my hands. "I'm thinking of Kansas City."

The silence was thick. I glanced up at my parents, who were doing some kind of mental telepathy over the tin of cookies. The coffee percolated in the background.

"I can't help but wonder if George has anything to do with this," my dad said. His voice gave little away as to his feelings, but his calmness seemed forced. My mom stood up, poured three cups of coffee, and set them on the table. I grabbed one and wrapped my hands around the mug.

"He does," I admitted. "But I'd like to mention some other reasons why it isn't a bad idea."

My dad raised an eyebrow. My mom smiled a little. "Go ahead, sweetie."

I laid out my argument: there were many more opportunities for jobs in Kansas City, the pay better than work I could get in Carlton. I opened a notebook in which I'd written down some examples of job openings from the newspaper, and some comparative jobs in Springfield, knowing one of them would mention the option of living closer to home.

I told them that George's parents were willing to rent me a room at their house. That it was something they did from time to time for extra money, and wasn't it better to rent from people we had connections to? I admitted that, yes, the fact that George was moving back to Kansas City was a big draw. But I liked George, and I wasn't ready for the relationship to end permanently. This seemed like a safe way to move beyond a long-distance relationship and get to know each other in a long-term, face-to-face setting.

At this, I stopped. I'd been as persuasive as I could be.

My parents looked at each other, communicating in the wordless way that only people who know each other really well can.

"I don't like it," my dad said finally. "But I know that's mostly just me not wanting you to grow up. You're 18, you'll be making your own living. We can't really tell you no. If this is what you really want to do, we won't try to talk you out of it."

My breath left me in a rush, and I grinned. "Thank you," I said, reaching across the table to give my dad a hug, then my mom. "Thank you, thank you. Yes, this is what I want."

"Well." My dad drained his coffee, set it back on the table, and stood up. "I guess that's it for tonight. I'm off to bed. Sun comes up early."

I smiled. My dad had ended almost every evening with the phrase "sun comes up early" for as long as I can remember. Sometimes I thought about cross-stitching it on a pillow.

My mom stood and grabbed the three mugs, taking them to the sink to wash. I sat a moment longer, relishing the sounds of home—the heavy sound of my dad's boot-clad feet overhead. The gentle rush of water and clink of a dish being cleaned. The sound of canned laughter coming from the living room, and the echoing real laughter of my brothers.

"I better tell your brothers it's time to turn off the TV," my mom said, shutting off the water and drying her hands on a tea towel. She walked to the hallway separating our kitchen and living room. I heard her give a 15-minute warning, and the resulting dramatic groans from my brothers. A second later she was back in the kitchen doorway.

"I think we need to buy you an interview outfit," she said, a small smile on her face.

"Let's go up to Springfield this weekend."

"Really?" I asked. "That would be great! I have a little of my babysitting money saved up."

My mom waved her hand. "Now, that won't do," she said. "I've got a little bit saved up, too, and you'll need your money to get you through until your first paycheck." She smiled a little, then walked over to me. She rested her hand on my shoulder and kissed the top of my head. "I won't get to do things for my girl much longer," she said in a sad voice. "My treat."

I reached up and squeezed her hand. "Thanks, Mom," I said.

It was too late to call George—on my end, not his. My parents had a very strict no-telephone-after-8:30 rule, and I didn't feel like pushing things. But I practically danced up the stairs, and it took me a long time to stop grinning and an even longer time to fall asleep.

The next day after school, I attempted to call George, but he wasn't in.

"Do you know when he'll be back?" I asked Dave.

"Um...no," Dave said. "Um...I haven't seen him all day...

but I know…some things have come up, and he's a little busy. So…yeah, I'm not sure."

I'd never heard Dave struggle so much through a reply.

"Well, just let him know I called," I said. "And tell him I have some good news."

"I will," Dave sounded sad. "Bye, Rosalee."

I hung up the phone and just stood there for a minute, my forehead furrowed, a frown on my face. That was hands down the strangest conversation I'd ever had with Dave.

It was 8:15 that evening before George returned my call. The phone rang, and I jumped up from the couch. My dad gave me a look.

"I've got 15 minutes," I said as I left the room.

"Hello," I was slightly breathless from sprinting across the hallway.

"Hi, Rosalee." George said.

"What's wrong, grumpy," I said. "Didn't Dave tell you I have good news?"

"No, he did," George said. "It's just…I don't."

My smile disappeared. "What is it?" I asked.

Silence.

"George?"

He sighed. "I'm just…not sure how to say it," he said.

I sat down at the kitchen table. "Like ripping off a Band-Aid," I said. "Get it over with quick. It can't be that bad."

"Oh, it is," George said, his voice thick with a mix of emotions I couldn't quite identify.

Anger, disgust, sadness. "But you're right. There's no easy way to do this."

I waited, my fingers twisting the saltshaker around and a round, my other hand clutching the phone.

"Rosalee, I..." He paused again. "Kansas City is off," he said at last.

"That's not the bad news," I replied. "I mean, that's bad news, because I was calling to tell you it's on. But it's the reason. What is it, George. Just say it."

"I...my friend Jeanette is pregnant," he finally pushed out, the words tight and rushed. "The baby is mine. We're figuring out what we're going to do. We might get married."

My body stilled, all energy rushing to my brain, which was whirling at an incomprehensible speed at his words. Jeanette. Pregnant. Mine.

"Rosalee?"

"I don't understand," I said. My voice squeaked, and I attempted to bring it down a notch.

"When...I...I just don't understand."

"It was back when you and I agreed to give each other some space for school and figuring things out. And...I was lonely, and frustrated, and drunk at a party. It wasn't...I didn't mean for it to happen. It was a mistake."

"Yeah, well. I guess so." Brilliant response there. I felt my eyes burn and my throat clench. The room was stifling. I was having trouble breathing.

"I am so, so sorry. I just...you have no idea."

"Oh, I have a pretty good idea," I choked out. "And you are sorry. A sorry ass who deserves to have all his precious plans come crumbling around him."

"I know." George's voice was quiet.

"I have to go," I said. I could feel the pressure rising in my chest, and I was pretty sure the sobs were coming.

"I know. I'm sorry."

"Good luck," I managed and hung up the phone.

I took several deep breaths, forcing my body to stand, forcing my tears back in place for a few more moments, forcing my voice to sound mostly normal.

"I'm headed to bed," I said from the hallway, one foot on the stairs, my hand on the banister. I had to stay out of sight, because I knew there was no hiding anything from my mom. "See you all tomorrow."

I ran up the stairs, not bothering to wait for any response. As I hit the top step, I made a detour to the bathroom. I turned the shower on full blast to cover up any noise, then threw up. I emptied my stomach, silent tears streaming down my face, while my heart shattered into a million pieces.

chapter *19*

November 2018

The next few weeks were full—family stuff, getting ready for Thanksgiving Day festivities, working a couple of extra shifts at work to cover co-workers who were getting busy for the holidays— and Rosalee found herself loving every minute of it. George came to Sunday dinner, a birthday party, and another soccer game. Rosalee was a bit surprised at his eagerness to jump into her family life. After the first soccer game he'd come to with her, she'd expected him to consider the meet-the-family box checked, but the week after the game, she and George were out having coffee and George had surprised her by asking if he could come to Sunday dinner.

"Really?" Rosalee asked.

"You can say no," George was quick to respond. "I'm sorry if I overstepped."

"No, no, it's fine that you asked. I'm just surprised, that's all. It's..." She couldn't find the right word. Bold? Weird? Indicative of stronger feelings than she was expecting?

"I've made you uncomfortable."

"No! Well...a little?"

"Maybe another time." George smiled and took a sip of his

coffee, clearly unoffended by her hesitation and confusion. They were quiet for a moment while Rosalee sorted through her thoughts.

"Why do you want to come?" she asked finally.

George thought for a minute. "A couple of reasons. I'm really enjoying spending time with you, and I want to do it more. I also really like your family. I don't have a lot of family nearby, and the big family atmosphere is nice."

When he put it that way.

"Please come," she said, reaching out her hand and squeezing his. "I'd like that."

Elizabeth hadn't been quite as excited when Rosalee had told her that George was coming, but she'd been a gracious if somewhat quiet hostess. Aside from that, family dinner was as lively and fun as always. George ended up sitting at the end of the table near Keira, Chris, and Austin—Rosalee was confident that wasn't an accidental seating arrangement, but she didn't make a fuss—and he made a point to ask Keira about what she was reading, ask Austin about soccer, and listen attentively as Chris described his new favorite video game. As everyone started to push back from the table and pick up empty plates, George stood up and rolled up his sleeves, grabbing a stack of dirty dishes and heading straight to the kitchen sink.

"Let me wash up," he said to Elizabeth when she walked up.

"Oh, no, you're a guest," she protested.

"I insist," he said. "Please. It was a lovely meal, and you are kind enough to let me intrude on family time. If you must, just grab another glass of wine and sit there to keep me company and tell me where things go."

Rosalee gently pushed Elizabeth onto a barstool and got

glasses of wine for them both, distracting Elizabeth with questions about work and what TV shows she was watching. George quietly washed and dried as mother and daughter talked, the gentle splash and swish and thunk of dishwashing a pleasant soundtrack to their conversation.

About the time George had dried the last dish, Rosalee's two glasses of wine were making her yawn.

"Are you ready to head out, or do you want to stay a while longer," George asked.

"I better go before I curl up on the couch and fall asleep for the night. I'll make the rounds."

The three of them made their way to the living room where Rosalee and George said their goodbyes. Rosalee was hoping Elizabeth would invite George back to another Sunday dinner, but while she was polite and thanked him for helping clean up, she didn't appear to have softened much. *At least everyone else seems to like him*, Rosalee thought as they waved one last time and walked out to the car.

"Thank you," she said as George opened her car door, waiting until she'd gotten settled before shutting it behind her.

A moment later he was sliding in next to her and starting the car.

"Well," he said smiling at her before turning his attention to backing out of the driveway. "I don't know if you noticed that I was on my best behavior. Did it work?"

Rosalee laughed. "I think the kids are fans, and I know Mary loves anyone who will listen to Chris talk about video games so she doesn't have to. Jonathan and Charles are usually on dish duty, so you've made two friends there."

"I don't think my charms worked on Elizabeth, though."

"No. Sorry, but not yet. Good effort, though."

George laughed, then sighed.

"I wouldn't worry too much," Rosalee said. "For one thing, you've only spent time with her twice, and she takes a while to warm up to people. For another, 'charming' doesn't usually work on Elizabeth. Sincerity, authenticity…that carries more weight with her."

"Good to know."

Rosalee glanced over at George, trying to read his expression. Was he upset by what she'd just said? It was hard to tell in the dark car, but his hands did seem to be gripping the steering wheel pretty hard.

"I wasn't trying to be offensive," Rosalee said. "Did something I say upset you?"

George's hands unclenched slightly. "No."

There was a long pause. Rosalee was starting to feel a little irritated—*not everyone has to love you at first sight,* she thought. She opened her mouth to say just that when his voice stopped her.

"I'm sorry," he said. "Even now it's a little tough when I can't win a person over right away." One corner of his mouth turned up in a half-smile. "Charming people is still my default, even at my age. Although—for the record—everything I did or said tonight really did come from a place of sincere interest. Even talking about video games."

Rosalee relaxed. "I guess we all have our armor."

They chatted about inconsequential things on the rest of the short drive to Rosalee's house, and he walked her to her door to say goodnight.

"Thank you for letting me spend time with your family," he said.

"Thank you for coming."

Rosalee unlocked the front door, pushed it open, and was immediately greeted by a happy dog.

"Hey, boy."

George leaned over and scratched Billy behind the ears before turning to walk back to his car.

"Have a good night," he said. "I'll call you this week."

Rosalee waved as he started his car, then sighed a happy sigh as she went in the house.

Rosalee and George talked quite a bit that week, usually in the evenings, and Rosalee realized how much she'd missed talking to someone at the end of the day, sometimes processing a bad day, sometimes laughing about nothing, and even once watching the same TV show with the phone pressed up to her ear. George left town Friday to visit his daughter for a few days, but it worked out, because Rosalee and Jessica were overdue for a Friday night movie night. Movie night had evolved a little, starting when Rosalee mentioned that Keira might like to start joining them. Rosalee and Jessica were having a quick weekday lunch near campus, and Rosalee watched Jessica's face carefully to gauge her reaction. She was happy to see genuine excitement.

"Great idea!" she said. "Keira's so much fun now."

That Friday, with Keira in happy attendance, Jessica was taking so long to get her stuff together at the end of the evening that Rosalee finally said, "Spill it, sweetheart. I can tell something's on your mind."

Jessica smiled sheepishly. "I've been wondering...my friend Margo has been really lonely lately. She misses her family and can't get up to Chicago to see them very often. I wondered if you'd mind if I invited her sometimes to Friday nights?"

"Of course!" Rosalee said, giving Jessica a hug. "One condition."

Jessica raised her eyebrows.

"Can I invite one of my own girlfriends sometime?" Rosalee asked with a smile.

"Gram, you have girlfriends?" Keira asked.

Rosalee rolled her eyes, "Yes, sweet and unbelieving granddaughters, your grandmother has friends."

"Well, it's not so much that you have friends," Keira said, a mischievous sparkle in her eye. "It's just...can you call them *girl*friends at your age?"

Rosalee laughed. "Well, I can't very well call them 'old lady friends.' Besides, we're all girls at heart."

Over the next few weeks, Friday night movie night became more consistent again and a lot more lively. The new mix of people also made for much more interesting movie choices. Rosalee would never have picked a movie about collegiate acapella singing groups, but found herself laughing until tears came out of her eyes. And the younger girls had never seen a Cary Grant romantic comedy, but admitted after it was over that they couldn't wait to see another. Rosalee and Caroline promised a December viewing of the original *Miracle on 34th Street*, which they were both appalled to hear that the younger girls had never seen.

She and George met for lunch a few times, he joined them again for Sunday family dinner, and one Thursday evening he

came over to help her babysit for the Blairs. He had called that
morning, wondering if she was free for a movie.

"Oh, that sounds lovely, but I'm babysitting for the Blairs
next door so Celia and Levi can go out for their anniversary."

"Another time," George said. "Although..." he added after a
moment. "How do you think they'd feel if you had a boy over?"

"Well, it would be kind of creepy if I had a boy over."

George laughed. "Okay, a gentleman caller."

"Well, that's a different story," Rosalee smiled. "I'm sure it
would be fine, but let me ask and give you a call back."

As Rosalee expected, the Blairs didn't have a problem with it.
George came over after dinner but before the kids were in bed.
Rosalee enjoyed watching him build Lego creations with Tripp
while she made sure Aislinn didn't put anything dangerous in
her mouth.

When Rosalee came back into the living room after getting the
kids settled, George was sitting on the couch reading a magazine.
He smiled as she walked into the room and patted the cushion
next to him. Rosalee sat down next to him and smiled back. "Do
you want some coffee?" she asked. "Or a soda or something?"

George shook his head. "No thanks," He leaned forward
and put the magazine back down on the coffee table then leaned
back against the couch. After a moment he slipped his arm across
Rosalee's shoulders and gently pulled her closer. "Thanks for
letting me crash your babysitting party," he said.

Rosalee leaned her head against George's shoulder with a
small sigh. "Thanks for crashing," she said.

He squeezed her shoulder but didn't say anything. Rosalee
closed her eyes, enjoying the comfortable silence of being in

someone else's company. Much different than the silence of being in one's own company, she thought. Not that she didn't enjoy her alone time as much as the next person—maybe sometimes more than the next person—but too much of a good thing was still too much. This silence was comforting, relaxing.

So relaxing, in fact, that when she heard a key in the front door, her whole body jerked and she sat up, feeling disoriented.

"Did I fall asleep?" she asked George, running her fingers under her eyes.

He grinned. "I think we both did."

She rolled her eyes. "Aren't we exciting." She stood up as Celia and Levi walked into the room.

"How was your evening?" she asked, stifling a yawn.

"Lovely!" Celia said. "We went to dinner and then went to get coffee before seeing a movie, but the coffee shop had this great guitarist playing, so we ended up just staying there and enjoying the music."

"Sounds nice!" Rosalee said.

"How about you guys?" Celia asked as she set her purse and keys on the small table by theentryway. "Anything exciting happen while we were gone?"

"Just the opposite!" Rosalee said with a laugh. "The kids were great. We played and they went to bed with no trouble. Then George and I fell asleep reading magazines. The perils of having elderly babysitters."

"Whatever!" Celia exclaimed. "You are far from elderly. I know how much of an early bird you are, so I'm guessing you're just up past your bedtime."

George raised his hand. "I know that's my problem."

They all laughed and chatted for a few more minutes before Celia went to peek in on the kids and Levi walked them to the door. Rosalee pulled her thick sweater tight around her as they walked through the yard toward her house. The night air was cool and crisp with a decidedly late fall feel. George put his arm around her shoulders.

"Sorry I wasn't exciting company tonight," he said.

"Nonsense," Rosalee replied. "You were the perfect company." She glanced up at him. "Everything just feels a little nicer when you have someone you care about to share it with." It felt like a bold thing to say—saying out loud that she cared about him seemed like it moved into territory slightly different than just "I'm glad we're friends."

It was something she'd only just realized for herself, something she'd only just admitted. A more cautious version of herself might have held that feeling a little closer to the chest for a while longer, but Rosalee had decided her grandson was right—she wasn't getting any younger. She'd earned the right to be a little bit bold in her life, and she did care about him. If she were perfectly honest with herself, the past few weeks had been some of the best she'd had in a long time, and while it wasn't entirely because of George, she knew their conversations and time spent together were definitely part of it. She still wasn't yet sure if her feelings were more tied to the George in her memory or the man who stood in front of her, but she was interested in finding out.

Rosalee pulled her keys out of her pocket as they climbed the front steps.

"So, clearly you're tired," George said. Rosalee raised an eyebrow and George laughed.

"Okay, clearly *we* are tired. I know tomorrow's movie night. What about during the day tomorrow? Do you work all day?"

"Just hoping to get a head start on Thanksgiving shopping."

"Excellent! You want to have brunch and then we can go to the store together? My fridge is pretty bare at the moment."

"So glamorous," Rosalee said with a smile, but reached out to take his hand and give it a squeeze. "But yes, that sounds nice. Thanks for the company tonight."

"Any time."

George took a small step toward her, and without thinking Rosalee lifted her face as he leaned down and pressed his lips against hers. The kiss was soft, almost tentative. A first kiss. But it made her smile, and when she didn't pull back, George slid an arm around her waist and kissed her again. This kiss was warmer, deeper. It was a kiss between lips that had met before. It was hello again. And Rosalee wasn't cold anymore.

George pulled back. "See you tomorrow."

"Tomorrow."

She unlocked her door as George made his way to his car, turning to wave as she stepped inside the lamp-it entry. She closed the door, locked it, and set her keys on the hall table. She went through her typical night-time routine: let Billy out, brushed her teeth, showered, and set a glass of water and her book on the bedside table. Only that night, she did it all with a big smile on her face, and a fizzy feeling in her stomach.

They tried a new place for brunch the next morning, about a mile from George's house.

He said he passed it almost every day on his way anywhere and it seemed a shame not to try it out.

The restaurant dining room was stunning, Rosalee thought as she looked around while George spoke to the hostess. It was almost entirely windows with bright white trim. The small amount of wall space was also painted bright white and contained brightly colored photographs of produce. Rosalee thought the photographs made the room seem fresh and inviting. The view outside the windows was of a garden, clearly both decorative and functional, the last of the winter squash and root vegetables sharing space with decorative shrubbery and ornamental grasses, freshly tilled earth marking the spots where she imagined summer vegetables had grown. The only downside that Rosalee could see was the fact that nearly every inch of floor space was covered in tables and chairs, making for a very crowded and loud environment. Hopefully some delicious food would make up for it.

The hostess sat Rosalee and George at a booth. Rosalee sat down, and George slid in beside her.

"I thought we might be able to hear each other better this way," he said, stretching his arm across the back of the booth behind her. Rosalee raised an eyebrow at the grin on his face.

"Good thinking," she said. But she had to admit that this way they could have a conversation without shouting.

They perused the menu for a few minutes. George said he'd heard that the French toast was amazing, and they discovered that they both loved Eggs Benedict. The waitress came with their water and coffees, and since neither one could make up their mind, decided to order the walnut bread French toast and classic Eggs Benedict and just share. The waitress smiled at them as she took their menus.

"You guys are as cute as my grandparents," she said. "They've been married 45 years, and I swear they act like a couple of newlyweds half the time."

Neither Rosalee or George bothered correcting her, just thanked her for the compliment as she walked off to tend to her other tables and enter their order. For a brief second, Rosalee contemplated feeling awkward, but as George turned his dark blue eyes toward her and they crinkled at the corners, she decided awkward was for teenagers and 20-year-olds.

"Do you think if things had worked out differently, we'd still be acting like newlyweds?" Rosalee asked.

George took her hand and squeezed gently. "I'd like to think so," he said. "But either way, I'm just glad we're here together now."

"Me, too," Rosalee said.

chapter 20

May 1974

The night after I talked to George, I told my parents that George and I had broken up, so plans had changed. I'd stick around Carlton after graduation, and see what happened on the job front. I might look for jobs in Springfield if nothing good popped up closer to home.

My parents asked what happened, but I told them I didn't want to talk about it. Of course, Dad was happy to leave it at that. Mom would have liked more details, I could tell, but there was no way. I didn't even really talk about it with Betty. Just told her that George had found someone else and was getting married. Betty suspected, I'm sure, but she knew me well enough, and she knew my stubborn face when she saw it. So, thankfully, she didn't push, just gave me a hug and told me anytime I needed to do a little George bashing she was up for it.

Betty and I spent most of our free time after school looking for jobs within a 30-minute radius. She ended up taking a job at the diner when one of the waitresses got too pregnant to keep working on her feet 40 hours a week. I wasn't having much luck, but, truthfully, wasn't looking all that hard. I didn't feel motivated to do much more than lie on my bed and listen to Patsy Cline. But eventually life caught up with me, despite my best efforts. I was in the drug store the Monday after graduation buying a couple of magazines, trying not to think about George, and ignoring the fact that I still didn't have a job. Tommy McDonnell was ringing me up and I was pretty quiet that day.

"I hear you're looking for a job," he said after asking for the $3.50 for my selection of magazines.

"Sure am," I replied, fishing the money out of my pocket.

"We're hiring a full-time clerk and potential store manager," he said. "Excellent pay, plus a 10 percent discount."

"Isn't that your job?" I asked with a small smile.

"I'm headed to pharmacy school in September," he said. "Dad wants me to have plenty of time to train my replacement."

I picked up my magazines and thought for a minute. My eyes caught the battered paperback he had tucked next to the register.

"Would I get to read as many books on the job as you do?" I asked with a nod at his book.

Tommy grinned, a dimple appearing in his right cheek. "Dad doesn't really care as long as everything and everybody is well taken care of," he said. "My guess is that you're a hard worker, so yeah, once you get in a groove, I imagine you would. Well," he added, "maybe not quite as many. I'm a pretty fast reader."

I laughed. "Challenge accepted, McDonnell," I said.

I asked him a few more relevant details about the job, then filled out an application. Then Tommy took me back to the pharmacy counter to meet his dad and hand him my paperwok. Mr. McDonnell invited me to come back to interview in a couple of days, and I agreed, writing down the time on a business card.

Tommy walked with me back to the front of the store.

"Thanks," I said. I pocketed the card and tucked my magazines under my arm.

"No problem," he said with another smile. "After all, I do have a vested interest on who I end up spending most of my summer with."

I smiled. "Good point. Well, see you Thursday." I waved and walked out the door.

My parents were pleased about the interview when I told them at dinner that night. I think Dad was just glad that I had a prospect for a full-time job, finally, and Mom was definitely hoping it meant I'd stick around for a few more years.

"Just think how much money you could save living at home!" she said while passing a bowl of mashed potatoes.

I nodded. "That's true."

"And maybe you'll discover you have an interest in pharmacy!" she went on. "Imagine that, a pharmacist in the family."

"I guess anything is possible."

My sarcasm was lost on her, although one of my little brothers snickered. I could see my mom's thousand-yard stare, and knew she was imagining many conversations that included the phrase "my daughter, the pharmacist."

I had been paying even less attention to my appearance lately than usual. My look that summer consisted of unwashed hair in a ponytail or braid, whatever jeans or cutoff shorts that weren't so dirty they stood up on their own, and a t-shirt or tank top. It drove Betty crazy, but I figured I didn't have anyone to impress, so why bother. But on Thursday, I talked myself into making an effort, because I knew deep inside my malaise that I really did need a job. So I washed and dried my hair, painted my nails, put on a little bit of makeup, and ironed my gray pencil skirt and a white oxford shirt. I found a small pair of silver hoop earrings, wrestled on some pantyhose, and borrowed a pair of my mom's heels before heading out the door.

Tommy was at the front register as usual when I walked through the pharmacy door, the bells jingling cheerfully in my wake. He looked up from a stack of papers spread out on the counter and grinned. "You look really nice," he said. "I don't think I've ever seen you that dressed up."

"Well, I figured it was a better look for a job interview than raggedy shorts."

"Hmm…well, my dad would probably agree," he said. "Although you do look good in a pair of raggedy shorts."

I blushed. Was Tommy flirting with me? I wasn't sure what to think about that.

"I'll tell Dad you're here," he said, stepping away from the counter.

I stood next to the counter, clutching my purse to my side and trying not to fidget. I glanced over at the stack of papers Tommy had been looking at. A list of store items stared back at me, subdivided into aisles and with a column for numbers. Must be inventory. I heard footsteps coming toward me and took a step back, not wanting to appear to be snooping. A moment later Tommy and Mr. McDonnell came out of one of the aisles. Mr. McDonnell was wearing tan pants, a light blue button-up shirt, and a white lab coat. A pair of reading glasses sat on his nose, and his smile was warm.

"Hello, Ms. Barnes," he said, extending a hand. I shook it, hoping my palms weren't too sweaty.

"Hello Mr. McDonnell," I said. "Thank you for meeting me today."

"Thank you for applying for the job," he said. "We haven't had too many applicants yet, and I know Tommy is anxious to train his replacement so he can start thinking about school and not this old place. Now, come on back to my office and we can chat."

He turned and started toward the back of the store. I glanced over at Tommy, who gave me a thumbs-up. I smiled and followed Mr. McDonnell to his tiny office. Mr. McDonnell pulled a small, wooden chair from where it sat in the corner of the room, then squeezed behind the huge wooden desk that took up almost every available space. I wondered if the office had once been a closet, because with the chair sitting in front of the desk, you couldn't close the door. There was a bookshelf behind the desk, and small filing cabinet as well, which Mr. McDonnell kept bumping into every time he leaned back in his desk chair.

"So, Ms. Barnes," he said, glancing at my application and peering at me over his glasses. "I see most of your previous work experience is in childcare. What made you decide to apply for a retail position?"

I checked my posture, making sure I was sitting up straight but keeping my soldiers relaxed. I tried to feel relaxed. "To be honest, sir, right now I'm simply looking for full-time work, something I can do to save up money and keep busy. Tommy's description of the job sounded like something I could do, and something that would provide low stress but enough variety and responsibility to keep me from being too bored. And he mentioned the possibility of promotion to an assistant management position, which is appealing on its own or as a step toward other things in the future."

"Hmm." Mr. McDonnell made a note on the application. "And tell me about the future," he said. "What are your goals, where do you want to be in five years?"

I hesitated, wanting to make sure I knew exactly what I was going to say so I didn't fumble around an answer.

"My greatest desire right now is to travel," I said. "Domestically, internationally…everywhere and anywhere. In five years, I would like to have a job that either includes some travel, or one that provides enough income and flexibility to travel regularly—not necessarily all the time," I said with a small laugh. "I'm realistic about real work. But if I were able to take short, weekend-length trips here and there, and then at least one longer vacation a year…well, that would be heaven. As far as what kind of career would lend itself to that…" I shrugged. "I'm still doing my research. I've thought of saving up for college and studying journalism. I've thought about pursuing administrative and secretarial jobs with the goal of one day working for an international company. I've also thought of going to college and earning a degree in French—I was pretty good in my high school classes—and seeing what kind of jobs that could get me."

I stopped, realizing I might have been dreaming my way out of a job. I bit my tongue, fighting the urge to add some kind of pandering "but-I-really-want-this-job!" statement.

"Sounds lovely," Mr. McDonnell said. "For you, of course." He smiled, and I saw Tommy in the twinkle of his eye. "Personally, I'm a homebody. A weekend in Branson is about as far as I'm willing to go. But everybody's different."

I returned his smile.

We talked then about more job-specific things. He asked me

what my strengths and weaknesses were, and had me do some basic math exercises. He went over the job duties and asked if anything sounded too overwhelming or beyond my abilities. Finally, he closed the manila folder containing my application, the work he'd had me do, and his notes.

"Well, Ms. Barnes," he said. "I will review this information along with our other applicants, and get back to you by the end of the week."

I stood. "Thank you again," I said.

He leaned over the desk and shook my hand. "My pleasure."

I made my way through the store to the front door.

"How'd it go?" Tommy asked as I passed by register.

I shrugged. "Pretty well, I think. Your dad's really nice. He said he'd review the applications and get back to me by the end of the week."

Tommy laughed. "By 'review the applications' he means 'double check your references and give you the job.' There are no other applicants."

I smiled. "Well, then, I'd say the interview went exceptionally well."

I turned to go. "I'll see you later," I said.

"See you Monday."

chapter *21*

December 2018

"He wants me to meet his daughter this weekend."

Rosalee and Caroline were sitting outside eating lunch at a picnic table in the library courtyard. Rosalee had started joining Caroline for a late lunch on Thursdays before her shift started, and since it was sunny and not too cold, they opted to eat outside.

"That feels like a big step," Caroline said. "Does it feel like that to you?" She unwrapped her sandwich and opened a small container of strawberries.

Rosalee nodded. She dragged a carrot stick through her hummus but just sat with the bite in her hand. "But am I being weird? We're adults. I feel like it shouldn't be a big deal. It's not like we're kids dating and meeting each others' parents."

"Maybe that's why it feels big," Caroline said. You ARE an adult. There's no…obligation to introduce each other to family. You're not taking each other home to meet the parents. You can date or whatever independent of anyone else."

That makes sense, Rosalee thought. "He's met my kids," she admitted. "It feels a little different because his daughter doesn't live in town. So it…it seems like more of an effort, I guess. It feels bigger."

"I can see that," Caroline said. She nodded at Rosalee's untouched lunch. "The back-to-work alarm goes off in 20 minutes."

"Thanks, Mom," Rosalee joked. But she pushed down her unsettled feeling and tried to eat something. Her practical side knew Caroline was right and she'd be hungry later if she didn't eat. They talked about a little work drama for a few minutes before revisiting Rosalee's dating dilemma. She sometimes referred to her and George in that way because it made her roll her eyes at herself. She was 63, for pete's sake! Too old for dating drama. She'd accepted the fact that she wasn't too old for dating but certainly too old for self-inflicted drama. It'd been three months since she and George had reconnected. Three delightful months of getting to know her first love, her first heartbreak, all over again.

"Does it make you feel like you have to define the relationship a little bit more?" Caroline asked.

"Yes."

"Well?" Caroline propped her chin in her fist, eyebrow raised, and waited. Her seemingly effortless ability to remain unruffled was settling and calming.

"I want to meet her," Rosalee admitted. She packed and repacked her lunch bag as she talked, her fingers unable to stay still. "I want to get to know her, because I hope we'll be seeing a lot of each other."

"You see things moving forward with George?"

Rosalee nodded. "I think…" She tested out the words in her

mind before speaking them. "I think I love him," she said. "Again. Still." She closed her eyes. "Again." Open. "Is it too soon?"

Caroline shrugged. "Only you know that. But for what it's worth, you're a grown woman, which means you know your own mind a lot better than you used to. You understand love more than you used to. And it's not like you and George are strangers. It's possible, that's all I'm saying."

Rosalee relaxed a little. It felt good to say it, to talk about it, when she knew she'd been thinking about it for the past few weeks. She hated needing validation for her own feelings, but sometimes it helped to know that at least one person didn't think she was crazy. Rosalee felt even more grateful for Caroline a few minutes later as they got up to walk inside and she reminded Rosalee about Caroline's Christmas dinner party next week to which she'd invited her and George. An actual adult dinner party, Caroline said with a smile, just friends. No family drama, no kids, no grandkids. The thought delighted Rosalee. As they went to their workstations, she promised to call with a meet-the-daughter update.

Two nights later Rosalee found herself with significantly fewer butterflies in her stomach as she stood in front of George's door, a bottle of wine in one hand as she rang the doorbell with the other.

She looked just like her picture, Rosalee thought, except so full of life and energy that it was almost like the picture was in black and white. In person, her blue eyes were so like George's that it almost took Rosalee's breath away. Her dimpled smile was as full of mischief and laughter as the first time Rosalee saw a similar smile in the makeup aisle of Mr. McDonnell's pharmacy.

"You must be Mrs. McDonnell!" the young woman exclaimed, immediately pulling Rosalee in for a hug. "I'm Kristen."

"Please call me Rosalee," Rosalee said returning the hug. "Too much formality makes me uncomfortable. I gave up Mrs. McDonnell when my kids and their friends started getting married."

Kristen laughed. "Done," she said. She shut the front door and gestured for Rosalee to follow her down the hall. "Come on back. Dad's in the kitchen."

Rosalee studied Kristen as they walked down the hall and into the kitchen. She was tall, with long, thick, curly hair. Rosalee noticed that what initially looked like highlights was actually graying hair. It made sense—Kristen was a few years older than Elizabeth, after all—but Rosalee didn't often meet women that age who chose not to color their hair. Kristen was dressed casually—jeans, a striped knit shirt, and stocking feet. She had a breezy, relaxed aura that immediately put Rosalee more at ease.

George was stirring something in a pot on the stove when they rounded the corner into the brightly lit kitchen. His face lit up and he set his spoon down so he could walk around the island and give Rosalee a hug and kiss on the cheek.

"Thanks for coming tonight," he said softly into her ear. "It really means a lot."

She smiled. "Of course," she replied, her nervousness beginning to abate.

Kristen started pulling wine glasses down from the top shelf of a cabinet. "I thought we'd go ahead and open the Shiraz that Rosalee brought," she said, nodding her head at the bottle she'd set on the kitchen counter.

"Sounds perfect," George replied, returning to his post at the stove.

Kristen uncorked the wine and poured it into the three stemless glasses she'd set on the counter, then picked up all three glasses like someone who spent a lot of time waitressing. She handed George and Rosalee each a glass before holding her own slightly aloft.

"Here's to old friends and new stories," she said.

"Cheers." She and George replied in unison. The clink of the three glasses against each other struck Rosalee in that moment as the most homey and friendly sound in the world.

"Your Dad tells me you've been thinking of moving down here," Rosalee said after a sip of her wine. "What put it on your radar?"

"I'm looking to cut my living expenses, basically," Kristen said, leaning one hip against the kitchen counter. "I'm a freelance writer and editor and do quite a bit of traveling for work. It's finally hit me that maybe I can save for retirement faster if my 'home base' expenses are lower. My closest friend from college has lived here for ages, so that's why I'm considering here. And it's not too far from a major airport, which is a requirement."

"That makes sense," Rosalee said.

"But who cares about me?" Kristen said smiling. "I've heard all of Dad's stories a million times. I need some new ones."

Rosalee had slipped around to the stove to peek inside George's pot. He handed her a spoon so she could sneak a taste, so thankfully her mouth was full for long enough to process Kristen's question for a moment.

"All of his stories?" she asked.

"Oh, yeah," Kristen replied. "And I think I heard the more embarrassing ones earlier than you'd expect. Dad was pretty intent on keeping me from making a lot of mistakes with deadbeat guys." A fond look at George softened her words. "So I know about how you met and how you broke up, and then I know about him and Mom and our life obviously. But I want to hear about you. Where'd you end up? What do you love? What are your kids like?"

"Wow," Rosalee said, sliding onto a bar stool at the island and taking a sip of wine. "Not sure where to start."

"How'd you meet your husband?"

Rosalee took another drink from her wine glass and told herself she needed to slow down before she ended up with a full glass on an empty stomach, but she also needed a minute to gather her thoughts. She admired Kristen's openness and forthrightness, but it was unexpected. And it wasn't that she minded talking about Tommy and how they met—or really, how they ended up dating and marrying, since they basically met in grade school—but she wondered how to tell the story with George standing right there. She glanced over at him where he was busy preparing a salad and checking on the risotto. He looked up, seeming to sense her gaze, and winked at her.

"Kristen's a writer," he said." She's always digging for a good story."

Kristen put one hand on her heart and held the other one up palm facing out. "I solemnly swear I am not mining your life for my own work. I just love learning about people."

"In that case," Rosalee began, "I suppose I should start with the fact that Tommy—my husband—and I started kindergarten together, like almost everyone in our tiny town, but we weren't really friends until I started working at his father's drug store after high school."

She told them about how she and Tommy had bonded over books, and how they got to be friends, even though Tommy claimed he was in love with her the whole time. She told them how patient he'd been, waiting for her to be ready to fall in love—tactfully skipping over the reason for her hesitation, which was understood anyway. She talked about their early marriage, saving as much money as they could, eating grilled cheese for dinner half the time so they could travel as much as possible—mostly road trip across the U.S., especially once the kids had come along. She talked about her kids and grandkids and the neighborhood she loved. She told funny stories about having a teenage granddaughter living with her, and she was able to stay pretty matter-of-fact about Tommy's long illness. She talked about her volunteer work at the elementary school and her part-time job at the library. By the time she was finished talking, they were scraping up the last crumbs of an apple pie, and the coffee was almost gone.

"I can't believe you let me talk this whole evening!" she said, "That was excellent pie, by the way," she told Kristen.

"Thank you!" Kristen replied. "Pie is my thing. Can't cook worth beans, but I can make a darn good pie."

"And don't worry about talking a lot," George said, standing up from the table and reaching around to gather the plates they had practically licked clean. "As soon as you leave, Kristen will tell me this was the most fascinating and wonderful evening. Hearing someone's life story is basically her favorite thing to do."

Kristen shrugged, conceding the point.

"Well, I love going to the movies too," she said. "But that's kind of the same thing."

Rosalee started helping clear the table while Kristen excused herself to the ladies' room. Rosalee set the dishes in the kitchen sink, then turned to find George standing inches away from her. Her heart lurched and her pulse quickened. "Hey there, Sneaky," she said, mentally rolling her eyes at her breathlessness. Like a teenager, she thought.

George rested one hand against the counter next to her, trapping her. "I liked hearing you talk, too," he said softly. His eyes were still so dark, Rosalee thought. And at that moment, they were full of openness and friendship and maybe a hint of the same thing that still had Rosalee's heart pounding.

"Thanks," she said. It wasn't exactly her ideal response, but it was the only thing coming to mind at the moment. Except for the thought that she'd really like to kiss George, and she wondered how long Kristen would be in the bathroom.

"Long enough," George said.

Rosalee's eyebrows shot up and he laughed a low, delighted, laugh that she felt from her head to her toes.

"You're not that good at hiding your thoughts," he said as he bent toward her.

"Apparently not," Rosalee murmured as his mouth settled on hers, and he wrapped his arms around her. He tasted like apples and coffee and butter, and the kiss felt like dessert. Slow, sweet, and something she wanted to savor for a long time.

"Break it up, kids."

Rosalee jumped away from George, but his arms stayed

around her so it was more like hopping in place. He laughed, and she wasn't sure if it was at her jumpiness or the grin on Kristen's face. Rosalee blushed, but it was clear that even though Kristen was teasing them, she wasn't surprised or shocked to find them kissing in the kitchen, and went right into a question about her and George's plans the next day as though seeing her dad and a woman she'd just met kiss in the kitchen was something she saw every day.

Rosalee leaned her head against George's shoulder as he and Kristen talked, and thought about how nice it was to not feel defensive or under inspection. How nice it felt just to spend an evening together. How it all felt pleasantly normal. She felt a yawn building up and knew she'd need to leave soon but was surprised to find how reluctant she was. Surprising, considering how reluctant she'd been to come in the first place. She couldn't think of a nicer surprise.

chapter 22

July 1974

The click of Mr. McDonnell's wingtips coming down the makeup aisle jolted me out of my reverie. I blushed, embarrassed to be caught staring into space. At least I'd just finished straightening the display.

"Good morning, Mr. McDonnell," I said as he passed by.

"Good morning, Ms. Barnes," he said with a smile.

I'd been working at the drug store almost two months and still stood up a little straighter every time my kind employer called me "Ms. Barnes." He called his own son "Mr. McDonnell" at work, and when I asked Tommy about it, he just shrugged. "Dad thinks it's important to be professional and courteous with all employees and customers—even in Carlton, where half the employers are related to you and half the customers changed your diaper when you were a baby."

I'd laughed, as I did at most of what Tommy said. We'd always been friendly—like he said, Carlton was a small town, and I was friendly with almost everyone—but he was usually quiet and reserved, especially at school. I'd never known how funny he was.

I took a slightly different route back to the front of the

store so it didn't look like I was following Mr. McDonnell. I straightened a few displays as I went and got to my register just as Mr. McDonnell was walking out the front door.

"See you all tomorrow," he called out with a wave. The door chimes jingled as the glass swung shut behind him.

I glanced over at Tommy. "Tomorrow?" I asked. "How long was I straightening eye shadow?"

Tommy laughed. "He has to head up to Springfield this afternoon and pick up my mom," he said. "She's been visiting her sister and the car broke down. Won't be fixed for a week, but mom doesn't want to stay that long. She says she has a church commitment, but really she can only handle visiting my Aunt Alice for a few days at a time."

I nodded. "Fair enough," I said. I pulled out my stool from under the counter and perched on top. "Anything else I need to do before you take lunch?" I asked. We staggered our lunch breaks so one of us could always be at the cash registers.

"Not that I can think of," Tommy said from his own stool. "Thanks," He smiled before punching a few keys on his register and grabbing a paperback from the countertop. "See you in 30 minutes."

I waved as he walked to the small break room in the back of the store and unlocked my own register, double checking the cash drawer. It was only 11, but one of the high-traffic times of the day was between 11:30 and 1, when most people around town took their lunch breaks. Tommy ate at 11 so we could both be available at 11:30, and I took a late lunch at 1:30 since I didn't come in until 10.

I pulled out a magazine and settled back on my stool. A few

minutes later the front door chimed and I glanced up to see two girls walk into the store giggling. I smiled and waved at them as they walked by. They were a couple of grades younger than me in school, but I'd had PE with them last year. They waved back with a "Hi, Rosalee!" and headed toward the magazine aisle. It reminded me of me and Betty and countless summer days spent looking at, and occasionally buying, magazines or makeup. I could hear the two girls chattering, although I couldn't make out what they were saying. Not that I was trying to eavesdrop.

I turned back to my magazine, and a few articles later the girls walked up. One of them set a lipstick down on the counter with a smile and a hello, and the flashback hit me hard and unexpected. I saw myself looking at lipstick and flirting with a tall, good-looking stranger. Paying for the lipstick without really paying attention. My heart seized up, but I smiled and made small talk with Karen—that was her name—while I rang her up. But as they walked out the door, I felt limp and shaken. George was in the past. Even though my logical mind told me it was going to take more than a few months to get over him, my emotional mind hated every second I wasted grieving the loss of our relationship.

I heard Tommy walking through the store a few minutes later and tried to make sure I had a neutral expression on my face.

"Finish your book?" I asked.

He shook his head as he unlocked his register. "Almost," he replied. "So is it terrible that I'm kind of hoping for a light afternoon crowd?"

I laughed. "You could always go restock toothpaste."

He smiled. "Tempting."

"Restock toothpaste" was our code for taking a quick break. Toothpaste was shelved in the back corner of the store, so it was easy to hide out there for a few minutes if you needed a breather.

Instead, Tommy looked at me in that way that I knew meant he could tell I wasn't as cool and calm as I was pretending to be.

"Something happen while I was at lunch?" he asked.

"Darn your perceptiveness," I said, trying to deflect by making him laugh. Then I shook my head. "No. Just something that made me think of...someone I'd rather not be thinking about."

He nodded and let it be. That was one of the great things about Tommy. He was perceptive enough to ask if something was wrong, but also to drop it if you didn't want to talk about something.

The rest of the day passed uneventfully and surprisingly busy enough that by the time Tommy went over to the front door to lock it, I was feeling pretty much like myself again.

"So I'm heading over to the diner for supper," Tommy said as he turned the key and flipped the Open/Closed sign. "Not in the mood to cook for myself. Want to join me?"

"Oh," I said. "Umm..." I was a little taken off guard and was stalling, trying to gauge whether or not Tommy was asking me on a date. Because while eating dinner with Tommy sounded enjoyable, I really didn't want to go on a date with anyone.

"You'd be doing a friend a favor," Tommy said, and I wondered if his perceptive radar was picking up on the reason for my hesitation. I kind of thought so, since he slipped the word "friend" in there. Don't worry, Rosalee, no romantic intentions here.

"Okay, sure," I said. "Sounds good. I could certainly go for a big plate of fries right about now. Let me just use the phone in the back to let my mom know I'll be home later."

Twenty minutes later we were settled into a booth at the diner, menus open in front of us.

"Well, hey there, you two." Peggy walked up to our table, coffee pot in hand, apron firmly tied around her waist. "Haven't seen you in a while, Rosalee."

I flipped over my mug and answered while she poured. "Been busy with graduation, and my new job," I said. "I'm working at the pharmacy now. With Tommy."

Peggy raised an eyebrow.

"My parents are out of town," Tommy explained. "My friendly coworker here took pity on me so I wouldn't have to eat alone or try and cook for myself."

"She is a sweet girl," Peggy said with a smile. "You kids know what you want?" We both nodded, and she set the coffee pot on the table to pull out her order pad. We ordered without opening the menus, and Peggy pocketed her pad and picked up the coffee pot. "I'll be back with that coke," she said. Tommy leaned back against the red vinyl.

"So." He said. "I think you should talk about it."

"Excuse me?" I said.

"I'm pretty sure you broke up with..." He paused.

"George." I was shocked enough at this blunt conversation that I supplied the name without thinking."

"Right, George. So yeah, I'm pretty sure you broke up with him, and I'm also pretty sure you're just trying to shove it away like it never happened. I'm guessing you haven't really tried talking about it with anyone, even Betty. So. I think you should talk about it. And maybe a neutral third party would be better than a best friend."

I just stared at him. "I don't even know what to say right now," I said. "Number one, I guess you don't believe in small talk? And number two, you're pretty confident in your opinion, aren't you?"

He shrugged. "Number one—no, I'm not that great at small talk. Plus, I figure we've been small talking for weeks at work. What's the point now? Number two, I have two older sisters. I've seen my fair share of breakups, and I've done my fair share of listening."

It was quiet for a minute as I thought about what he said.

"Just listening," he said. "No analyzing, no judging, no commentary, no fixing. But I know from experience that sometimes talking it out helps. Not just with breakups, but I'm guessing that's where you're at."

I sighed, all the way from the bottom of my feet.

"Darn your perceptiveness," I said, smiling a little. "But who am I to argue with the logic of a younger brother?"

"It's useless," he said, his smile softening the matter-of-factness.

I started at the beginning but stuck pretty much to facts not feelings, since I was talking to a boy after all. Our food came and we dug in, me continuing to talk. Tommy would interject a question here or there, but mostly he nodded and made sympathetic faces. We ate our dinner and drank a lot of coffee. And wouldn't you know it, he was right. As I talked, I felt the hard, hard part of my heart relax just a little. I gave myself permission to get angry, and true to his word, Tommy offered no commentary or advice. Just listened.

Peggy was slipping the check onto the table when I finally finished talking. I grabbed it before Tommy could.

"My treat," I said. "Let's pretend I'm a feminist. You deserve it after listening to all that."

He shook his head with a smile "My mother would kill me if she knew I let a lady pay for my dinner."

"Well, I don't feel much like a lady, and I won't tell if you won't."

He laughed.

"Seriously though," I said. "It's the least I can do. You were right…I needed that. And your sisters taught you well. You're a good listener, Tommy McDonnell."

"Thanks," he said. He opened his mouth again but closed it without saying anything. I wondered if there really were opinions and commentary lurking inside his head. But true to his word, he didn't offer them. *Maybe one day I'll ask him,* I thought.

chapter 23

December 2018

"Well, isn't this the best surprise!"

Betty's voice hadn't changed one bit in the past 40 years, and if Rosalee didn't know better, she'd think she was sitting on the couch at her parents' house, her 17-year-old self talking to her best friend.

"I got your Christmas card today and felt embarrassed over how long it'd been since I'd called you," Rosalee said. Billy jumped up next to her on the couch, and she shoved her cold feet underneath him.

"Well, the phone lines go two ways, so don't be too embarrassed," Betty said with her characteristic frankness. "But let's just forget all that. How in the world are you? How are the kids?"

Rosalee caught Betty up on all the family news, on upcoming Christmas plans, and heard all of the news from Carlton where Betty still lived, married to Phillip, her high school sweetheart. After Rosalee's brothers had moved to Kansas City with their elderly parents, Rosalee had lost touch with most people in her old hometown except Betty, but it was always nice to hear who was still around, who was married, who had kids and grandkids.

"You still working at the library?" Betty asked after giving Rosalee the town rundown.

"Sure am," Rosalee said. "I've finally started making friends with a few of my co-workers, too."

"Good for you!" Betty said.

"Yeah, I didn't realize how antisocial I'd gotten until recently. And speaking of making friends…" Rosalee hesitated. "You'll never guess who's moved up here."

"You know I hate to guess," Betty replied.

"George Bowen."

The silence on the other end of the phone stretched. Rosalee looked down at her cell phone to make sure the call hadn't dropped.

"I'm sorry," Betty said eventually. "I thought you said George Bowen."

"I did. He'd been living in Chicago recently and retired. Decided to take a break from big city life."

Rosalee paused, but Betty didn't say anything. Rosalee checked her phone again. Yep, still connected.

"You're going to have to get a little more talkative, hon," Betty said. "I'm reading the silence here, and you're holding out on me."

Rosalee told the whole story, and, as always, Betty was a great audience. When Rosalee wrapped up the past several weeks, she waited, prepared for another long pause. But Betty's mental processors had fired up.

"I feel like we're back in high school," Betty said. "So I guess kissing means dating, right? It feels weird. I feel like I'm supposed to ask you if you trust him and why you'd take him back, but I guess it's not like that anymore. Forty years and two marriages later…still feels funny though."

"Oh, it feels funny to me too," Rosalee said. "Some days I wonder what I'm thinking, and other days it almost feels like we're two completely different people, so why not date?" She sighed. "I just…it's fun. I'm lonely. He's still ridiculously handsome and charming."

Betty laughed at that. "Just take it slow, old friend," she said. "Watch your heart."

"Don't worry."

Rosalee heard a faint doorbell sound over the phone, and Betty said someone was at her door. They said goodbye and hung up. Rosalee sat for a while longer on the couch, watching the neighbors' Christmas lights turn on as the daylight waned.

"Merry Christmas!" Rosalee called out her front door. Elizabeth, Jonathan, Corbin, Keira, Jessica in her own car, and Charles and Mary and their kids had all pulled up and were starting to pile out and unload their trunks. She walked down the porch steps, shivering just a little as she hadn't grabbed a coat, and gave Corbin a hug, despite his gift-laden arms.

"Welcome home, college boy!" she said.

"Hey Gram," he replied with a grin, kissing her on the cheek. "Good to be home."

He headed toward the house, and Rosalee went to Elizabeth's car to help carry food into the house. Among them all, they managed to get everything in one trip. It was a suitably cold Christmas Eve, but Rosalee was sad to see such a clear sky. They weren't expecting a white Christmas this year, which was actually typical in Missouri. But everyone still hoped for it every year.

Because both of her kids married into families that also lived fewer than two hours away, everyone had fallen into the habit years ago years ago to spend Christmas Eve at Rosalee and Tommy's house. They'd exchange gifts and bake cookies for Santa, and then watch a Christmas movie with popcorn and hot chocolate. Rosalee helped Mary and Elizabeth arrange food on the table, buffet style. Rosalee put out a platter of sliced ham and a basket of hot yeast rolls, with some fancy mustards, pickles, relish, and a bowl of olives. The girls set out a cheese tray, crackers, green salad, and a couple of delicious-looking hot dips. Mary had brought her famous chocolate pecan pie, and, of course, they'd make cookies later. There was a fresh pot of coffee, a simmering pot of spiced cider on the stove, and a carafe of mulled wine.

When the kids were small, they'd usually eaten while opening gifts—the benefit of finger foods after all. Now they all loaded their plates, poured drinks, and settled in around the tree in the living room, but by the time Austin said, "Hey! Are we opening presents or what?!"—much to the chagrin of his parents, who told him now he was going last—they realized they'd been talking for over an hour. So Jessica quickly volunteered to play elf and passed out the gifts.

A short time later Rosalee and the kids—even the college kids—were gathered around the flour-covered kitchen table decorating cookies and placing them on parchment-lined baking sheets. It was Rosalee's favorite holiday tradition. She took pictures of some of the finished products each year and loved watching the kids' decorating skills and tastes evolve over the years. Plus, something about busy hands meant everyone was more talkative.

While the cookies baked, Mary and Elizabeth helped the kids clean up the mess, and Rosalee started popping popcorn and making homemade hot cocoa. Before too long, the living room coffee table was laden with a big plate of cookies, chocolate and marshmallow-filled mugs, and two huge bowls of popcorn.

"Ready?" Rosalee asked before dimming the lights and pressing play on the remote. She smiled as the opening credits of this year's movie selection rolled, illuminating her favorite people in the world, curled up on the couch, in the big leather chair, stretched out on pillows on the floor. The Christmas tree twinkled quietly in the corner, and Rosalee sank into a corner of the couch.

chapter *24*

August 1974

The doorbells jangled, and my internal self groaned while my mouth said, "Good morning!"

I stuck a gum wrapper into the worn paperback in my hand and slipped it under the counter, glancing toward the front of the store as I did.

"Well, if I'd known it was just you, I'd have finished the chapter," I said.

Tommy's dimple appeared as he walked over to my register. "Enjoying it, are you?"

I shoved his shoulder. "You win, smarty-pants," I said with a laugh. "It's so good."

"And you'll never doubt my taste in books again."

I rolled my eyes. "One good recommendation goes a long way, but I don't know that I'd go that far just yet."

I'd given Tommy a hard time once about the fantasy books he read in between the more classic literature he picked up now and then. He'd gotten on a bit of a soap box then, going on for almost a whole shift about how genre fiction wasn't taken seriously, and how fantasy fiction had some of the best writers around, and how you shouldn't disregard something you had no firsthand experience with. A few days later I'd come into work to find a paperback sitting at my register: *The Wizard of Earthsea*, by Ursula le Guin. A scrap of paper taped to the top. "Just try it. If you don't like it, the next order of fries is on me."

"So, how's shopping going?" I asked Tommy as he leaned against the counter in front of me. He and his mom had started buying things he'd need for his dorm room and other first-year-of-college supplies.

He shrugged. "My mom's been having a good time, I guess. When she's not sniffling because 'her baby's going off to college.'"

I laughed. We chatted for a few more minutes about the rest of Tommy's to-do list for the week as he prepared to leave for school on Monday. When the door chimed again, Tommy straightened.

"Well, I'll let you get back to 'work.'" He grinned and patted the book on the counter. "I just wanted to make sure we were still on for tonight," he said.

"It's Thursday, right?" I said. "Of course. I'll see you there."

A week after that first work trip to the diner, we had been closing out our registers at the end of the night and Tommy had asked if I wanted to grab a burger. I'd said "Sure" without even thinking. Then as I finished counting my drawer and packing up my purse, I started having second thoughts, my mind going into overdrive with questions like: Is this a date? Does he think it's a date? Will people talk? But I knew backing out or making it a big deal would then make it a big deal, so I just called my mom to let her know I'd be eating with a friend and walked with Tommy the short distance down Main Street to the diner.

It turned out that my first response—Yes—was the right one. Because it wasn't weird at all. He didn't try to pay, there were no awkward looks, and when he asked again the next week, it already seemed like the normal thing to do.

Every Thursday—because that's the only day we both closed—Tommy would lock the door and we'd walk down the street to the diner. Peggy would wave to us as we came in and sat in a booth halfway along the big front windows. A few minutes later she'd set a coffee, coke, and plate of fries on our table and ask if we wanted the usual (scrambled eggs and toast for me, a burger for Tommy). We'd inevitably say yes, she'd smile and go put in our order, and we'd get back to whatever serious or silly topic we'd started talking about on the way there. And sure, Peggy seemed curious about why we kept eating together once a week but paying separately, but never said anything. I managed to keep it from seeming like a big deal to my mom, who would have read a lot into it for sure. Betty was the only person who I ever had to set straight.

"So, it's not a date?" she asked when I told her why I couldn't go see a movie with her that Thursday.

"No. Not a date."

"But you have dinner together? Every Thursday?"

"Yes. We're friends. Like you and me."

She raised an eyebrow. "Um, I don't really believe that, but sure, whatever you say."

I felt myself get defensive and opened my mouth to argue but closed it again without saying anything. I knew Betty well enough to know that getting worked up would only prompt a "Methinks-she-doth-protest-too-much" response from her. So I played it cool and just changed the subject.

"Okay, be honest," I said to Tommy as he grabbed a few fries from the plate. "Pharmacy school. You said you wanted to go, but I want to know if you REALLY want to go, or if you mostly just want to make your parents happy."

He chewed and swallowed. "Both. Dad's always joked about the 'like father like son thing' and Mom's mostly just wanted me to have a nice, respectable career. I've spent some time actually watching Dad do his job so I know what it's like, and I love science so...I can't think of any reason why not."

"What about pharmacy are you looking forward to the most?" I asked, grabbing my own handful of fries.

"The science part," he said. "Chemistry, biology. I like the idea of learning about how it all works, how it all fits together. Getting to buy a lab coat, obviously."

I laughed and tossed one of my fries at him. "Weirdo."

He grinned.

We talked about his roommate whom he'd only talked to on the phone, and if all the necessities were within walking distance since he didn't have a car.

"A neighborhood grocers, a movie theater, the public library, and a church. So I think I have the most important things covered."

"Leave it to you to list the public library under most important things."

"You know you would, too," he said. I laughed and agreed, because it was true. Our love for reading was definitely something we had in common. Which led to a lengthy discussion of the Ursula le Guin book that I'd finished that afternoon.

Eventually we each pulled out our wallets and started

counting out the amount we now knew by heart—tip included. Tommy set his money on top of the check that Sally had left on the end of the table, then pulled a piece of folded notebook paper out of his wallet.

"Here," he said, handing it to me. "It's the address and phone number at school. I...I'm going to miss working with you. And our Thursdays. I was hoping maybe we could keep in touch." He laughed a little and looked out the window. "That sounds pretty corny."

I opened up the paper and pulled a pen out of my purse. The sound of paper ripping pulled Tommy's gaze away from the street view, and I handed him a square of his own notebook paper.

"It's my address and phone," I said with a smile. "You're a little bit corny, but it's a good idea. I'm going to miss you, too."

He smiled back, a big, friendly, relieved grin. I slid toward the end of the booth and he followed. We left the diner, waving to Sally as we left, and began walking toward our cars. This walk was quieter, just the sounds of Carlton around us. The occasional car driving down the street, music playing at the movie theater, kids playing on the residential street one block over, a dog barking. Tommy walked me to my car and I pulled my keys out of my purse.

"Well," I said. "It's been fun." It sounded awkward, but I realized I was at a loss for what to say. I hadn't really thought about this being the last time I'd see Tommy for a few months. I hadn't realized how much I really was going to miss him. Our friendship had surprised me.

We stood awkwardly for a moment in that conversational space normally reserved for hugs. But Tommy seemed to be waiting for me to make the first move, and now that I'd thought about it, the time for a natural, non-weird hug seemed to have passed, at least in my mind.

"Well, see you around," Tommy said finally with a smile, his hands stuffed in his pockets.

"See you," I replied. "Behave yourself."

He laughed and began to back away. "No promises."

I unlocked my car door and slid inside, watching as Tommy walked around to the driver's side door of his mom's car. I waved as I pulled out and headed toward my house. My eyes stung with surprising emotion, and I reached forward to turn the radio on, not really in the mood to analyze my feelings but hoping for a sad song on the radio.

chapter 25

January 2019

Rosalee never tried to eavesdrop on people at the library, but sometimes it was really hard to ignore conversations people were having just a few feet from her. People who sat tucked back at a table, or who were browsing through the book stacks. It was like they thought the books insulated them from anyone else who might be around. Like the books just absorbed their words before they could go out into the world. Penelope, the student worker who did most of the shelving, wore earphones while she worked and listened to audio books or podcasts. Rosalee thought about doing the same, except then she'd have to admit that deep down she found these little snippets of other peoples' lives endlessly fascinating.

"Dump him," a girl's voice was saying. Two college-aged girls sat at a table, books, paper, and laptops spread out between them. One of the girls was short and curvy, with blond hair pulled into a messy ponytail. Her heart-shaped face drooped, and her makeup-free eyes looked red.

"I know. You're right, of course," she said. Her fingers drummed against the table. "But he's apologized and he knows what he did was wrong. I believe that he won't do it again."

Her advice-giving friend was short and thin with long red hair pulled into a braid. She was typing furiously into her laptop but paused and reached a hand across the table to grasp the blonde's.

"Look," the redhead said. "I'm sure he is sorry. And I'm sure he doesn't intend to do it again. I like Gavin. I don't really want you to break up either, but in my experience, once a cheater, always a cheater."

"People can change," the blonde said, her voice watery. "I really believe that. Maybe you just have trust issues."

The redhead shrugged. "Maybe I do. Maybe I have forgiveness issues, too. And, yeah, people have to earn my trust—guys especially. Once that trust is broken, it just takes a long time to earn back. Even if you don't break up per se, things aren't going to be the same for a while. You're going to second guess everything he does. And he's going to get tired of you not trusting him. And then he's going to seek out someone who isn't harping on him all the time. And then you're right back here, crying over your statistics homework."

The blonde managed a smile. "I'll think about it," she said. "You make some good points."

Rosalee frowned on the other side of a stack of books, her eyes absently searching for the right spot on the shelf. Good points indeed.

The books took Rosalee away from the two girls, but the conversation kept running over and over in her mind. When her cart was empty, she wheeled it back to the main desk and sat down next to Caroline, who was on the closing shift. Caroline glanced up from the document she was working on and smiled at Rosalee.

"Hello, there!" she said.

Rosalee glanced around. The few patrons in the computer and reference area were deep into their tasks. Regulars that Rosalee knew were unlikely to need immediate help.

"Do you have a second?" she asked, gesturing at the computer screen. "If you're in the middle of something, it can wait."

Caroline glanced at the screen herself. "Well...I'm almost done with this and I'd love to finish it tonight. You want to go get coffee after we close?"

Rosalee nodded and stood up. "Yes, sounds perfect. Good luck!" She said with a smile. She headed to the children's room to see what she could do down there. When she got to the bottom of the stairs, a group of children exited like a litter of puppies. Two chatting mamas followed, tote bags stuffed full of books. Rosalee smiled, both at the always enjoyable site of families enjoying the library and at the knowledge that there was sure to be a lot of straightening and scanning and sorting to keep her occupied until closing.

An hour later Rosalee waved goodbye to the other library staff and walked down to the library coffee shop where she and Caroline had arranged to meet. Rosalee was thankful to see that the place wasn't full, and that there were even two soft chairs empty tucked back in a corner behind a display of mugs and coffee beans. Caroline walked in as Rosalee placed her order, and in a few minutes the two settled into their chairs, steaming mugs in their hands.

"So, what's up?" Caroline skipped the small talk, one of her more endearing qualities in Rosalee's opinion.

"Do you think I'm making a mistake starting a relationship with George after all this time?" Rosalee asked.

Caroline took a sip of her tea. "What kind of mistake are you concerned about making?" she asked. "Is this about your family? Your husband?"

Rosalee sighed. "No. It's not about starting a relationship in general. It's more…well, I'm a little embarrassed to admit this, but it has to do with a conversation I overheard while I was shelving."

Caroline laughed. "I can't even tell you how many conversations I listen to every day," she said. "Don't worry about that. Tell me what it was about."

Rosalee related the conversation. "I just…I wonder if I'm making a mistake just believing George when he said he made a mistake, that he regrets it, and that he's not the same person."

"What do you think?"

"I don't know!" Rosalee said. "I thought I did. On the one hand, so much time has passed. Who *wouldn't* be a different person now? *I'm* a different person now. And just spending time with him I can tell he's…a more mellow version of the George I knew. More thoughtful and mature, as you would expect. But how well do I really know him now?"

"Well," Caroline said. "I mean, how well do we really know anyone, right? If it were me, I'd trust my instincts. Keep spending lots of time together, spend time with each other's friends and families. All the typical dating stuff, you know?"

Rosalee nodded. "Yes, that all makes sense. I guess I'm just trying to decide how much I trust my gut."

Caroline set her cup down on the low table between them and

rested her elbow on the arm of the chair, chin in her hand. "It's harder because if this was you dating him a year or two after... you all broke up, then I might be saying something different. I'm thinking the girl in the library should probably be cautious." Caroline paused. "Is it more than just that conversation that's bothering you?"

"I don't know...maybe? My daughter hasn't been the most supportive—maybe that's getting to me." Rosalee groaned and covered her face with her hands. "I wasn't even worrying about this until tonight. But now I just..." She sighed. "You're right, I know. I just need to trust my gut."

"For what it's worth, my gut has a good feeling about George," Caroline said. They had gone out with Caroline and her husband for New Year's Eve. They'd all gotten dressed up and made reservations at a swanky restaurant. It had been really fun. "And I think even if I hadn't spent any time with him, I wouldn't think you were making a mistake. It's been a long time. People are allowed to move on. And I say that knowing you have."

Rosalee nodded. It was true. She had forgiven and moved on a long time ago. Caroline was right, she just needed to trust her gut.

Rosalee changed the subject at that, thankful for Caroline's advice and happy to have a girlfriend again. She laughed inside thinking about the alternative—talking to Elizabeth. She knew exactly what her daughter would say. But she was pretty sure Elizabeth was biased.

They finished their drinks and headed home, and Rosalee thought she had worked it all out in her head. She was pretty sure, anyway.

A few days later Rosalee was sitting on a barstool in George's kitchen, drinking a glass of red wine and watching him chop vegetables for a stir-fry. He had been telling her a funny story about his neighbor, but they were now in a comfortable pause in the conversation.

"So you mentioned a while back that you don't have close family nearby, but I never really asked any follow-up questions," Rosalee said. "You have a sister, right? Where does she live now?"

George scraped the vegetables into a saucepan with hot olive oil in it. They sizzled and he stirred.

"A younger sister, yes. Karen. She moved to Milwaukee when her oldest daughter got married and moved there. My younger niece lives in New York. I have one cousin who lives about 30 minutes away."

"Hmmm…are you and your cousin close?"

George shrugged, pouring his sauce onto the chicken and vegetables, an amazing-smelling steam rising from the pan as he stirred. "Sure, I guess," he said. "But we're men. We don't talk on the phone regularly or anything. We go camping and fishing together once a year, sometimes twice, but that's about it."

"You don't have dinner together or anything? He only lives 30 minutes away?"

"He's been divorced for a while," George said, "and, like I said, his girls are grown and live out of state, so no, we don't do regular dinners or anything. Men, remember?" He smiled.

"What about your sister?"

If George felt like he was being grilled like a suspect in a murder investigation, he did a good job of hiding it. He pulled the stir-fry off the stove and turned off the burner. "We spent more time together when they still lived in Kansas City and we lived in Chicago. Holidays, birthdays, that kind of thing. We talk on the phone every couple of months."

He put two plates on the counter, pulled chopsticks out of a drawer and held them up, eyebrows raised.

"Chopsticks?"

"Yes."

He slid one of the plates and a set of chopsticks toward her. "Do you want to move to the table?" he asked, "or just stay here at the bar?"

"Here's fine."

He topped off Rosalee's wine glass, grabbed a stool, and settled down at a right angle. As soon as he was settled, they both dug in. Rosalee realized that not only was she hungry, she'd made short work of her first glass of wine. Probably a good idea to absorb some of that alcohol with some food.

They ate in silence for a few minutes, then Rosalee asked George about the music playing, an attempt to break a silence that should have been comfortable but tonight was making her antsy. He asked about work, but her minimalist reply shut down that conversation topic pretty quickly as well. The rest of their meal was a similar exercise in stilted, staccato conversation. Rosalee had little to say, and eventually George seemed to get tired of trying to carry the conversation. A part of Rosalee cringed, even as the other part found everything George did irritating or suspicious.

Eventually they finished eating and Rosalee's good manners prevailed enough to prompt her to clear the plates and help wash up. Usually George brushed her help aside, but tonight he didn't object.

"Everything all right this evening?" he asked as he put the leftover food into smaller containers.

"Of course," Rosalee said. *Lie.*

"You just seem…like maybe something is bothering you."

Rosalee stiffened. "No, everything's great," she said, her voice daring him to challenge her statement. "Just don't feel like talking, I guess. Maybe I'm fighting off a cold or something."

"Okay." George did not accept the dare.

They finished cleaning up in silence, and Rosalee said she'd probably better get home. George's eyes were sad, but he just went and got her coat and scarf.

"Thanks for supper," Rosalee said after she'd buttoned her coat.

"Any time," George said. He leaned in for a kiss, but Rosalee turned her face, his lips landing on her cheek.

"See you."

"I hope soon."

chapter 26

October 1974

A window-shaped patch of afternoon sun warmed my legs as I lay stretched out on our living room couch. I was waiting for Betty to stop by with some magazines she'd finished reading so we could do our semi-regular magazine swap. It was Sunday afternoon, but I had the house to myself. Mom had gone to visit a friend and Dad and the boys were on their way home from a weekend camping trip. A book sat on my chest, but I mostly stared out the window at the blue sky and bare tree branches waving slightly in a breeze. I thought about the unopened letter sitting on my desk in my room and tried to decide how I felt about it.

A ringing phone cut into my self-analysis and I debated just letting it ring, but curiosity and my mother's voice in my head prompted me to get up and answer.

"Hello?"

"Took you long enough," the voice on the other end teased.

I smiled. "Well if I'd known it was you, I'd have just let it ring," I said.

Tommy laughed. "Hey," he said. "How's it going?"

"It's…good," I said.

"That's not very convincing," he said.

"No, really. Same ol' same ol.'" I wrapped the phone cord around my wrist. "I, uh…I got a letter yesterday. From George."

The silence stretched.

"What did it say?" Tommy's voice was neutral.

"Don't know. Haven't opened it."

"Are you going to?"

Tommy knew me well. He knew there was a part of me that knew it would be easier and cleaner to just ignore it. The past is the past.

"Probably."

The silence stretched.

"So what's up with you?" It was an awkward segue, but it did the job. Tommy talked about classes and midterms and his crazy roommate's weirdly large collection of rabbits feet. I told a few stories from work, and we talked about the books we were reading. It was our usual Sunday conversation, a habit we'd fallen into, similar to Thursday night dinner.

The first few times he'd called, my mom had given me a "look"—like she wanted me to fill her in on what was going on. But I could tell the fact that most of the time I just stayed in the kitchen at the table, unconcerned with who might overhear our conversation, threw her bit. It was like talking to Betty, and after a few weeks it stopped being a big deal. Tommy and I usually only talked about 10 minutes, and I'd started calling him about half the time—it was long distance after all—but it was nice to chat, even briefly. Sometimes I still marveled at the difference between a guy friend and a girl friend, but I could honestly say that there was something about getting a guy's perspective on life that made things feel more well rounded.

We chatted for a few more minutes, then said goodbye. I hung up the phone and went back to my spot on the couch. I tried to zone out again, but the sunshine and blue sky had lost their magic. My brain was engaged, and stuck in a loop:

Are you going to open it?

Probably.

With a deep sigh, I stood up and walked upstairs to my room. I retrieved the slightly crumpled white envelope and walked back down the stairs and out to the front porch, where I sat on the glider. I needed fresh air and chirping birds for courage. I set the envelope on my leg and smoothed a hand over it. Betty would be here soon. I needed to get this over with.

I slid my finger under the flap of the envelope and loosened it, pulling out a single sheet of notebook paper.

Dear Rosalee,

I hope you read this letter, although I understand if you don't. It's easy to see now how stupid my decisions were, and I am truly sorry that those decisions hurt you.

I'm writing because I don't want you to be caught off guard by gossip. We're getting married next month and moving to California. I've been working this semester and taking time off school, but I'll be transferring to a university in San Diego in the spring. We both wanted a fresh start, and a cousin of my mom's lives there so we'll have family around.

It's too late to change anything now, but I'm trying to learn enough to not repeat the same mistakes in the future. Know that loving you has and will make me a better person. I just wish I hadn't ruined things between us in the learning process.

I wish you lots of adventures and good things.

Love,
George

I re-folded the letter and lifted my head. A few tears slid down my cheeks, but I was pleasantly surprised to realize that the knot in my chest wasn't nearly as painful as it had been a few months ago.

I was still staring at the oak tree in the front yard when Betty sat down next to me on the glider, her stack of magazines in her lap.

"What have you got there?" she asked, nodding at the letter still resting in my lap.

"Letter from George," I said.

She raised an eyebrow. "So how is it?"

"Not terrible."

"How are you?" she asked next.

I shrugged. "Not terrible."

"Well," she replied, "progress."

I smiled at her and asked if she wanted some coke, then went inside to grab a couple of bottles. I brought them back onto the porch along with some blankets from the couch. We settled into the swing with our blankets and magazines and drinks, but as I stared at the glossy brown eyes of a model advertising shampoo,

I found myself having trouble focusing.

First, my mind would settle on George's letter. It was nice of him to keep me from finding things out through the grapevine, and his apology seemed sincere. I pushed on the bruise a bit more, and found that the ache that had been my constant companion for the past few months had diminished quite a bit while I wasn't paying attention. Then I wanted to know why and how. Was it simply time? Distance? It hadn't been that long, relatively speaking. I mean, the baby wasn't even born yet. And even that thought didn't hurt as much as I would expect it to.

So there it is again—why? How? A series of images sprung to mind, and I wasn't quite comfortable with them. The diner and a plate of French fries. The afternoon sun streaming in through plate-glass display windows. Dog-eared paperback books. Letters that were a minimum of two pages and kept me laughing or thinking or sometimes both. The fact that what I really wanted to do right now was go back to the phone and talk to Tommy about George's letter.

So, yeah. Tommy. Somehow Tommy had sped up my recovery timeline. Was I falling in love with him? No. That made me nervous. It was too soon for love. Friendship then. I just needed a new friend, someone to shake up the status quo.

Friendship fit, and it felt comfortable, right. But maybe the idea of love didn't seem so bad anymore.

chapter *27*

February 2019

Rosalee pulled into a parking space just as her phone started ringing from the inside of her purse. She put the car in park, turned off the ignition, and grabbed the phone. "G. Bowen" stared at her. Rosalee hesitated, then swiped her thumb to the right.

"Hello," she said, forcing a cheerful lilt to her voice.

"Well hey, stranger," George's deep voice replied. Rosalee smiled despite herself. She loved that voice, she really did. It's why she'd been ignoring his calls the past week. The last time they talked on the phone, everything had been normal; then as soon as she'd hung up she'd felt irritated and angry at herself.

"How are you?" Rosalee asked, wedging the phone between her ear and shoulder as she gathered up her purse and keys and slid out of the car.

"Can't complain except I miss you. Where've you been hiding?"

"Oh…here and there," Rosalee said. *In my house. At work. Definitely hiding, though.* "Work stuff. Coffee and lunch dates with Caroline."

"You busy today? I thought you might like to take Billy down to the riverside trail. It's such a beautiful day."

"Oh, that sounds so nice, but I'm actually meeting Elizabeth right now to do some shopping," Rosalee said, relieved she had a good excuse, because she did love taking Billy down to the trail.

"Oh," George said, his voice heavy with disappointment. "Well, another time then."

"Definitely," Rosalee said. "I hate to do this (*Not really*), but Elizabeth's here now. Can I call you tonight?" She was really being kind of a jerk, and she really should stop completely ignoring him.

"Sure, that sounds great. Have fun."

"Thanks! Bye."

Rosalee slid her phone into her purse as Elizabeth joined her.

"Hey, Mom," Elizabeth said, giving her a quick hug. "Who was that?"

"Not your business, last I checked." Rosalee cringed and Elizabeth stepped back, her eyebrows sky-high. "Sorry, sweetie," Rosalee said. "It just slipped out. I'm…in a mood I guess. It was George."

"Oh." Elizabeth's voice was flat. "Him."

Rosalee sighed and rolled her eyes, slipping her arm through Elizabeth's and guiding her toward the door of their favorite department store. "And that's why I wasn't going to say anything," Rosalee said. "Because as much as I love you, darling, I get tired of those judgy eyes."

"Sorry." Elizabeth sounded halfway sorry at least.

They headed for the shoe section first, which was their habit, taking their path through accessories. Their conversation fell into the comfortable rhythm of talking about kids and work. Their focus shifted once they started trying on shoes—Elizabeth was looking for a comfortable pair of low heels, and Rosalee's walking shoes were starting to wear out—and they spent quite a while sending the salesperson on trips back to the storeroom. Eventually they each ended up with what they needed, and Elizabeth added a pair of clearance boots for Keira.

"She still lets you buy her shoes?" Rosalee asked as they walked to the register to pay.

"Most of the time," Elizabeth said. "We actually wear the same size shoe, so what I usually do is find a pair that I like, too, so if she doesn't want them, I keep them."

"Clever."

They paid for their shoes then made their way to the women's section. As they started going through the clothing racks, Elizabeth told Rosalee about a new book series she'd found. It was a typical shopping conversation, easy and meandering. Rosalee felt her tension from earlier ease up, at least, until they started trying on clothes.

"Really?"

That was Elizabeth's response to a top that Rosalee was actually kind of excited about. It was a little different than what she normally wore—a simple blouse, but with some modern lace details that gave it a bit more flare and style.

"What? I like it."

"It looks so...I don't know. Something. It's not really you."

Rosalee bristled. "Well, does it look bad?"

"No, it fits nicely."

"Fine, then I'm getting it," Rosalee said, turning back toward her dressing room without commenting on Elizabeth's outfit—which looked fantastic, but Rosalee suddenly wasn't in a complimentary frame of mind. "I have a lot of tops that look like me. Something different isn't going to turn the world off its axis."

"Don't be so dramatic, Mother."

Rosalee knew their morning had taken a turn now that Elizabeth had called her "Mother." She only did that when she was irritated. Usually Rosalee just brushed it off and knew that whatever had gotten to Elizabeth would fade soon enough. But today...well, Rosalee wasn't in the mood. They tried their clothes on in silence, each only emerging once more to double check fit with another pair of eyes. Rosalee ended up keeping the lace top and a pair of slim gray pants. Gray was not a typical color she chose, but it was a nice, soft gray, and she just liked it. She didn't ask Elizabeth's opinion, but she could feel Elizabeth's skepticism as she watched Rosalee pay for them.

"Lunch?" Elizabeth asked once they were done.

"Are you going to let me order my own food?" Rosalee asked.

Elizabeth sighed loudly and rolled her eyes. "Yes, Mother. When have I ever ordered for you?"

Rosalee refrained from bringing up all the times that Elizabeth did, in fact, tell her what to order. Instead she just suggested a restaurant they both enjoyed that wasn't too far away, and they headed that way.

By the time they were sitting at their table with glasses of water with lemon in front of them, the tense atmosphere had eased.

"I haven't seen George lately," Elizabeth said as she looked over the menu. "Has he been traveling?"

Her tone was stiff, but Rosalee could tell she was attempting "friendly interest" rather than "accusing interrogation." However, since Rosalee knew that George's absence was due more to Rosalee's ignoring him and not his own choice, she still bristled.

"No, he's just been busy. I haven't really seen much of him either." Half-truth. He wasn't busy, but she hadn't seen much of him.

"Well. I can't say that I'm sorry to hear that," Elizabeth said.

"Oh, for the love!" Rosalee said. "I thought we'd covered this topic extensively, Elizabeth. What exactly is wrong with George?"

Elizabeth looked taken aback. Rosalee usually just quietly changed the subject whenever Elizabeth made remarks about her dislike of George or—more accurately—how much time Rosalee spent with him. Elizabeth was not used to Rosalee being in any way confrontational, but Rosalee was on edge and didn't feel like deflecting the topic yet again.

"Nothing specific," Elizabeth said, "but I don't want you to get hurt, and I'm not sure what he's got in mind, that's all. I don't...I'm not sure, to be honest. I just don't trust him."

"Fine," Rosalee said. "But do you trust me? Do you think I can look out for myself?" It was ironic, Rosalee thought even as she asked the question, because lately she wasn't quite sure she trusted herself.

"Of course I trust you!" Elizabeth said. "I just..."

"I appreciate your concern," Rosalee interrupted her. "I really do. But I'd like you to just leave it at that right now, okay? Trust me. I'm done with the criticisms. Your concern is noted."

For once, Elizabeth was silent. A moment later, Rosalee thought thankfully, their waitress returned for their orders, and once she'd walked off with them, Rosalee deliberately turned the conversation to a television show they both enjoyed watching. It wasn't the best mother-daughter day they'd ever had, but they stayed to safe topics, and at least it ended well.

Later that night Rosalee completed every conceivable before

bed routine she could—even decided to do a five-minute face mask, for crying out loud—before finally accepting that she'd put off her promised phone call long enough.

"Hello."

"Hey, George, it's me," she replied.

"Rosalee! Hi! I was afraid you'd forgotten to call."

"No, just a busy day, that's all."

"Tell me about it."

It was not an unusual request. They often spent their time on the phone just chatting about the mundane details of the day, the little things that weren't really interesting to most people. But today Rosalee's answers were short, lacking any color or life. She didn't fill in any details, and despite George's continued attempts at a normal conversation, it clearly wasn't. Finally, there was an awkward silence.

"Have I done something?" George filled the black hole masking as a conversation. "And please. Do me the courtesy of being honest, Rosalee. I know you've been ignoring me, and you've been acting distant." His voice finally lost its congeniality, an edge of frustration hardening it. Oddly enough, it was this edge that loosened Rosalee's own tension just a little, like he was finally giving her permission to be openly—frustrated? confused? irritated? unsure?—about whatever it was she was feeling.

"No," Rosalee said. "Not really. And I'm sorry, I know I've been a jerk." She searched for the words and sighed, deciding the conversation had moved beyond tactfulness. "I think that the novelty of getting to know you again is wearing off, and I think I'm just re-processing the past. But processing the past in light of a possible future. Does that make sense?"

"You're trying to decide if you've really forgiven me."

"No." Her response was quick and sure. "No, I absolutely have forgiven you. A long time ago. I'm trying to decide if…if I really trust you. Enough to be more than just friends."

He was silent so long, Rosalee started to get nervous.

"That's fair," he said finally. His voice was quiet and sad and still a little hard, but had lost its jagged edge. "It's…" he sighed. "It's disappointing, I guess, that consequences can reach so far. But it's fair."

"I'll…can I call you later this week?" Rosalee asked, finding that just talking honestly with George about what she was feeling made her less anxious about talking to him in general.

"Sure," he said. "I'm around."

They said their goodbyes and hung up. It wasn't the best end to a conversation, but it would have to do for now. Rosalee felt like at least she'd bought herself a little time. A little time to hopefully get her head on straight and figure herself out.

chapter 28

December 1974

"What's wrong with you this morning?" my brother Lloyd asked as he walked into the kitchen. His hair defied gravity, and he still had on his pajamas.

I laughed. "What, because I'm awake before noon? Dressed? Alive? Getting ready to go to my gainful employment?"

"You're humming," he said, grabbing a box of cereal from on top of the fridge and the carton of milk from inside it.

I shrugged and took another sip of coffee. "Whatever, bro. Just a beautiful morning, I guess."

He grunted, shook his head, and started shoveling cereal in his mouth.

I continued to drink my coffee and attempted to read my book. I *was* in a good mood, and as much as I tried to pass it off as just a nice day or a good night's rest, the truth was that Tommy was home for semester break and working at the pharmacy today. Lloyd's spoken observation had killed my mood, though, and I couldn't get back into my book. So I downed the last of my coffee and took the mug to the sink. I lightly swatted the back of Lloyd's head as I walked past on my way to the stairs.

"Hey!" he protested, mouth full of corn flakes.

"Later, kid."

Lloyd hated it when I called him kid, and maybe it was mean considering he didn't realize he'd irritated me this morning, but I decided he'd get over it. I brushed my teeth and put on some lip gloss, grabbed my bag, and ran down the stairs, stopping to say a quick goodbye to my mom in the laundry room. I rolled the windows down even thought the morning air was cold and cranked up the radio, so by the time I got to work, my good mood had been restored and I felt a little more like myself.

I let myself into the store, stashed my purse and coat in the tiny break room, and began my opening routine. Coffee (a full pot, because Mr. McDonnell was as much a coffee drinker as I was), lights, double check that the displays were full. Pour a cup of coffee and get the cash register drawer out of the safe. Often, these morning rituals were redundant. If I closed, I did it all the night before—well, not the coffee. But Mr. McDonnell appreciated attention to detail, and it was good to double check. And sometimes Julie Smith closed up, so I just got in the habit of doing it every morning. Most mornings I would hear Mr. McDonnell come in the back door as I was counting the money in my drawer, sipping my coffee, and getting ready to unlock the front door and flip on the Open sign.

This morning I heard the back door chime right on cue. Only this morning I smiled at the sound of two people talking in the back room and the sound of footsteps making their way to the front of the store.

A moment later Tommy emerged from the aisles, a big smile on his face. "Good morning," he said, walking up to my register.

I walked around the counter. "Hey stranger," I said, and reached out for a hug. "It's good to see you."

There was a half-second delay as Tommy processed my greeting. We'd never hugged before, and, honestly, we'd barely touched, something I was just now realizing. But in that moment, before I had time to overthink or overreact, I just thought: I want a hug from my best friend. Tommy wrapped his arms around my back.

"Yeah," he said. "It's good to see you, too."

We stood there for longer than I'd expected, but it felt right. It felt good. I'd read somewhere that there's science behind the way humans crave physical touch. That hugs in particular release chemicals in our brain that make us healthier, safer, and less stressed. Well, I believed it now. And more than that, it just felt like I was exactly where I wanted to be, and exactly who I wanted to be with.

Finally Tommy pulled back and glanced up at the big clock on the wall.

"Guess it's show time."

I smiled and walked over to the front door.

"So where are you working this morning?" I asked as I unlocked the front door and turned on the sign.

Tommy nodded toward the back of the store. "With Dad," he said. "I think his plan is to keep me back there most of break, except for the week before Christmas." The week before Christmas was typically pretty busy, so there were always two cashiers working, and occasionally someone on the floor for a few hours a day, too.

"Makes sense," I said. "Shame, though. I was looking forward to some catch-up time."

Tommy ran his hand through his hair. "Yeah, me, too," he said with a sigh. "But, you know, at least I'm around for a few weeks." He grinned. "I won't be hiding."

I laughed. "See that you don't."

"Anyway, just wanted to say 'Hey' before I got started. But I better head back. I think Dad's got a full day of exposition planned." He rolled his eyes, but I could tell he didn't mind.

"Have fun!" I waved as he walked back toward the pharmacy counter.

It was an uneventful day, but it already felt like Christmas, and I know it was having Tommy back. We spent our lunch break talking and made plans to spend time later in the week after work. Tommy said he should probably stick around home for a few nights to make his mom happy, which I totally got.

So it happened to be our previously regular Thursday night that we locked up the pharmacy door and walked over to the diner. We slipped into our regular booth without pausing our conversation, and when Sally came over to take our order, she set two cups of coffee in front of us and asked, "Long time no see, kids. The usual?"

We looked at each other and laughed.

"Guess so, Sally," Tommy said. "No sense in getting crazy now."

It wasn't quite like our usual Thursday night dinners. For one thing, I talked about George. Tommy asked about the letter, and it all came spilling out: the backstory, the betrayal, and my complicated feelings about everything.

"Getting his letter…it makes me realize that I have forgiven him. But does it seem so soon? I feel like if I really loved him, then maybe I'd still be more upset. And if I didn't love him…

that's frustrating because then I feel like I don't even know my own mind, you know?"

Tommy nodded. "I think…" He paused and laughed a little, running a hand through his hair. "I think I don't have much experience at love," he said. "But I watch people, and I read a lot, and it seems to me that every love is different. There's no hard and fast rule for how long it takes to get over 'real' love. There's no algebraic formula, or easy definition. If you loved him…you loved him. And if your heart has moved on, well, then it has. You don't need to explain it, or qualify it, or defend it."

He smiled at me before picking up his coffee mug and looking out the window. I don't know if he was trying mentally to give me a little privacy or was just a little embarrassed about the subject, but I appreciated the moment to think about what he had just said.

"Thank you," I said finally. I reached across the table to where his free hand rested and wrapped my fingers around his. "You're pretty smart, you know. And you're a good friend, Tommy McDonnell."

He turned his hand slightly so he could give mine a gentle squeeze. "Thanks." He opened his mouth as if to say more, but shut it with another smile.

"What?" I asked. I was very aware that we were still holding hands but felt no interest in changing the situation.

"Sometimes less is more," he said. "Not every thought needs to be spoken, you know?"

I raised my eyebrows. "How mysterious."

"Maybe I was just thinking you need a haircut, but I didn't want to hurt your feelings."

I reached across the table and smacked him on the shoulder. "You dork," I said, laughing. "I can see it's time to go home if we've resorted to attacks on personal appearance."

"Hey, you asked."

I smacked him again, and we gathered our coats and hats, put cash on the table, and slid out of the booth. As we walked back across the town square and toward our cars, I looped my arm through his and stuffed my hand in my coat pocket, leaving our elbows linked. It felt weird, but right. Warm and cozy and friendly. A few minutes later we were standing at my car.

"See you tomorrow?" I asked, untangling my arm from his.

"See you tomorrow."

chapter 29

March 2019

Rosalee wheeled her empty cart behind the children's desk at the library and waved goodbye to Stephanie, heading toward the employee break room and her things. She gathered up her purse, slipped on her jacket, and pulled out her car keys. But a few minutes later, she was standing in front of Caroline's desk.

"Do you want to go on a road trip?" Rosalee asked.

Caroline looked up from her computer screen. "Yes," she said. "Absolutely."

Rosalee smiled. She had a small suspicion Caroline thought she was speaking hypothetically.

"I was thinking next weekend. Still interested?"

Caroline arched her eyebrows. "Yes," she said, her own smile a bit mischievous. "Absolutely. Bill's due for a bachelor weekend, and I'm 99 percent sure I'm not on the schedule here. Let me double check that, but otherwise, I'm your wingwoman."

Rosalee felt like bouncing in excitement but decided it was not something a 60ish-year-old woman should do out in public.

"Fantastic!" she said. "Give me a call when you know for sure, and when you think you can leave next Friday?"

Caroline nodded. "Of course. I'll call you tonight. So… where are we going?"

"Home," Rosalee said. "Or rather, my home. Down in the country, the hills, the old homestead. I just need…" She paused, trying to identify what it is she felt like she needed. But Caroline just nodded.

"I get it. Sometimes we need to go home."

"Exactly," Rosalee said, grateful for such a sympathetic friend and wishing not for the first time that she had gotten to know Caroline much sooner. Caroline's phone rang, so Rosalee waved goodbye and headed out to her car. She'd been feeling antsy all day. For a few weeks, if she was going to be honest. Antsy at Sunday dinners. Antsy with George. Antsy talking to her grandkids. Antsy on walks with Billy.

But as she was pulling on her jacket—an old corduroy blazer of Tommy's, an item of clothing she'd appropriated long before he'd gotten sick—the idea had hit her and with it, an instant feeling of calm. How long since she'd been down home? How long since she'd climbed the hills, and sat by the creek, and breathed in the smell of wood smoke and earth and water and sunbaked rocks? Too long.

Rosalee went home and walked Billy, then sat down to make a list. She needed to find a place for them to stay, pack a weekend bag, and call Elizabeth to tell her she'd be out for the weekend. She should call Jessica, too, just to confirm there would be no Friday night girl's night. Although she could tell her tomorrow. Maybe she should call her anyway, just to make sure Jess was still planning on coming over tomorrow. Now that she thought of things that way…Rosalee turned her pencil around and erased one of her list items—she could just talk to Elizabeth on Sunday. She'd see if the Blairs could keep an eye on Billy. Rosalee smiled. Maybe she could offer to pay Tripp five dollars to feed and play with him. She'd ask Celia. Rosalee glanced over the short list, then added one more item. She also needed to call George.

"Why don't you come over Monday night?" Rosalee was saying to George over the phone. She held the phone with one hand and scrambled some eggs with the other. "I can make dinner." She turned off the burner and slid the eggs onto a plate next to two pieces of buttered toast, then picked up the plate. She laughed.

"Yes, I will make something other than scrambled eggs," she said. "But be nice, or it might just be grilled cheese." She sat down at her kitchen table and leaned back in her chair with a smile, listening to George on the other end of the phone. "No, no," she said. "Nothing against grilled cheese. But speaking of scrambled eggs, my dinner's hot, so I'll let you go. Yeah. Talk to you soon. Bye."

It was weird, Rosalee thought as she ate her eggs and toast. She'd been feeling awkward around George for a few weeks now—ever since that overheard library conversation and the subsequent awkward conversation they'd had the next night—but never over the phone. On the phone she could talk to him all day or all night and feel relaxed and happy and normal. But anytime they were together, it felt off. She felt off. Well, that's what her weekend away was all about, wasn't it?

As Rosalee pulled up to Elizabeth's house a few days later, she regretted her decision to let the family know in person that she was going out of town for a few days. On the phone, it was easy to just find an excuse to hang up. Here, she had no escape. Well, maybe she was overreacting. It's possible her daughter would treat her like a grown-up. Rosalee smiled to herself. There was a chance.

After greetings and hugs, Rosalee washed her hands and started helping chop up vegetables for a salad. Charles, Mary, and the boys still hadn't arrived, but Jess and Keira sat on barstools and kept Elizabeth and Rosalee company. Jonathan was out on the patio, grill tongs in hand.

"I won't be here next week," Rosalee said as she sliced through some carrots.

"Oh?" Elizabeth turned from where she was mixing up salad dressing. "What's going on instead? I hope you aren't ditching us for George."

It was possible she was joking, but Rosalee didn't detect much humor in her statement.

"I'm going out of town on Friday," she said. "Taking a little trip down south with my friend Caroline."

"Fun!" Jess said. "Good for you, Gram. Will you guys go antiquing? Canoeing on the lake? Hiking?"

Rosalee smiled. "You are too sweet, Jess, thinking that two old ladies like us are going canoeing or hiking. Actually...we probably will do a little hiking. But nothing too intense. More like nature walking."

"This is a little out of the blue, isn't it?" Elizabeth said.

"Yes," Rosalee agreed. "It is. But I'm a grown-up. I have few commitments, and only a part-time job. Might as well take advantage of that for a spontaneous girls' trip, right?"

"Hmmm. I guess." Elizabeth said, her face still set in a frown.

Rosalee sighed. "Look, Elizabeth. As I just said, I am a grown woman. I'm sorry if it upsets you that I have friends, and interests of my own, and a new interest in actually doing things I want to do. But, the fact is, all that is true. And I think it'd be nice if you stopped making your judgy face, and using your judgy voice, and just back off a little."

Well. Speaking of being on edge lately.

Jessica looked back and forth between the two of them, her eyes dancing as though she was watching a particularly interesting television show. Keira sat frozen, a cherry tomato halfway to her mouth. Both of them waited to see what was going to happen.

Rosalee kept chopping vegetables and throwing them into the salad bowl, but from the corner of her eye she could see Elizabeth stiffen. Rosalee could feel Elizabeth fighting her urge to respond to irritation with her own hard-edged irritation, but at that moment, Jonathan opened the sliding glass door, bringing with him the smell of charred meat and a welcome dissipation of the prickly atmosphere.

"Hey, Mom," he said, walking up to Rosalee and kissing her cheek. "How are you?"

"Oh, she's just fine and dandy," Elizabeth said, moving to the oven to check on the baking sweet potatoes. "In fact, she's so fine and dandy she's planning a little weekend trip with her friend Caroline on Friday."

"Good for you!" Jonathan said, echoing his older daughter's earlier enthusiasm. Rosalee smiled. A casual observer would think Jonathan was oblivious to the slight sarcasm in his wife's voice, but Rosalee knew he was just ignoring her, knowing that once

Elizabeth processed things, she'd be fine. He winked at Rosalee while Elizabeth's back was turned, and Rosalee reached out a hand and patted his face gently. "You're my favorite," she whispered.

Jonathan grinned, then announced that the burgers would be ready in five minutes. Keira and Jessica took their cue to set the table, and in eight minutes, Elizabeth was setting the last of the food on the big dining room table right as Charles' family walked through the door.

"Sorry we're late," Mary said, giving Rosalee a hug before shoving the boys into chairs at opposite ends of the table. "We got hung up in traffic. An accident had half the road blocked."

Everyone took their seats, and after a few minutes of shuffling and commenting on the accident, they all grabbed hands while Jonathan prayed over the food. Rosalee held a small bit of hope that maybe Elizabeth was getting used to the idea that she didn't have to hover over her anymore, that the status quo was different.

It was just after lunch on Friday afternoon when Rosalee pulled up to Caroline's bright yellow bungalow. Caroline must have seen her pull up, because she opened the door while Rosalee was still on the sidewalk.

"Just throwing a few last-minute things in my tote bag," Caroline said, holding the front door open. "Come on in and wait. It'll just take a second."

Rosalee followed Caroline through the entry and into the cozy living room dominated by a huge picture window and stone fireplace. The room was mostly white and cream, but with splashes of color in pillows, accent rugs, and gorgeous art covering the walls. There were bright modern paintings, a few muted watercolors of what looked like the sea, and a couple of portraits with pleasantly oversaturated colors. A set of three black-and-white architectural photographs hung over the fireplace, and there was a small bookshelf holding a jumble of pottery, some fine and delicate and some rough and purposeful-looking, and just about everything in between.

Rosalee had seen some of the art at Christmas, but the photographs were new. "These new works are wonderful!" Rosalee said.

"They're Bill's. He's had them for a while, but we finally got them framed a few weeks ago."

"They're fantastic," Rosalee said, walking closer to look at them.

"Thank you," Bill said, walking into the room. He was carrying a book, reading glasses shoved on top of his head. "Seeing them hanging up has been inspiring me to get out with the camera more again."

"You definitely should, you have a great eye."

"I'm ready." Caroline stood in the hallway now, a small rolling suitcase in one hand, her purse and a tote bag on the opposite shoulder.

"Great!" Rosalee felt slightly giddy, almost like her first road trip.

Bill walked them out to the car and waved as they pulled out of the driveway and down the street.

Caroline pulled a pair of sunglasses out of her bag and put them on, then leaned back. "Is it bad that I feel a little bit like Thelma and Louise right now?"

Rosalee laughed. "Well, I'm not planning on doing anything illegal, immoral, or fatal. But if you're identifying with a spirit of freedom and carefree-ness, then I can totally get on board with that."

Caroline laughed. "That's fair. So. Tell me what we're doing this weekend."

"I am really impressed that you have left every detail about going out of town in my hands. I never even told you where we are staying!"

"Carefree! Thelma and Louise!" Caroline replied. "I mean, I figured you asked me, so you must have an idea of what you wanted to do. And I think I know you well enough by now to know that you're not one to do something like this without at least a bare minimum of a plan."

Rosalee smiled. "Caroline, I don't know if I've mentioned it before, but I am just really glad that we've become friends. Not to get cheesy on you, but I don't think I realized how much I missed having friends. Not just the kind of long-distance old friend that you talk to occasionally and send Christmas cards to. But real-life, talk-more-than-once-a-week, spend-time-together-regularly friends."

Caroline nodded. "Me, too. Get as cheesy as you want. Making friends—or maintaining friendships even—just gets harder as you get older. Especially if you have a family. Your friends are other parents, or your spouse's co-workers. You're busy with keeping up schedules and work and school and just life. It's not as natural or easy as when you're young and carefree."

"And yet, looking back, I can say I probably needed those friendships more when they were harder to come by," Rosalee said. "But anyway, you asked me what we were doing. Bed and breakfast in a little town on Table Rock Lake. Then some antiquing, maybe low-key hiking around a great trail on that side of the lake, and, if you're up for it, a drive out to the middle of nowhere and an old family cemetery. I plan on going out to the cemetery regardless, but you're welcome to stay behind if you want."

"No way! I love family history and country drives. Sounds perfect."

They drove for a few minutes in a companionable silence. Rosalee handed Caroline her phone and told her to pick some good road trip music, and they spent the next hour singing along to Fleetwood Mac.

chapter 30

January 1975

It was an unseasonably mild January day, so when Tommy called me up on my day off to see if I wanted to go hiking down by the creek, I said yes with no hesitations. I was working the next day, and he was going back to school the day after that, so it was really our last chance to spend time together. We'd seen each other nearly every day of his break, minus a couple of days around Christmas when his family went to visit an aunt out of town. I was dreading his absence.

We walked for a while, talking sometimes and sometimes just listening to the crunch of dead leaves and the low whooshing sound of the nearby creek. Running water didn't really freeze around here, but it was a little more subdued than in the warmer months, and there were some frozen patches here and there. After a while, we both got hungry and found a sunny spot on the trail with a big, flat rock to perch on while we ate the peanut-butter-and-jelly sandwiches I'd brought.

It was a big enough rock to sit on, but not so big that we weren't sitting right next to each other, our hips and arms and shoulders pressed against each other. After we'd finished eating, we still sat talking, enjoying the feeling of being a sunning cat. At a pause in the conversation, I leaned my head on Tommy's shoulder.

"I'm going to miss you when you go back," I said. "I've just gotten used to having you around again."

He wrapped his arm around my shoulders and squeezed. "Me, too."

We sat that way for a while, our breathing slowly syncing. I lifted my head but didn't pull away, and when he turned his face toward me in response to my movement, our faces were inches apart.

"Tommy," I said quietly.

He raised his eyebrows in a silent "Yeah?"

"I…" My brain was skittering in a million different directions. "I always thought your eyes were brown."

The corners of his moss-green eyes crinkled. "Nope," he said softly.

I opened my mouth, trying to search from some witty or funny reply. Instead, I kissed him.

For just a second, Tommy was completely still, frozen in what I assumed was surprise. But then he shifted his body toward me, wrapped his other arm around me, and kissed me back like it was something he'd been wanting to do for a long time. He kissed me with his full attention, like it was the only thing he wanted to be doing at that moment, or any moment. Every nerve in my body sizzled, hyper aware of his hand pressed against my lower back, his fingers in my hair, and the taste and feel of his lips. I was over-aware of the rough texture of the rock we were sitting on, the feel of the breeze against my skin.

When he pulled back, I felt like I'd just stepped on land after a day out on a boat. We were both a little out of breath, and I rested my forehead against his, my eyes closed as I searched for my bearings.

"I'm sorry," he whispered.

I opened my eyes and pulled back so I could see him better. "I'm not," I said. "And...you could have fooled me."

He laughed a little, untangled his hand from my hair, and reached down to hold one of my hands. "I'm not sorry because I didn't want to kiss you," he said. "Believe me, I really, really did. In fact, I'm pretty sure that 90 percent of me is thinking about doing it again right now."

My face flushed, because 100 percent of me was wishing he would. "Only 90?" I said instead.

His dark eyes were sad. "Rosalee, you are...I really like you, Rosalee. I've liked you for a long time. And there is nothing I want more than to be with you. All the time. But I..." He hesitated, searching for the words. "...I want you to be sure. I don't want to be a rebound, or a fling, or a way to pass the time until you move on to bigger and better things." He hesitated. "I don't want you to think of him when you're with me."

I jerked away, nearly falling off the rock.

"I would never do that! How could you even think that about me?" I asked.

He sighed. His eyes were sad, but there was a firmness in his gaze. He understood my reaction, but he wasn't backing down. "I don't think you would deliberately hurt me, or lead me on, or mess with me. It's just...I was there, Rosalee. I watched you fall in love, and I watched your heart break.

"You are not a rebound," I say. Words pour out, words that I hadn't given voice to but that I knew were true as I said them. "You are my best friend. You're the first person I want to talk to every day. All day long I ask myself what you would think about one thing or another. You challenge me, and make me laugh, and inspire me. I don't know what I would do without you."

Tommy looked into my eyes, searching for the truth behind my words.

I reached forward and grabbed one of his hands, holding it tightly in my own. "You're not wrong, Tommy," I admitted. "Yes, I fell in love. Yes, my heart broke. But it was a clean break. No regrets, no looking back."

"But what do you want now?" he asked.

It was a good question. It's what he was getting at all along, really. I looked into his eyes, and I knew that what he'd said was true. He had been hoping for this for a long time. He was all in. But he was guarding himself, too, because who wants a broken heart? I thought about his question. What did I want? I took a moment to think, because he deserved the full truth, not what I wanted to be true.

"I'm going to be really honest," I said. "I just don't know. I know that I'm ready to move on. I know that I care about you. I know that it hasn't even been a year and my heart is still tender, but I can't think of anyone better to entrust a tender heart to than you. I can't give you promises, or guarantees. But I can tell you that my feelings are 100 percent about you." I reached up and framed his face with my hands. "I see you, Tommy."

The middle of his forehead creased, and eyes—those amazing green eyes, why had I never noticed?—were cloudy with conflict and doubt. He gently took my hands from his face but continued to hold them. My heart pounded, and all of a sudden I felt nervous. What if I'd ruined everything?

Finally Tommy let out a huge sigh. "Screw it," he said. Then he reached out and took my face in his hands and kissed me, and it took my breath away. It was as if before he'd been holding back, and this time the kiss was a force crashing down on us. I lost all awareness of anything but his lips on my lips, his hands on my face. It was longing and promise and heat.

When we broke apart, I kept my eyes closed for a minute, letting the world settle back around me, feeling flustered and slightly off balance. Tommy cleared his throat.

"So," he said, "want to finish this hike?"

Absolutely yes. Or no. Maybe we should just sit here on this rock kissing forever. Which meant, yes, we should go.

"Probably a good idea," I said, opening my eyes.

chapter *31*

March 2019

Rosalee sat on one end of the twin beds in the blue-and-white room of the Big Rock Inn, her feet resting on a low, padded bench, with a bottle of deep burgundy nail polish. Caroline lounged on a mound of pillows in the other bed, a remote control in her hand. After asking for recommendations from the innkeeper, they had ordered pizza from a local shop down the road, and were searching for a movie on TV.

"Not even a sappy made-for-TV movie," Caroline said, giving up and turning off the television. Good thing I brought some books with me!"

Rosalee laughed. "Me, too. I can't go anywhere without one. Or my e-reader these days."

Caroline picked up a magazine and opened it, but before she could have read much of anything, she looked up again.

"So," she said. "Feel free to tell me to mind my own business, but I'm curious about your sudden desire for a getaway. Not that I'm complaining!" she said, "Just curious. I just get the feeling there's more to it than meets the eye."

Rosalee smiled and dipped her nail brush in the bottle. "You are quite perceptive, my friend," she said. "And I don't mind. It's basically man trouble, which sounds ridiculous coming out of my mouth. I feel like a 20-year-old."

Caroline shrugged. "I don't think you're ever free of man troubles unless you completely abstain from male company," she said. "We...experienced women just talk about it differently. You were married for a long time. You know. It just looks a little different."

"True," Rosalee admitted. "But this isn't exactly old-marrieds kind of trouble. It's dating trouble...anyway, I just thought I'd left this part of life behind along with a smooth skin and brown hair."

Caroline laughed. "For what it's worth, you have fantastic skin. But on to the point...lay it on me."

Rosalee smiled. "Thanks, friend. Well, you remember the conversation we had the other day about history repeating itself? Once a cheater, always a cheater? Well, that little doubt is still nagging at me. And it's growing new doubts—am I betraying Tommy? Am I just grasping at companionship because I was so lonely?" Rosalee sighed. "It may be a little bit of Elizabeth sneaking into my head too. She—a lot of the family really, but mostly Elizabeth—keeps acting shocked that my life has changed slightly in the past year. Friends! A social life! Romance! My rational brain can smack down every single one of my irrational concerns, but I'm just weary of fighting myself."

Caroline nodded. "I get it. You don't trust yourself, and your family and friends are making everything muddy. Being in the middle of the moment makes everything less clear."

"Yes!" Rosalee said. "Exactly." She finished brushing polish on her last nail and screwed the cap back on the bottle. "I needed some space to breathe. And I really just needed to find myself again." She shook her head. "No, not find myself...more like... get back to myself." She gestured out the window at the trees and hills and tiny sliver of lake in the distance, glinting in the setting sun. "This is me. I love my home and I love the community I live in now, where I learned how to be a wife, and raised my kids, and grew and changed and became a grown-up. But my roots are deep here. I think this is where I can think clearly again, and, yes, like you said—I think I can re-learn to trust myself again here. Because I *know* this is me." Rosalee laughed and flopped back on the bed. "I sound like a lunatic."

"No way," Caroline said. "A bit dramatic maybe, but not a lunatic." She smiled "I get it, though. It was a good idea."

"Thanks."

They chatted for a little bit longer, talking about what books they were reading and funny things their grandkids had done. Caroline had Rosalee crying with laughter at a reference desk story, and by the time the two had settled in with reading lamps and the previously discussed books, Rosalee felt calm and happy and exceedingly glad she'd invited Caroline to join her this weekend. Glad that she'd invited herself on this weekend. It was good to put it into words. She wasn't looking for a sign from Heaven or anything earth-shattering. She just needed to hear her own voice.

The next morning was as beautiful as Rosalee had hoped it would be. The first thing she did after getting out of bed was step out onto the room's tiny balcony. She took a deep breath of cool, damp morning air, relishing the scent of honeysuckle from the garden and grass that had been mown yesterday. A perfect day for a morning of hiking, a trip to the cemetery, and an afternoon of antique shopping. They ate breakfast in the inn's dining room, and picked up the box lunches they'd ordered the night before. Caroline peeked at hers as they got settled in the car.

"I know I just ate enough Eggs Benedict and skillet potatoes for three people, but this lunch looks good enough to dive into immediately," she said.

Rosalee laughed. "Then please, let me save you from yourself. It'll be extra delicious with a fresh-air-and-exercise-induced appetite."

Caroline conceded that this was probably true and tucked the box back into the adorable basket the inn had sent with them.

A few hours later the two were sitting on the hood of the car, boxes next to them, mouths full of baguette, sundried tomato spread, mozzarella cheese, and fresh arugula. The boxes had seemed almost too full when they got them, but after hiking for a couple of hours, they both agreed there wouldn't be a crumb left.

Rosalee smiled. It had been many years since she'd been down to Blair Creek and explored the trail that ran mostly alongside the rocky creek bed. While she was hiking, she'd been trying to remember the last time she'd been down there, and the best she could come up with was sometime after the kids were in elementary school but before her parents had passed away and Tommy's mom had moved into the nursing home up in Springfield.

She had a memory of coming down one summer with her brother and his family, probably for the Fourth of July, and taking all the kids down to the swimming hole. She remembered the kids having fun, and she vividly remembered her, Tommy, and her brothers having even more fun. Something about the creek bringing out the kid in everyone.

Today Rosalee was happy to find out that the old trail still looked familiar. She recognized the lookout points and could picture the view around every bend in the trail. She knew which oak tree had the best position for a rope swing—and the tree had, in fact, had a rope swing dangling from its lowest branch. It felt good to know kids were still swimming there.

She and Caroline didn't talk much while they walked. Occasionally Caroline would ask Rosalee about a house tucked up in the trees, or an unusual plant by the side of the trail. Rosalee felt herself relax with each step and each breath of the damp, earthy scent of an early summer woods. A scent with that unique twang that she thought must come from the rocks that made up the Ozark hills.

Rosalee did her best to turn her brain off, to just watch and listen and smell the woods around her. For weeks, she'd been worrying about her family, her relationship with George, and her muddled feelings. But as she focused simply on breathing in and out, putting one foot in front of the other, she found herself finally able to shut out the noise, and finally able to feel a sense of release.

"I feel 30 years younger," she said to Caroline a few hours later. She sat on the hood of the car, leaning back on her hands, face turned up to the sun, eyes closed.

"I'd take some ibuprofen tonight," Caroline said, reaching into her lunch box for the huge chocolate chip cookie. "You won't feel 30 years younger tomorrow, I can almost guarantee it."

Rosalee laughed. "Good point."

They were quiet again for a few moments, listening to the

leaves rustling in the wind, the water trickling down the rocks, and a distant tractor.

"You know," Rosalee said, "George and I used to come to this spot to swim a lot that summer we met." She opened her eyes and glanced over Caroline. "This is where we kissed for the first time. And…we may have come down here just to make out a few times."

Caroline laughed. "I love slightly naughty memories," she said. "Especially someone else's." She grinned as Rosalee swatted at her halfheartedly. "What about your husband? Did you guys come down here, too?"

Rosalee shook her head. "We hiked down here quite a bit, but by the time we started dating, he was in college and only home for the summers, and we were both working full time." She grinned. "We'd just make out at work."

"I think the rest of the day is going to have to include plenty of stories," Caroline said. "I'm finding so much out about you!"

Rosalee grinned. "Well, only if you reciprocate."

"Deal."

Rosalee glanced at her watch, and they decided it was time to hit the road if they wanted to drive out to the town cemetery. They packed up their trash and stashed it in the back seat, then headed down the one-lane road back toward Carlton, windows down. The drive only took about 15 minutes, mostly through the woods, since Rosalee decided to head the back way.

The cemetery sat on the edge of Carlton, right next to the oldest church in town. It backed up to the woods—the better for bored children to scare each other with ghost stories—but the church kept it maintained and kept the woods at bay. It was shady and green, hemmed in by a low stone wall with an old, wrought-iron gate on one side, and had a stone path that wound between the rows of gravestones. Rosalee pulled her car up to a small gravel parking area by the gate and shut off the car but didn't get out. She listened to the wind in the trees…a bird singing nearby…someone playing the piano inside the church. She took a deep breath in, exhaled slowly.

"About two years after Tommy's diagnosis, the kids sent me on a cruise. They were worried about me, about my health. Elizabeth had gone with me to the doctor—had nagged at me until I made the appointment—and he'd told her I was basically just exhausted and needed some real rest. That first year-and-a-half after we found Tommy's cancer had been brutal—doctors and treatments and side effects. And brain cancer…it can alter a person's personality. Not always but…Tommy wasn't quite the same."

Rosalee smiled, but wiped her face as tears began rolling down her cheeks. "Tommy was the kindest, most patient person I knew. He was funny, but in a quiet way. Unexpected. He was really observant and thoughtful. Once I told him about an article I'd read in some magazine about this ancient Roman road that crosses Great Britain. I didn't even say anything about wanting to visit it, or walk part of it. But I love to travel, always dreamed of it even as a kid, and for our anniversary the next year, he surprised me with a trip. Almost two years after I'd mentioned it! But he remembered, and squirreled away money to take me on a trip. He would take a sandwich to work every day for lunch so we could save just a little bit extra for vacations and trips."

Rosalee's voice caught. "He was just…the best, you know? But that tumor. He became moody and forgetful and…mean sometimes. I went on that cruise and slept and slept and sat out by the pool and ate food someone else fixed for me. The last night I went to a show—a piano player, I think—and I sat in the back in the dark and just cried and cried. Because he was gone. My Tommy was already gone, and I knew it." Rosalee sniffed, and Caroline handed her a tissue.

"Thanks," Rosalee said, wiping her nose. "I'm sorry, I hadn't intended to…well, get emotional, I guess."

Caroline waved away the apology. "It's part of the process."

Rosalee nodded toward the cemetery. "The day of his funeral service, I felt so relieved. Relieved for him, because he wasn't suffering anymore, because he could finally be himself again— the truest version of himself. And I felt relieved for me. I was so, so tired. Physically, of course, but I was frankly tired of being a caregiver to someone I used to know. I think it would have been easier caring for a stranger rather than a stranger wearing my husband's body."

Rosalee shook her head. "And of course…I felt guilty because of that. Ashamed."

"You had nothing to feel guilty about or ashamed of," Caroline said. "Absolutely nothing. But I know, grief is not logical."

"I finally got to the point that I realized that, too," Rosalee said. "A good grief counselor helped, and a lot of time in prayer." She smiled. "And I think that's one of the benefits of age. If you let it, time, and experience give you a much better perspective on life and the big picture."

"So true."

Rosalee wiped her nose again, then sat up straighter. She unbuckled her seat belt and opened the car door.

"Want company?" Caroline asked.

"Either way," Roslaee said. "I'm fine if you want to stay here, but you're welcome to come along."

The slam of the single car door startled a few squirrels snacking under a nearby oak tree. Rosalee walked through the gate and followed the stone path to the middle of the cemetery, then turned right down a row of newer gravestones. She glanced at the names as she walked by. Most of those on this row were Tommy's great-great-greats. Aunts and uncles and cousins generations removed. Then grandparents, then parents. She paused at the double marker for Tommy's parents, reaching down to pull a few dead leaves off of the rose bush they'd planted there years and years ago. She then walked just a few more feet down the row. She kneeled down and rested her hand on the sun-warmed stone.

Thomas Patrick McDonnell

1956-2015

"Life, with its rules, its obligations, and its freedoms,
is like a sonnet: You're given the form, but you
have to write the sonnet yourself."

She smiled as she read the *Wrinkle in Time* quote. She and Elizabeth had fought about what to put on the gravestone. Elizabeth had wanted something unimaginative about fathers and friends and husbands. But Rosalee had dug in, knowing that one of Tommy's favorite quotes from one of his favorite books said more about him than any pithy descriptions anyone else could come up with.

I feel like I'm in a novel, Tommy, she thought. *But not one of yours. Too much relational drama.* She smiled, knowing that, had she actually been talking to Tommy, he would have immediately accused her of not understanding the science fiction and fantasy books that he loved so much. Tears stung her eyes and clogged her throat. *I miss you, friend,* she thought. *But I have another chance to…another chance for love. Companionship. Don't worry, I'm not doing anything so clichéd as asking for permission from a dead man, I'm just…I don't know. Asking myself for permission, maybe?*

She sat thinking about that, and realized that was the thing. The reason she'd felt such a strong need to get back in touch with herself. She needed to ask 18-year-old Rosalee for permission to love George again.

Rosalee sat on the stool for several more minutes talking about her kids and grandkids, knowing that she was talking to herself but still finding comfort in drawing together her present and her past, in honoring one of the most important people in her life by acknowledging their life and legacy and the part of her heart that would always belong to Thomas Patrick McDonnell.

chapter 32

March 2019

The early morning sun slanted in through the open kitchen window while Rosalee brewed a cup of coffee and buttered her toast. She slid the sunny-side up egg onto her plate, grabbed her mug, and nudged open the back door with her elbow. It was already open slightly since she'd let Billy out earlier. She saw her morning-loving dog standing by the gate to her fence, nose pressed between the chain links and tail wagging as he watched kids walking to school, neighbors walking their dogs, people heading to work, and runners getting in a few miles.

Rosalee set her plate and cup on her small patio table, sat down, and took in a deep breath. Why had she only just now realized how delightful eating outside could be? Well, better late than never, she supposed. She opened a magazine and took a bite of egg and toast. She and Caroline had enjoyed their last breakfast of the weekend out on the patio of their bed and breakfast, and Rosalee had not realized how perfect the combination of coffee, toasted bread, bacon, freshly cut grass, flowers, and dew-damp earth could be. Caroline was not a morning person—something Rosalee had seen first at work—so they each brought something to read to breakfast, Rosalee knowing Caroline did not want to talk first thing in the morning, and Caroline not talking out of habit. Rosalee had quickly discovered that Caroline's tendency to bring a magazine to breakfast was brilliant, since it was much easier to read with no hands.

Rosalee was finishing the last of her coffee when Billy stood up from where he'd been lying at her feet and ran over to the gate of the fence, tail wagging furiously. He barked his I-know-you bark, bounded away from the gate, only to rush back again. Rosalee stood up, wondering whose attention Billy was trying to get. She got to the gate just as George rounded the corner of the house. He was wearing jeans, a gray pullover shirt, and a pair of aviator sunglasses, and was carrying two cups of coffee and a paper bakery bag.

"I'm sure you've already eaten," he said as he walked up to the gate, "but I'm hoping you still have room for a cappuccino and some cinnamon sugar donut holes."

"Always," Rosalee replied, unlatching the gate and opening it to let him in. Billy's training kept the bakery bag safe, but he was sitting on George's feet and practically shoving him over with his excited, whole-body-tail wagging.

"Let me free you to greet your best friend," Rosalee said, taking one of the cappuccinos and the paper bag. George knelt down to give the old dog some love and accept a few doggie kisses in return.

"You'd think he was a puppy sometimes," Rosalee said as George stood up and the now-satisfied Billy trotted over to the patio to resume his morning nap, "not an old 10-year-old dog."

"No harm in feeling young sometimes," George said. He

took a step toward her, his body angled for the usual hug or kiss on the cheek, but he stopped short, arm dropping down to his side. He stuffed his hands into his pockets. "Did you have a good trip?" he asked.

"Wonderful," Rosalee said, leading him toward the patio. "Go ahead and sit down," she said, placing the bag of donut holes and her drink on the table. "Let me get a few napkins."

While she grabbed a few napkins from the kitchen counter, she glanced out the door's window. George had leaned down and was petting Billy, and Rosalee was quite certain Billy would have purred if he could have. She wished she could see George's eyes better behind the dark shades, but she could see seldom-appearing frown lines around his mouth.

She stepped outside and walked over to George, placing a hand on his shoulder and leaning down to kiss his cheek. "Thanks for the treats," she said, before sitting down in her own chair and putting the napkins on the table. George's frown lines immediately transformed as he smiled. He caught her hand in his and gave it a squeeze before letting go to dive into to the bag that smelled of that heavenly mixture of fried dough and cinnamon sugar.

They munched in a companionable silence until the silence stretched just long enough to include the return of awkwardness that Rosalee had allowed to creep into their interactions lately.

"I'm sorry things have been kind of…off lately," she finally said. "It's entirely my fault, I know."

George shrugged. "I'll be honest, it's not easy to just ignore it or brush it off when I feel like I've done something wrong but have no clue what." One corner of his mouth turned up. "It's like flashbacks of the worst kind of married-life fight."

Rosalee cringed. "Yikes, you're right. I promise I'm not usually so passive-aggressive."

"Yes, I remember a much more candid Rosalee."

"Well, I found that girl again, don't worry," she replied. "Or at least, the older, tireder, and more prone to aches and pains version."

George laughed, a tension in his shoulders easing as he did. "So, it was a good time away?" he asked, fishing in the bakery bag.

"So good," she said. "Just what I needed."

She told him about the weekend, from sharing childhood stories and memories with Caroline to the balm of being in a place that felt more like home than anywhere else on earth. She tried to explain to him how it made her feel more like herself than she'd felt in a long time. Like moving all the furniture out of a house before you redecorated, so you could get a sense of its bones, its character. And then you can fill it back up in a way that celebrates and highlights the beauty of the house rather than masking it or trying to make it something it's not.

George nodded. "I think I understand what you mean," he said. "I had a similar moment in my life when I realized that I didn't even recognize myself anymore. But it was fatherhood that really shook up my ill-fitting status quo. I saw myself in her, and it was…well, you said it already."

Rosalee asked him about his own weekend, and their conversation turned naturally to friends, and George's consulting client. Rosalee told library stories and laughed at George's crazy neighbor stories. Their coffee and pastries were long gone when Rosalee's phone rang.

"It's Elizabeth," she said, glancing at the caller ID. "I should probably take it. You're welcome to stick around, but she and I haven't talked for a while, so it might be a longer conversation."

"I'll just call you later," George said, standing up. He leaned over to kiss the smiling mouth that Rosalee turned his way. "Bye."

Rosalee waved with one hand as she swiped up to answer with the other. "Hi, sweetie," she said.

"Hi, Mom, how was your weekend?"

Rosalee gathered up the trash and put it on her empty plate as she told Elizabeth the less philosophical version of her weekend. The hiking and good food and antiquing portion of the weekend. It wasn't that she didn't want to have more of a philosophical discussion with her daughter, but the recent months had just emphasized the fact that Elizabeth wasn't really into the idea that her mom was an actual person. And that was okay, there was time for that. There was no reason that Rosalee's personal life should come between them. After all, their relationship had already weathered decades of change, from preschool tantrums to teenage hormones, and the surreal experience of watching a child grow into a parent. Rosalee reminded herself that Elizabeth wasn't just her daughter anymore, she was her friend. Rosalee knew she'd come around eventually.

"Hello?"

"Hello, beautiful. What are you up to?"

"Mmm...staring at old things."

Rosalee smiled at George's belly laugh. It was 8 o'clock that night, their usual time for chatting each day. Even if they'd seen each other earlier in the day, it had become a bit of a ritual—a post-dinner, pre-bed conversation.

"Any elaboration on that, or are you just going to play enigmatic tonight?"

"Tempting," she replied. "I read in a magazine once that it's important to be mysterious if you want to keep a man interested in you."

"Unnecessary."

"If you must know, I'm in the study. I came in here looking for a book I can't find, and I realized it's the last shrine."

"I don't understand?"

Rosalee sighed. "It's Tommy's room. And it's...still Tommy's room. I think I need to take it over, and I'm just not sure where to start. So right now, I'm just...staring at old things."

"Sorry, hon."

"Eh. It is what it is. I'll figure it out, and probably be better off for it. Repaint, maybe. Add some bookshelves so it feels like a library and less like an office."

"Sounds like a good plan."

Rosalee asked George about his day, and listened to him while she moved slowly, touching items as she circled the room. Tommy's framed degree. A world map with not as many little green pushpins in it as she'd once dreamed of, but enough to make a lot of good memories. She ran her fingers over the spines of Tommy's medical reference books and gardening books. Little mementos here and there, scattered among the heavy doorstoppers on the shelves—rocks the kids had given him as children, seashells, tacky bobble-heads he couldn't help but buy on family road trips. One shelf crowded with his favorite science fiction books.

She stopped at the desk, her hand grazing over a heavy glass paperweight with "World's Best Dad" engraved on the top. She remembered Elizabeth seeing the glass engraving kiosk at the mall the summer she was eight, and begging to buy Tommy something from it for Father's Day. And sitting on the corner of the big oak desk, a dark gray milliner's head with a straw fedora perched on top, its blue band as bold and crisp as the day he bought it.

George was asking if she wanted to see a movie this weekend. "That sounds great," Rosalee said. "Maybe an early Saturday show, and then we can eat after?"

They made plans, even though Rosalee knew they'd probably talk tomorrow.

"Before you go," Rosalee said, "would it be all right if you skipped family dinner on Sunday? I love it when you come, and I want that to be as regular as possible, but I think I need to bring the kids some of this stuff and..."

"It'll be easier," George finished her sentence.

"Thanks."

They said their goodbyes, and Rosalee wiped tears from her cheeks. That was one thing she was learning about grief: you didn't say goodbye just once. And even when the goodbye got less painful, you still felt it. Not always in sadness. Sometimes it was just an ache, or the memory of pain. Grief wasn't getting over the goodbye, but learning how to live with it.

chapter 33

April 2019

Rosalee was typically the first one to Elizabeth's house on Sunday afternoons, but she made sure to get there early this week so she could pull up to the top of the driveway, as close to the house as she could get. She got out of the car and waved to Keira curled up in her usual spot with her usual book resting on her knees.

"Come help me with something," Rosalee called, shutting the driver's side door and walking around to the trunk. None of the boxes was particularly heavy, but there were three, and she thought it would be nice not to have to make multiple trips from the car to the house.

She gave Keira a quick hug before stacking the two smaller boxes into her outstretched arms. She pulled out the third box and shut the trunk before following her into the house.

"Where to?" Keira asked.

"Let's set them in the living room," Rosalee answered, nodding to the archway across the hall from the one leading to the kitchen. "We should save them until after dinner." They caught Elizabeth's eye as they walked into the living room.

"Moving in, Mom?" she asked as she stuffed lemon halves into a chicken.

Rosalee smiled as she set down her purse and walked into the kitchen. "Tempting, but not just yet," she replied, moving around the counter to plant a kiss on Elizabeth's cheek. "It's just some things of your Dad's I thought you and Charles might like to have."

Elizabeth's busy hands stilled. "Why are you getting rid of Dad's things," she said, a layer of tension underneath her calm tone.

"Not really getting rid of," Rosalee said, "more like, passing on. It's not like I'm dropping it all off at a thrift store." She washed her hands in the sink, then moved over to where a cutting board was set out with carrots, onions, and potatoes. She picked up the vegetable peeler and slid a scrap bowl nearer to the cutting board.

"Of course, but…" Elizabeth's hands resumed their work double time. "It just seems a little abrupt, that's all."

"Darling, I have a lifetime's worth of mementos and memories. Giving you and your brother and your kids a few things isn't a great purge or anything. I just…I don't need a houseful of your Dad's things. I want to be present in my life."

Elizabeth rolled her eyes. Rosalee stiffened but kept peeling. "There's no need to be condescending."

Elizabeth ducked down to place the two chickens in the oven. "I didn't say anything!"

Rosalee waited until Elizabeth was visible again. "I've watched you roll those eyes for 40 years, darling, and I know when I'm being condescended to."

"It just sounds very…self-help section to me, that's all."

Rosalee slammed the vegetable peeler down on the counter. "And so what if it is," she said, her voice rising a bit. "What is the big deal, Elizabeth? I love you and Charles and our family. With my whole heart. But does that mean I can't have friends? A life?"

"Of course not, Mom, that's not what I meant."

"Well, what did you mean? Tell me. I really thought we'd had this conversation already, but you're still giving me pursed lips and eye rolls, so let's just get it all out!" Rosalee picked up the knife and started chopping vegetables, partially because it still needed to get done, and partially because she hoped trying to avoid cutting herself would help her calm down.

Elizabeth sighed. "It's just...I don't even know anymore. At first, I didn't trust George, and now...I thought you were happy. I guess I feel foolish, and I hate feeling foolish. And we all know how well I process change. It's all just a big change, Mom."

"I know," Rosalee said, her voice soft. "I *was* happy, sweetheart, especially all the times I was with all of you. I was probably the most myself with my family. But then I'd go home or to work, and I wouldn't talk to anyone, or go anywhere different or new. There were days where the only living thing I'd talk to was the dog."

Elizabeth winced. "I had no idea."

"I know, that's why I've been cutting you some slack," Rosalee said with a small smile. "Do you remember when you were a kid? Camping trips and picnics and dinner parties?" Elizabeth's hands stilled for a moment, her gaze softening as she went back through memories.

"Now that you mention it, yeah, I guess I do. We had that camper you bought when Dad got promoted, and we went out to the state park almost every month except the dead of winter.

And you were always dragging us to the art museum up in Kansas City every time we went to visit Uncle Daniel."

"But you loved playing all over that big lawn," Rosalee reminded her.

"And I do remember the dinner parties," Elizabeth said. "I remember getting to eat takeout pizza on a blanket in the living room while we watched movies and all the adults got to eat fancy food in the dining room."

"And then you were so thrilled when I finally let you eat with us."

For a while, there was just the sound was Rosalee's knife gently slicing through potatoes, carrots, and onions. Eventually Elizabeth sighed.

"Okay, if I really think about it…you're right. Things before Dad got sick were definitely different. You were different, I can see that now," she said.

"The cancer overshadows everything, I think," Rosalee said. "And now we tend to think 'before death' and 'after death,' and we forget that there was a 'before cancer,' too."

"I'm really sorry, Mom. And…thanks for bringing over some of Dad's things. It'll be nice to go through them."

Rosalee set down her knife and walked around the counter to give her daughter a hug. "Thank you."

Charles and Mary arrived just a few minutes later. Elizabeth took the chopped vegetables and tossed them with some olive oil, salt, and pepper, then spread them in a roasting pan and put them in the oven with the browning chicken. The boys talked over each other, telling Rosalee the latest about sports and school and the newest superhero movie they'd seen the night before.

Corbin called while they were setting the table, and everyone took a turn saying hi. Rosalee was the last to get the phone.

"You're probably about talked out now," she said.

"A little," Corbin admitted. "But this way I only have to make one phone call instead of feeling pressure to call everyone individually. It's a bit of an easier way to get the mega brownie points."

"Smart boy," Rosalee said with a laugh. "And I'll just bet with your mom that means literal brownie points?"

"She did promise a care package next week," he replied. Rosalee could hear the grin in his voice, and could picture his lopsided dimple. The one that gave him a particularly mischievous look, and always made it nearly impossible to tell him no. She talked to him for a few more minutes, then hung up and headed over to the table that was now full of delicious-looking food and surrounded by hungry faces.

After dinner, the kids were tasked with clean up—supervised by Keira—while the adults went to look through the boxes that Rosalee had brought. Rosalee was expecting to feel emotional, especially after her conversation with Elizabeth in the kitchen, but it turned out to be a delightful end to the evening. Instead of feeling morbid, going through the boxes felt like the best kind of storytelling and remembering. Charles had everyone crying with laughter when he told a story about using Tommy's favorite paperweight as buried treasure in a neighborhood game of pirates, or the time in high school he borrowed Tommy's Rolex watch—a pharmacy school graduation gift—to impress a date and then ended up losing it halfway through the night.

"I'd forgotten that!" Elizabeth exclaimed through her

laughter. "You dragged me out of bed at two in the morning and begged me to go around town with you and find it."

"So did you?" Mary asked.

"No way!" Everyone died laughing again. "I mean, not that night. I told him there's no way we'd find it at that time, and I'd take him out in the morning."

Charles held up the watch. "We searched for three hours, drove to the restaurant and the movie theater. I spent the whole time with my head hanging out the window looking for it on the street or in a parking lot and hoping a car hadn't smashed it. We came home and I was practically crying..."

"Practically?" Elizabeth said, raising an eyebrow.

"...and we found it lying on the front porch. Must have fallen off when I came home."

"I made him pay me back big time for that one," Elizabeth said. "He did my laundry for a month."

Later that night, after Rosalee had driven home and gotten ready for bed, she retold the story to George over the phone. He laughed as hard as the rest of them.

"Classic guy move," he said.

Rosalee's laugh turned into a yawn. "Guess that's my cue to hang up," she said. "Billy's already snoring."

"Got any breakfast plans?" George asked. "We haven't been to Ida's in a while."

"No plans," Rosalee replied. "And that sounds nice. I need to swing by the hardware store tomorrow, so I'll meet you there."

"8:30?"

"See you then."

They hung up, and Rosalee got up to plug her phone into its

charger on her dresser before walking over to the window and raising the shade halfway. She slid into bed, turned off her bedside lamp, and rolled over to the side of the bed by the window where she now had a perfect view of the cloudless night sky. She could see the edge of the moon rising over the trees across the street, its light bright enough that it obscured any stars visible in the city lights. She tucked on arm under her pillow and yawned again. She felt tired, happy, nostalgic, hopeful, and a bit like crying, although she couldn't exactly put her finger on why.

It had been an emotional few weeks, to be sure. Among her angst over George, the trip down home, cleaning out Tommy's office, and her conversation with Elizabeth…now that she thought about it, her mixed bag of emotions made sense. She remembered a conversation she had with Jessica once. Jessica had been through a rough couple of months: bad breakup with a long-time boyfriend, a less-than-stellar semester at college, lots of fighting with her mom, and the growing pains of friendships changing. She was emotional and upset, which just made her more emotional and angry at herself.

One night when they'd both been at the house—Jessica had been staying with Rosalee at the time—Rosalee had made cups of strong tea and a batch of cookies, and curled up with Jessica on the couch after dinner. They'd shared a long hug, and then the tea and cookies, while Rosalee explained that it was okay to feel lots of feelings sometimes. That our emotions were a gift, reminding us of things like compassion and joy. That emotions helped cement memories and lessons into our brain so that maybe we wouldn't make the same mistakes twice. And that our emotions helped remind us that we're alive.

Rosalee smiled at the memory and reminded herself that it was okay to feel emotion. To feel happy and sad and hopeful and nervous and nostalgic and excited all at the same time. To lean into this moment and let it remind her that she was alive.

chapter *34*

May 2019

Rosalee had just poured coffee into her to-go mug when she heard a knock at her front door. She set down the coffee pot, walked toward the door, and wondered who it might be. George often came over on Saturday mornings, but he was visiting his daughter today. It might be Elizabeth, but they were going to see each other at Austin's baseball game later. Rosalee opened the heavy wooden front door and smiled at the face on the other side of the screen door.

"Well, hello, neighbor," she said to Tripp. He was wearing kneepads and a bright green bicycle helmet.

"Hi, Mrs. McDonnell," he said. "I got a new scooter and we're taking it for a ride, and Mom wanted to know if you and Billy wanted to come with us."

Rosalee peeked over Tripp's head and saw Cecilia standing at the end of the driveway with Aislinn in a stroller.

"I would love to," Rosalee said, "and I know Billy would, too. Let me grab his leash and I'll meet you outside in just a minute."

She left the front door open as she walked back toward the kitchen where Billy lay in his dog bed. Her walking shoes sat in

the mudroom. Rosalee slipped on her shoes and grabbed Billy's
leash. She shook it gently by the dog bed.

"Billy! Walk?"

The big dog's head immediately lifted and he wagged his tail.
Rosalee clipped the leash onto the dog's collar and grabbed the
coffee she'd conveniently already put into the mug. She'd had a
thought to run a few errands before the game, but a walk with
her neighbors sounded better. She and Billy stepped onto the
front porch into the summer heat. Rosalee locked the door and
pocketed the key, then turned and joined Cecilia and the kids at
the sidewalk.

"Thank you so much for asking me to join you!" Rosalee
said. "It's been weeks since we've chatted. Too long."

"Agreed," Cecilia said. "We were out of town, and then the
kids were sick, and Levi's been busy at work, and…you know, all
of a sudden, it's been three weeks since you had a cup of coffee
with your favorite neighbor."

Rosalee marveled that it had really been that long. "Well, tell
me all your news," she said, pausing to let Billy sniff a rose bush.

Cecilia called out to Tripp, who'd raced ahead on his scooter,
telling him to stop at the stop sign to wait for them. "Sorry," she
said to Rosalee. Rosalee waved away her apology. Cecilia told her
about their weekly adventures at the park, and Aislinn's newly
discovered love of playing in the mud. Cecilia also mentioned she
was thinking of starting a neighborhood book club but hadn't
quite committed enough to invite anyone or set a date.

"Well, obviously, I would sign up in a heartbeat," Rosalee
said. "And I'd even help you plan the first one. So if you really
want to, I think you should go for it."

"Yeah, I think I will," Cecilia said with a bright smile. "I was thinking we could have the first meeting at the beginning of August. Most people are back from summer vacations, but haven't gotten deep into school activities yet. And it gives me plenty of time to plan and get the word out. Do you think I should pick the first book before the first meeting?"

"Definitely," Rosalee said. "That way the first meeting is less awkward. I'm assuming most people who come won't know each other, and having a purpose and topic to start out with will help minimize awkward conversation."

"Good point," Cecilia agreed. They'd caught up with Tripp, and Ceclia gave him another landmark to use as a don't-go-past-this reference. Then they started discussing which book would make a good pick for a first read for a fledgling book club made up of strangers.

"But what about you?" Cecilia asked as they collected Tripp and turned the corner again. "I'm still seeing a lot of that fancy gray Acura."

Rosalee laughed. "Yes," she admitted, "George and I are still seeing a lot of each other. We had a bit of a rough patch but…it's good now. Really good."

They talked about George the rest of their stroll around the block—much to Rosalee's chagrin—but Cecilia seemed genuinely interested, or at least didn't seem to mind. They stood at the end of their driveways for a few minutes while Tripp scooted up and down the sidewalk, revisiting the upcoming book club and making plans for how to invite people and what they should eat. Eventually Aislinn got tired of sitting and watching her brother, and Rosalee glanced at her watch. "Oh!"

she said. "I've got to get going. Baseball games don't wait for tardy Grandmas!"

She gave Cecilia a hug, kneeled down to kiss Aislinn on the cheek, and waved goodbye to Tripp before hurrying up the sidewalk and into her house. She gave Billy a hug and got him settled with a dog bone, made a quick pit stop in her bathroom, and grabbed her purse.

Austin's team had just scored, and the McDonnells were all on their feet cheering. Rosalee felt a hand on her arm and glanced at Jessica, who was standing on her right, and squinting at something over Rosalee's shoulder.

"Is that George, Gram?" she asked, pointing toward the parking area.

Rosalee turned. "Oh!" she exclaimed. "I was not expecting this."

It was, in fact, George.

"Who is he with?" Jessica asked.

"That's Kristen. His daughter."

Rosalee's stomach flipped, something she was also not expecting. She was happy to see both George and Kristen. Her kids—well, Elizabeth—were finally all acting more normal and welcoming and comfortable around George. In fact, he was usually with Rosalee at most of the grandkid sporting events and concerts. But Kristen had never met Elizabeth or Jonathan, Charles, and Mary. She was pretty sure it would all be okay, but she still grabbed Elizabeth's arm and leaned close to her ear.

"George is here with Kristen—his daughter," she said. "Don't. Be. Weird."

"Mother!" Elizabeth exclaimed with a frown. "Really? You have to say that."

Rosalee raised her eyebrows. Elzabeth sighed.

"I'll be good, I promise."

Rosalee left the row of camp chairs and walked toward George and Kristen.

"What a surprise!" she said, reaching out to hug Kristen and then George.

"A nice surprise, I hope," George said, kissing her cheek as she hugged him.

"Of course!" She smiled and kept her arms wrapped around him. "But I'm a little surprised you dragged Kristen out to watch little league with a bunch of people she doesn't know."

Kristen smiled, the charming and lopsided grin she'd inherited from George.

"I actually asked Dad to bring me," she said. "He's been talking about your family now for months, so I thought it was time to meet everyone. I have serious FOMO. I need to know what someone is talking about. Plus, it was a good chance to see you again."

Rosalee tilted her head up to George and raised her eyebrows.

"Fear of Missing Out," he said.

"Okay, that makes sense."

And Kristen did look like she was ready for a couple of hours of outdoor sports-watching: jeans, tennis shoes, navy blue t-shirt, her long curly hair pulled up in a ponytail, sunglasses on, cup of what looked like iced coffee in her hand. Rosalee slid out of George's arms but kept hold of his hand and linked her other arm through Kristen's.

"Let's go make new friends," she said.

Despite her effort at appearing nonchalant, Rosalee felt

nervous as they approached her family. It wasn't even that she was nervous things would go wrong or be awkward. George was a fixture these days—he knew the names of almost all of the other kids on the team, and a few of their parents. Her family was wonderful and welcoming, and anyone who met Kristen fell in love with her instantly.

Rosalee decided that maybe her nervousness was just a reaction to what felt like another step forward in her and George's relationship, another milestone she hadn't quite prepared herself for. Family mingling meant…family mingling. It opened the door to shared holidays and celebrations and memories. It was like adding a new color as you knit a sweater—once you got to a certain point, you couldn't take out or change the color without unraveling the entire project.

They arrived at the group of chairs and blankets just as one team called a time out, so Rosalee was able to make quick introductions before everyone's attention was split between conversation and game action. Kristen jumped right into game mode, asking Elizabeth questions about what the score was, what position Austin played, how the team looked. Rosalee settled into her chair and George opened his own up next to her. She commented that she'd had no idea Kristen knew so much about baseball, and George reminded her that she'd grown up with a Dad who was really into sports.

"It wasn't inevitable, of course," he said. "But I think she had a higher-than-normal chance of being a sports fan."

Rosalee's butterflies settled, replaced by a warm feeling of contentment as she processed the moment. Yes. This was a good idea. Why hadn't she thought if it before? By the time they'd all eaten lunch and were saying goodbye in the pizza place parking lot, Kristen had exchanged phone numbers with Elizabeth and Jessica and Kiera, and Rosalee heard her promise to text Keira with the name of a book series they'd been talking about at lunch, and make plans with Elizabeth to go shopping before she left town on Thursday.

George walked Rosalee to her car after she'd said her goodbyes.

"Kristen's got a movie night planned," he said as he opened her door. "Want to join us?"

Rosalee tossed her purse into the passenger seat. "I don't want to intrude on father-daughter time," she said.

Just then Kristen walked up. "Has Dad talked you into movie night yet?" she asked. "He said we could watch an arty independent film if you came and he was outnumbered."

"Well, in that case, count me in!" Rosalee said.

George sighed a huge sigh, but then he winked at Rosalee. "I guess if I get to spend the evening with my two favorite women, it'll be worth it. I'll just bring my travel pillow in case I get bored."

Rosalee rolled her eyes and Kristen smacked his arm. "Rude," she said with a smile. "I'll meet you at the car. See you this evening, Rosalee!"

George and Rosalee made a plan for which theater and time, picking one close to one of their favorite restaurants so they could go out to eat after the movie if Kristen was up for it. George glanced over at Kristen, who was leaning against the hood of the car talking on the phone.

"It went well today, don't you think?" he asked.

Rosalee agreed. Kristen was a natural people person, with all of her father's charisma and charm and with a genuineness and authenticity that was nearly impossible to resist. Rosalee and George continued chatting, George keeping an eye on Kristen but not making any moves to go join her. Rosalee wasn't in any hurry either, but kept thinking she really should let George go. *I need to get home anyway*, she thought, *and…and what? Walk the dog?* Billy was always up for that, but he was an old dog and it wasn't urgent. Clean something? There was probably some deep cleaning she could do, but to be honest, the house was pretty clean. There were plenty of things she would enjoy doing at home—reading her new library book, taking Billy to the park, calling Jessica or Caroline and see if they wanted to go to the flea markets with her before the movie. All enjoyable, all perfectly fine, but today the thought of getting in her car and going to do any of those things just left her feeling…restless. Lonely.

She looked up at George, half-listening to the story he was telling and half-watching the way he constantly fidgeted as he talked—jingling his keys, pushing his sunglasses up on top of his head, then back down over his eyes, and tapping the edge of her car door. She was listening to the sound of his voice as much as the words he was saying, and wanting nothing more than to be sitting next to him on a couch or puttering around the kitchen making sandwiches for lunch and listening to a podcast or watching college football or talking about nothing much. She wanted to be walking aimlessly through a neighborhood garage sale or big, rambling flea market—and while those were both fun things to do alone or with friends or one of her granddaughters or Elizabeth, she wanted to be doing it with George.

When Rosalee thought about what she wanted to do with the rest of her afternoon, she kept coming back to that thought: that she wanted to be doing nothing special, just living life, enjoying a Saturday. With George. She felt like going home. With George. Her breath caught in her throat. George stopped mid-sentence.

"You all right?" he asked, putting a hand on her shoulder.

"Yes, fine," Rosalee said quickly. She nodded over to Kristen, who'd ended her phone call and was sitting in the car. "Looks like we should get going," she said. "I'll see you at the theater." She reached up for a quick kiss, then slid into her seat. Rosalee gave a little wave as George shut her door, feeling a little bad for the puzzled look on his face, but she really needed to be alone with her thoughts for a moment. She put on her sunglasses, buckled in, and waved as she drove out of the parking lot and straight to her favorite nature trail.

chapter 35

May 2019

Rosalee slid into a seat at the small, wrought-iron table and thanked the hostess as she handed Rosalee a menu. The hostess asked Rosalee if she'd like a glass of water while she waited for her granddaughter, and Rosalee smiled and said, yes, please. She adjusted her sunglasses as the hostess walked off, and glanced around. Rosalee was meeting Jessica for lunch. Jessica was taking a class that met on Tuesdays, and had mentioned to Rosalee that past Sunday that she usually ate a late lunch at a little cafe near campus and then camped out with her books, laptop, and free coffee refills to get some studying done.

Rosalee immediately told Jessica they should have lunch together that week, since it had been way too long since they had spent any lengthy one-on-one together. Between Jessica's school and work schedules and Rosalee's new social life, Friday movie nights had become more occasional than regular.

The café was only a mile or so down the road from the college, sharing their block with a bookstore, a few other restaurants, a small pharmacy, a couple of bars, a laundromat, and a vintage clothing store. The café and restaurants all had small patios in front of the store, shaded by the big trees that lined the street and providing excellent people-watching opportunities. Rosalee had to laugh to herself at how young most of the pedestrians looked—mostly college students, naturally—a visual reminder that even though she'd been feeling quite a bit younger lately, she was well past the fresh-faced stage.

Was that a bad thing? No, not really. Did she miss the energy and metabolism and naturally brunette hair? Of course. Did she miss the sense that her whole life was ahead of her, full of possibilities? Sometimes. Did she miss the insecurities, the trap of sometimes trying too hard, the search for identity? Not for one minute. Nor did she miss the hard and sleepless work of taking care of babies and toddlers.

She remembered her late thirties and early forties, which had been a time of transition. The kids were moving on, moving out. Several of their neighbors who had become their closest friends had moved when their own kids had moved out, and their community and family had been reduced. Even though they had always loved just being together, Rosalee remembered she and Tommy feeling quite lonely for a while. Rosalee started missing the busy and full days when her kids were little, and started resenting the physical changes that were also accompanying this new stage in life.

But slowly her mindset shifted, and Rosalee realized that this new season of life also included more confidence and a more well-developed sense of self. She wasted less time on things that didn't matter to her, because knew with more surely what she valued. She didn't care as much what other people thought about her, and started relishing that freedom.

Rosalee's cell phone dinged and she glanced at it, then smiled. *Hey you.* The text message read. *Still coming over tonight? Of course.* She typed. *Want me to bring anything? Ice cream. You know what kind.*

Rosalee shook her head. A new ice cream shop had opened up between her house and George's condo, and he was obsessed. Anytime she came over, he asked her to stop and pick some up. She teased him about it mercilessly, but he only shrugged and kept asking.

"Hey, Gram, sorry I'm late."

Jessica slid into the seat across the table, her backpack thudding to the ground next to her chair.

Rosalee shook her head, sending a smiley face emoji back to George before putting her phone in her purse. "I've been daydreaming anyway," she said. "Didn't even notice."

She asked Jessica what she liked on the menu, and a few minutes later their server arrived with water glasses.

"So," Jessica said as the server walked away with their order. "I've been dying to talk to someone and it's too soon to tell Mom and Dad, but I've met someone. You know...a boy kind of someone."

"You know I love being the first to know," Rosalee said.

They'd met in her anatomy and physiology class, Jessica said. He was also in the nursing program, so she'd seen him around, but they hadn't talked until they joined the same study group. Jessica said Kellen—that was his name—was pretty awesome. Funny, smart, cute, thoughtful. A great study partner because he took it seriously, but also knew the importance of study breaks, coffee, pizza, and the perfect studying playlist.

"He sounds pretty great," Rosalee said. "Have you gone on a date?"

Jessica sighed. "Sort of?" she said. "Here's the problem. We went out for a post-test celebratory ice cream once, and met to see a local band we both love play a few weekends ago. But neither one seemed very...date-like. I'm dropping as many hints as I can, so I'm not sure how interested he is. I know he's not dating anyone, so that's not it."

"You may need to take a less subtle approach," Rosalee said. "Some people just don't pick up little clues, you need to be more direct. It may be that he doesn't want to date or it may be that he's shy, or it may be that he's clueless."

"You're probably right," Jessica said. "I have to say, Gram, people these days don't know how to date. No one's willing to put themselves out there anymore. One of my friends said that a guy asked for her number at a show the other night, and she felt like he was stalking her. And it's a guy she sits next to in one of her classes! So like...not even a stranger." Jessica shook her head. "How did I get to be so old fashioned, Gram?"

"Spending too much time with your grandmother," Rosalee said wryly.

Jessica reached over and squeezed Rosalee's hand. "Never. But I do think you're right. I'm going to have to just woman up and ask him out on a date."

Their lunch arrived then and they talked about other things: Jessica's classes, the book club Rosalee and Cecilia were starting, family gossip. They lingered over their lunch until Rosalee finally told Jessica that she should probably let her do some studying. As she walked to her car, Rosalee glanced at her watch and realized it was only a few hours until she was supposed to be at George's house. She thought about errands she needed to run. She thought about the book in her bag. She thought about her conversation with Jessica. After she got into her car, she pulled out her phone and sent him a text:

Mind if I come over early? Can I bring Billy?

The answering "ping" was almost immediate:

YES

A couple of hours later, Rosalee was curled up on George's couch, her big dog curled up on her feet, her book in her lap, and a glass of wine on the coffee table next to her. A pot of something delicious-smelling simmered on the stove, and George sat in the wing-backed chair that sat perpendicular to the couch, his reading glasses perched on his nose while he read on his tablet. Rosalee had perked up when he'd pulled it out, asking him what he was reading. George had gotten a sheepish look in his face before saying "ESPN. Sorry, Rose, some things never change. You're going to have to save the book talking for your friends."

"This is really nice," Rosalee said, setting her book down on her lap.

George glanced up from ESPN. "It is," he said with a smile, "I'm glad you came over early," then he dropped his eyes back to the tablet.

Rosalee picked up her book again but stared at the words without seeing them. She thought again of Jessica, pulled her feet out from underneath Billy, and sat her book down next to her wineglass. She reached over to George and pushed his arm gently, moving his tablet to his lap and causing him to look at her again. She smiled at the tiny irritation in his eyes at being interrupted.

"No," she said. "This is really, really nice." She scooted to the edge of the couch so she could reach him better and put her hands on either side of his face. His cheeks were scratchy with stubble and his eyes were still deep blue, with a few more smile lines these days.

"I love you."

She smiled at him and said it again.

"I love you."

He covered her hands with his own, and turned his face to kiss her left palm, then rested his forehead against hers.

"Me, too."

Rosalee closed her eyes. For a moment they just sat, their breath mingling. He leaned toward her and pressed his lips against hers, then sat back.

"Don't go away," he said, walking down the hallway.

She rose from the couch, walked across the room to the French doors, and stood looking out over George's patio and the big green space beyond. She smiled, since it was impossible not to notice how bare George's patio looked compared to all the others that surrounded the common area. Every other patio was covered with potted plants, but George's simply contained a small wooden table, two charis, a grill, and an open ice chest.

Rosalee heard a noise behind her and turned to see George coming back into the room. He came to stand next to her and Rosalee nodded her head toward her view.

"One of these things is not like the other," she said.

George looked confused. "Come again?"

"Your patio. It's…you're not much of a gardener, are you?"

"No," George said. "Definitely not. Never had time, never cared."

Rosalee smiled at how unapologetic he was about it, too.

George shook his head. "But that's not what we're talking about," he said.

"You just walked into the room. We're not talking about anything yet."

George sighed. "You know what I mean. Just...hush for a minute."

Rosalee obediently closed her mouth, and George reached for her hands.

"When I married Jeanette I knew I'd made some big mistakes. My life was just one big reaction to things going on around me, and getting Jeanette pregnant was a big wake-up call to the fact that it was past time for me to start acting like a grown up. I did love you, in my own immature way. I regretted hurting you, and I regretted never knowing if what we had would have grown and matured into something lasting. I'm not going to lie—as much as I regret my past actions, my life turned out pretty great. I had a good marriage, and I have an amazing daughter." He squeezed her hands gently. "I know your life turned out pretty great, too."

"Yeah," she said softly, "it really did."

"When I saw you that night at the pizza place, it was such a surprise. I thought I could see my life stretching out in front of me pretty clearly. I knew what was coming. But then it was like God said 'guess again.' You were such a surprise. A wonderful, wonderful surprise." He paused and she smiled at him and squeezed his hands but stayed quiet, since she could tell there was more to what he wanted to say.

"Let's get married."

Rosalee blinked. Once. Twice.

"I can see I surprised you," George said, laughter and doubt mingling in his voice.

"A little," Rosalee managed. "I just…it wasn't what I was expecting to talk about today."

George's mouth turned up slightly at the corners. "I'll admit, I'm being a little bit spontaneous. But not entirely."

He reached into his pocket and Rosalee's heart lurched. *A ring? Really?* Nothing like a legitimate marriage proposal to make an AARP member feel like a teenager again.

George opened his palm. Inside sat a delicate gold braided band with a row of small alternating diamonds and emeralds across the top. It was beautiful and unique and exactly what someone who wasn't a teenager and had been married before might want.

"When you called this afternoon about coming over early, I thought to myself, *Yes, that's perfect.* Before you called, I'd been doing the same thing—reading, puttering around the house, wondering if I needed to run any errands. But I felt restless. And here you are, and I'm doing the exact same thing, but I feel settled and peaceful and like there's nothing I'd rather be doing. When I'm not with you, I wish I was. All the time. I love you. I love the girl that's still inside you, and the woman you are now. I love your family and want nothing more than to completely win Elizabeth's heart to my side." Rosalee laughed at that and George grinned. "And there's no reason for you to say no. So say yes. Let's get married."

"Yes."

Now it was George's turn to look surprised.

"Did you think I would take more convincing?" Rosalee asked.

"To be honest, a little."

Rosalee smiled and leaned forward, rising up on her toes to kiss George's still-surprised mouth.

"Nope," she said softly. "I'm in."

Six months later, Rosalee stood in the entryway of her house, her eyes taking in the bittersweet sight of rooms that were still full of history and memories and love, even if they were empty of furniture and knickknacks and photos on the wall. A memory came to mind of herself standing in almost this very same spot, seven months' pregnant and listening through the open back door to Elizabeth exploring their brand-new backyard.

"Mr. McDonnell, I have a proposition for you," she'd said, watching Tommy set down the last box from the truck.

"What's that?" he asked, straightening with a sigh.

"Let's never, ever move again."

He'd laughed and walked over to her, putting one hand behind her back and resting the other lightly on her huge belly.

"Deal."

Rosalee blinked back tears as the memory faded. She heard the front door open, and turned to see George come in. He walked over and put his arm around her shoulder.

"We could still stay here," he said. "I'd be happy to move all that stuff back inside. My muscles probably wouldn't be quite as happy."

Rosalee shook her head. "You're sweet," she said with smile, "but no. I think we're better off without quite so many ghosts around."

George squeezed her shoulder and kissed the side of her head. "Need a few more minutes?" he asked.

"Not in here," she replied. "But I want to make sure to say goodbye to the Blairs."

She glanced around one last time, taking it in, the sight of the home where she'd spent the past 30 years, every corner familiar, every ding and scrape with a story. Finally she turned toward the front door and followed George outside. As she passed through the doorway, she patted the wood frame.

"Thanks, house," she said. "You've been great. Thanks for being a good home all these years." She closed the door and locked it, pocketing the key. They'd drop the keys off at her realtor's office on the way to the condo.

The past six months had been a whirlwind—she and George had talked late into the night after he'd asked her to marry him, making plans and dreaming about the next steps. Rosalee had been firm even then that she wanted to move in with George, although he'd made her take a couple of weeks to be sure before they moved forward with selling the house and telling her family. Once they'd told everyone, Rosalee had started putting things in motion, hiring a realtor, scheduling an estate sale, and packing up what she planned to take with her to George's condo.

She and George decided on a simple, family-only ceremony on a Saturday afternoon, then rented out the banquet room at their favorite Italian restaurant for a big dinner afterword. Caroline and her husband, the Blairs, and a few other friends joined them for dinner. As she had gotten ready for bed the night before the wedding, she mentally patted herself on the back for the way they'd planned things. A small ceremony and restaurant meal certainly meant a lot less planning, and meant that while she was tired from all the packing and sorting and selling, she wasn't absolutely exhausted. More emotional than she'd anticipated— but thankfully she was staying at Elizabeth's, and she and Jessica and Keira had made it a really special evening.

As Rosalee walked down the porch steps of her house— not her house anymore, she reminded herself, but the Finch's house—she saw Celia and Levi and the kids walk over across the lawns. Celia opened her arms to Rosalee and wrapped her up in a big hug.

"I promise I'm happy for you, but I'm very sad for me," she said.

Rosalee hugged her back. "I know. I'm sad, too." She pulled back to look at Celia. "But I am 100 percent coming to your new book club. And you still have my number for babysitting or coffee or whatever. I'm just a few minutes away."

Celia wiped away a tear but smiled. "Well, it's not perfect, but I'll practice being content. Oh, and here," she pulled a small canvas tote bag off her shoulder. "I didn't have time to get a wedding present before last weekend, so there's a little something in here to celebrate that. Plus…" She reached in and pulled out a book. "Our first book club book! So, no excuses."

"Oh, thank you!" Rosalee said. "You're the sweetest!"

They hugged again, then Rosalee gave Levi and the kids hugs before scheduling a date to have the family over for dinner in a couple of weeks. Finally, she followed George down to the moving truck and climbed inside. They both buckled up, and George started the truck, the engine rumbling loudly.

"Well," he said, looking at her. "Anything else?"

Rosalee shook her head. She'd spent the past week going around and saying goodbye to the neighbors she still knew. Billy was already camped out at George's—their—condo, and everything she needed was packed up in the back of the truck.

No, that wasn't true. Rosalee reached over and squeezed George's hand. Everything she needed was right here. She looked into his midnight eyes, her heart clenching. How did she get so lucky? She'd thought Tommy had been her second chance at great love, but turns out life had one more surprise for her.

"I'm ready."

acknowledgments

The first thank you goes to my parents—for helping me to grow up loving books and reading, and for teaching me that making up stories in my head is a great way to fall asleep at night.

Thank you to Shannon, Carolyn, Margaret and everyone at Orange Hat Publishing—for being encouraging and kind, for making this dream become reality, and for helping this little novel to be better than I could have made it on my own.

Thank you to Nicole, Camille, and Jeanette—When I told you "I'm going to write a novel" you believed me and you believed I would finish it, even when my progress was almost imperceptible. I don't know what I'd do without your friendship.

I literally never would have finished this book without Doc and Julie Reed. One New Year's Eve you asked me about my writing. When I answered honestly that I was struggling to keep going and thought maybe I should just give up writing altogether, your genuine distress at that thought and heartfelt plea to keep writing and creating were exactly the encouragement I didn't know I needed. Thank you for teaching me the importance of art and the value in creative community.

Thank you to my kids, for enjoying twice-a-week preschool so Mom could write her book, and for the crew at Barbarossa

Coffee for a welcoming place to write that doesn't have a view of my dirty dishes or unfolded laundry.

Last, but certainly not least, thank you to Jeremy, for always believing in me and supporting me, for loving the people around you with your actions, not just words, and for helping me to not take myself too seriously.

Amanda Waters is a former journalist-turned-librarian. She's a midwestern girl who, by the fault of her husband, has become a naturalized Texan. When she's not writing or hiding from the Houston humidity, you can find her reading, drinking way too much coffee, or playing endless games of UNO and Go Fish with her two children. You can also find her online at www.amandawatersauthor.com.

CPSIA information can be obtained
at www.ICGtesting.com
Printed in the USA
BVHW061219210120
569695BV00007B/60